Masters
of Desire

Masters of Desire

Myla Jackson
Layla Chase
Shayla Kersten

APHRODISIA

KENSINGTON BOOKS
http://www.kensingtonbooks.com

APHRODISIA BOOKS are published by

Kensington Publishing Corp.
850 Third Avenue
New York, NY 10022

ISBN-13: 978-0-7582-2549-8
ISBN-10: 0-7582-2549-0

First Trade Paperback Printing: January 2009

10 9 8 7 6 5 4 3 2 1

Printed in the United States of America

CONTENTS

Pirate of Mystique Island

Myla Jackson

1

"Wait!" Lord Rafe Herrington yanked his cutlass from the pirate's chest and leaped to the quarterdeck. All around, his men waged a fierce battle with the crew of the pirate ship *Nomad*. The fight was all but over, the pirates dying or surrendering one by one.

With blood dripping from his sword's edge, Rafe strode across to where an older man with steely gray hair and a scruffy beard held the end of a hangman's rope. Seumus Mackintosh, the boatswain of his own pirate ship the *Serpent's Curse*, loved a good hanging.

"He's the capt'n. Soon as he's dancin' the hempen jig, the rest'll lay down their weapons."

"I have use of him alive." Rafe wiped the blade of his cutlass across the doomed man's trousers, leaving a long streak of blood on his dirty rags.

"He's a bloody pirate. I t'ought ye wanted to rid the seas of sech vermin." Seumus leaned into the rope enough to make the man on the business end of the noose stand on his toes to keep from choking.

"I want answers." Rafe took control of the rope from Seumus and loosened it. Then he stood in front of the filthy pirate who'd plagued the waters surrounding Mystique Island for the past month. "For whom are you working?"

"I work for meself." The man's gruff voice rattled like bones in a tin cup.

"Then why do you only target some of the ships leaving Port Newton and not all?"

"Why should I tell you? Yer nothin' but a pirate yerself."

Rage burned in his chest. The man spoke truth. Rafe was no better than a pirate, no thanks to the witch Busara. Yet he felt a misguided sense of obligation to protect his island from marauders such as this. "I shall make it simple to the point even a filthy, bilge slime pirate like you can understand. If you don't tell me, you die." Rafe handed the rope back to Seumus.

The burly Scot leaned hard on the rope, jerking the pirate off his feet.

With his hands tied behind his back, the pirate kicked at the air, wheezing unintelligible words out of his constricted throat.

"What's that? Now you wish to talk?" Rafe blinked and Seumus let go of the rope.

The captain of the *Nomad* dropped to his feet, his knees buckled and he crumpled to the hard wooden deck. "The governor," he gasped.

Rafe lifted the man by the collar until they were eye to eye. He held his breath in order to avoid gagging on the stench of the man's unwashed body. "The governor, what?"

"I pay him a cut of me booty, he gives me certain information." The man shrugged a ragged shoulder. "Works to both our benefits."

Heat rose beneath Rafe's blood-splattered white shirt. "Governor Lord Sheldon Braithwaite?" The bastard who'd driven him off the island was responsible for this cutthroat's reign of terror on the hapless ships entering and leaving Mystique Island's only port.

"Aye."

"So you murder innocents and steal from them to pay your debt to the good governor?"

The man's face split into a gap-tooth grin. "Right ye are. I'll give ye a cut as well, if ye set me free."

Rafe stared hard into the man's black eyes, and then in a deadly calm voice said, "Hang 'em high, Seumus."

"Gladly, Capt'n." Seumus leaned on the rope slowly hefting the man up the mast. The Scot was soon joined by Murphy Reid, the first mate. Shirtless and sweating, they applied all their weight into raising the captain of the *Nomad* high above the melee.

Shouts of challenge turned to dying screams as the crew of the *Nomad* dropped from their wounds or threw their cutlasses and pistols to the ground when confronted by their captain dangling from the mast.

Rafe retired to his quarters aboard the *Serpent's Curse* where he stripped off his torn and bloody shirt.

Seumus barged through the door, carrying a jug of ale and laughing at Murphy, who entered behind him.

Naked but for the strap holding back his hair, Rafe stood with his feet spread wide, his hands resting on his hips. "Have you forgotten common courtesy?"

Seumus stared at Murphy and Murphy back at him. "Me pardon, Capt'n." He shoved the jug out in front of him. "After you."

Manners were lost on his boatswain and first mate, but they were true and loyal men. Rafe shook his head.

"The prisoners are secured in the hold and the *Nomad* set afire. 'Tis time to celebrate with the men," Murphy insisted.

Rafe waved aside the jug and stepped to the trunk containing clean clothing. He opened it and shut it without retrieving a single item. "I'll not be celebrating this eve."

"Why ever not?" Murphy slapped Rafe's back. "The inhabitants of Mystique Island will be forever in your debt for ridding them of that plundering cur."

"Yes, but you heard the man—Braithwaite is responsible for allowing the pirating to continue."

"What do ye care, Capt'n?" Seumus tipped the jug and downed a lusty swallow before continuing. "Yer not the gov'nor anymore. The people of the island shunned ye fer the curse."

"Damn and blast the curse!" Rafe lifted his cutlass and jabbed it into the wood flooring. "I'm going ashore tonight to break the bloody curse, once and for all."

"And how would ye be doin' that, sir?" Seumus set the jug on the table that served to hold the maps of the Caribbean Islands. "The Obeah woman refused to cure ye. Do ye propose to force her?"

"If I have to . . ." Rafe pulled the cutlass from the wood planking and stared at the razor sharp blade. "I'll kill her, if I must."

Seumus's eyes widened. "Ye know the penalty fer killing a witch, don't ye?"

Murphy shook his head. "The locals say you'll be cursed forever to a life worse than death if you kill an Obeah."

He dropped the cutlass onto the table, lifted a dagger from the table and slung it as hard as he could. The blade thwacked against the cabinet next to Seumus, embedding two inches into the wood. "My life is worse than death. While I'm out cleansing the waters of pirates, Braithwaite is breeding more. If the people of Mystique dare to speak out against their new governor, they're murdered. How can I stand back and let it happen? These are my people."

"Not anymore, Capt'n," Murphy said quietly. "Not anymore."

Barefoot, Rafe paced the length of the cabin and back. "I can't stand by and do nothing."

"You're doing everything you can." Murphy tugged at the dagger on the wall beside Seumus. The weapon didn't loosen from its mooring.

"It's not enough. I can't rest until Braithwaite is replaced by someone of morals and integrity."

"That rules me out." Seumus grabbed the jug and tipped it again, swallowing a huge gulp of ale. He swiped his arm over his mouth. "Ach! I can no' see ye blastin' away at an old woman, Obeah or no. Ye don't have it in ye to kill a female."

"I'll do what I have to do in order to save the island from the devil himself."

"How do you propose to get to the witch?" Murphy asked. "She's nigh on impossible to find by land. The only way in to her is by sea, if you can find the entrance to Siren's Cove."

"I'll find it." He strode across the floor and yanked the dagger from the wall. "I'm thinking that if I kill the Obeah woman, her curse will be broken."

Murphy shook his head, a sorrowful slant to his brows. "And if your curse worsens, then what?"

"What's a little more hardship when I don't have much of a life as I am?"

"What's so bad about your life?" Murphy waved an arm at the interior of the captain's cabin. "You have everything you need. Food, clothing, a ship, a profession, and friends." He patted his chest, a smile spreading across his face.

Rafe snorted. "I'm no better than the man we hanged today. I steal from other pirates to make a living, and I spend half my time in the ocean, like a bloody fish."

"But yer not a fish. Yer a magnificent monster." Seumus cringed at his own words. "Well now, I'd give me balls to be as fearsome."

"You can keep your balls. It's no life for a man who once was the governor of this island."

"Even if you break the curse and remain human, what

makes you think you'll regain your governorship?" Murphy asked. "As you said, you've been nothing but a pirate since you were run off the island by Braithwaite and the superstitious natives."

Rafe had thought of that, but he still didn't have an answer. All he knew was that he was powerless as long as he was only human half the time. He turned to Murphy and placed a hand on his shoulder. "If I don't return, the ship's yours. Take care of my crew."

Murphy nodded. "Aye, Captain."

Melodie stared at the scattered bones, trying, to no avail, to see what the old woman saw. For the past week, she'd lurked around the Obeah woman's living quarters on the slim chance of receiving a spell that would make her whole. "How soon until you finish the spell?"

"Takes much time. Much t'ought to make a spell dat strong." She gathered the bones of cats and other small animals into her hands and shook them gently, the sound like reeds rattling in the wind. "Why you want always to be part of the sea?"

"It's the only place I don't feel like such an oddity." Melodie shrugged. "Humans wouldn't understand my life and they fear what they don't understand."

The old woman nodded, her bone earrings bobbing with the movement. "You can no find love. Love is what keeps us young."

"It's more than that." Melodie pushed to her feet and paced in front of the thatched hut where the witch lived. She'd been inside only once before. Movement was difficult among the myriad of items she had in stock. The Obeah had everything from rags, feathers, balls of clay and glass beads, to cat skulls and earthen jars with mysterious contents of which Melodie could only guess. The place reeked of dried vegetation and decaying animal parts and it gave Melodie the chills. For all she knew, the woman could have human body parts in there.

Melodie shuddered at the possibility. Still, she endured the long wait for a spell to cure what Melodie considered her affliction. After twenty long years of dealing with her birthright, she was ready to trade her feet for fins permanently. "In the sea, I'm free. No one judges me based on my family lineage or the color of my skin." She glanced down at the light mocha shade that had been her bane in the human world. Neither Carib, nor English, she was a freak and didn't fit in either society.

"What makes you tink the merfolk won't have de same prejudices?"

"I spent time with them when my father was still alive. They didn't make fun of me or shun me because I was different."

"And how long did you spend wit' dem?"

"A few days at a time. When Mother would let me go with Father."

The old woman nodded, her gray brows dipping low. "Are you sure you not be tradin' one difficulty for another?"

"I don't know." Melodie flung out her arms. "I just don't want to live two lives. I want to be normal in whatever world I live in."

A young version of Busara rounded the corner of the hut with an earthenware jar perched on her hip, water sloshing over the top. "If you leave de island, who will I talk wit'?"

Melodie took the jar from Kanoni, Busara's beautiful daughter. "I'll always come back to visit, as all the merfolk do. We can't stay away for long. You know that."

Kanoni's gaze swept the cove where the water shimmered like sparkling jewels. "No, you will not stay away long." She dragged her gaze back to Melodie, her eyebrows furrowing. "I will miss you, girl."

"You know how I feel. I want more from life. As it is, I'm on the edge of two worlds. I just want to belong in one."

"She be needin' a man, Mamma." Kanoni laughed. "Can't you give her a love spell to catch one?"

"I don't need a man. I need to be either all mermaid or all human and my preference is to remain in the sea." She felt less constrained by custom and man-made obstacles when she floated among the coral and sea creatures.

The old woman ignored their chatter. Squatting on her haunches, Busara cast the bones in the dirt in front of her shack and sat back, her dark forehead wrinkled in a frown. "I will make de spell."

Melodie turned to the woman and dropped to her knees in the sandy soil. "You will? When? How soon?" She clasped the old woman's gnarled hands in her own, tears springing to her eyes. "Oh, thank you."

"First you must do something for me." Her old fingers clasped Melodie's in a surprisingly strong grip.

"Anything, just name it," Melodie promised.

"A man comes to Siren's Cove. You must stop him."

The intense look in Busara's eyes struck sudden fear in Melodie's soul. "Who is he? What does he want?"

"He's de pirate of de *Serpent's Curse.* His name is Lord Rafe Herrington, de former governor of Mystique Island. He is come to kill Busara."

Melodie perched on a flat rock, near the entrance to Siren's Cove. Like a shroud, darkness settled over the sea and the shore. One by one, the stars blinked to life in the sky, their reflection shimmering across the placid ocean's surface, like so many jewels on a black, velvet carpet.

How would she know when he came ashore? Would he be in a boat? Would he choose to swim ashore to avoid detection? From where she sat, Melodie could see the beach on either side of the cove's entrance. If anything stirred, she'd know.

Busara had told her he would be there within the hour. It was up to Melodie to stop him from killing Busara. If the old witch died, Melodie would never fully belong to the sea and the inhabitants of the cove would be in danger.

A light breeze stirred Melodie's hair about her face. Soon, he would be upon her. If she wanted to distract him, she had to start now.

Melodie closed her eyes and lifted her face to the sky. When she opened her mouth, she sang the songs of her ancestors. The sirens for whom the cove was named. The sound was of the sea, the sky, the island. Hers was a melancholy song of love, loss, and rebirth.

Her voice swelled and retreated with the tide, flowing over the shore like a breeze. As she sang, she opened her eyes and scanned the shoreline. So far nothing moved. If he was out there, he'd fall under her musical spell and come directly to her. If he were in a ship, he'd run aground and maybe save her the trouble of killing him. But she figured he'd come ashore in a much smaller craft and survive despite her siren's song.

A jeweled dagger lay beside her on the rock. Once she had him close enough, she'd stab him through the heart. A chill slithered down her spine. Melodie had never killed another living soul. But she had to accomplish her goal or risk the death of a great Obeah witch, her friend, the protector of innocents and the only person capable of freeing her from her human form.

Her own freedom wasn't worth killing another person for, but saving the lives of countless others was. But still . . . to kill someone? Guilt warred inside, her troubled spirit reflected in her song.

Maybe she didn't have to kill him. If she wounded him, perhaps he'd go away and leave the witch alone. Unskilled in the art of war, Melodie feared she wouldn't have the heart to stab a blade into living breathing flesh. If she didn't, Busara would surely die. One life for another.

Her song died down to a whisper, her confusion robbing her

of her voice. Why couldn't she disappear into the sea and let fate decide whether she was to be a mermaid or a human?

Because fate and her parents had predetermined her life as part human and part mermaid to spend half her time on land and half in the water. She stared out at the indigo sea bathed in sparkling diamonds of starlight.

Something moved in the corner of her vision. Far out from the shore, a figure slid along the surface, gliding through the water with the steady flowing movement of an eel or a serpent. From the direction it was headed, it wouldn't be long before it entered the mouth of Siren's Cove.

Melodie sat up. What was this? If the creature was the man destined to kill Busara, her time of reckoning was upon her. Not only was the great Obeah woman in danger, but many hundreds of small lives were at stake as well.

The voice that had faded out a moment before, grew strong and sure. She couldn't only think of herself, she had the cove, Busara, and Kanoni to consider.

As her song filled the air, the figure in the water neared the shore and drifted to a halt in the shallows below her rock. Then it disappeared altogether.

Melodie stood and peered over the edge of her rock into the inky darkness of the still water, but she couldn't see anything but ripples where the being had gone under.

Her heart thundered in her chest as she forced air past her vocal chords. Where had the creature gone? Had it ducked beneath the surface and swum off into the cove? Just as she made up her mind to climb down off her rock and check, a body materialized from the water.

He rose like Poseidon, water streaming from his shoulder-length hair, running in silvery rivulets down his torso like liquid mercury. His naked skin glowed deep blue in the light from the million stars twinkling in the heavens. Striding through the surf toward shore, more of his magnificent physique emerged with each step.

Dark, wavy hair hung in wet strands to his shoulders. His gaze fixed on her position. As he pushed through the water, he walked as if in a trance, intent on reaching the source of the music.

Melodie's gaze scraped over bulging shoulders, broad chest, and a muscular abdomen that narrowed to trim athletic hips.

Glorious in his animal strength and magnetism, he ascended the shore like a conqueror. In his next step, his cock sprang free of the surf.

With her breath caught in her throat, Melodie's song choked to a halt.

He was so big, so firm and erect. He stood in water up to his thighs, waves lapping at the base of his balls.

As soon as her music died away, the man shook his head, a frown pushing his brows together. He spied her perched on the rock and moved toward her. "What happened?"

For a moment, his overwhelming size and beauty froze her tongue.

"Who are you? Why are you here?" he demanded.

When he stood directly in front of her rock, she could stare down into his face. Even in the shadowy light from the constellations, she could tell his eyes were the deep blue green of the sea. Then starlight glinted off the dagger in his hand. A more beautiful and deadly man she'd never known. She could fall under his spell instead of making him fall to hers.

She slipped from the rock to land on the sand at his feet. The man towered above her by at least a foot, reminding Melodie of her vulnerability.

"I'm here to please you." *And to keep you from killing my friend.* She pressed her fingers to his chest, marveling at the steely strength beneath taut skin. Easing her hands lower, she skimmed across rippling muscles and down to the triangle of hair where his cock jutted out, hard and smooth.

His lungs filled and released before he grasped her arms, holding her away. The cold blade of the dagger lay against her skin, an icy reminder of his purpose. "I don't have time for this."

Oh, no. She wouldn't let him get to Busara.

Her voice lifted to the sky, in a soft, lilting melody. "You came to see me, to partake of what I have to offer," she sang.

"No." He shook his head, his eyes clouding with confusion. "I came to . . ." His gaze drifted to the dagger in his hand.

"To see me." She reached for the weapon and slid it from his hands.

"No. I came to kill the witch."

She tossed the knife into the jumble of rocks behind her. "No, you came to make love to me." Her fingers rested on the knot that held together the white cotton wrap she'd chosen to wear for her assignation with the killer.

Resisting propriety of the gentile English women of the island, she preferred the light, flowing garments of the native Caribs. Kanoni had loaned her the wrap, but Melodie had put her own twist on the fabric, cinching it over her breasts so that it fell to midthigh. With one hard tug, she had the knot loose and the wisp of fabric drifted to the sandy shore. She stood naked in the starlight, her skin kissed by the night air. How glorious to be free of the constraints of human society, to revel in the caress of the ocean's breeze. She lifted her voice, singing of her joy for living.

The man covered his ears with both palms, blocking out her song.

No.

If he didn't hear her song, he'd get past her and kill Busara. Melodie pushed at his hands in an attempt to open his ears and mind to her siren's spell.

But he held firm.

Fear licked like fire at her belly and she sang louder.

Finally, the man dropped his hands from his ears, and spun her around. A large palm clamped over her mouth, the other reached for the dagger she'd left lying on top of the rock.

With the jeweled dagger pressed against her neck, Melodie fought panic. This wasn't supposed to be the way it happened. She was supposed to kill him.

"I didn't come to make love to you. I came to kill the witch."

2

The siren's song had lured him off course; now Rafe could barely seem to recall what his path had been. What manner of witch had Busara sent to detour him from his purpose?

Her long, golden tresses lay like silk against his skin, her tender lips moving beneath his palm lit a fire in his loins. She'd said he'd come to make love to her. With her rounded bottom pressed against his cock, he could well imagine how wondrous a ride the siren might be. But would he lose his soul to her devilry?

While one hand covered her mouth to stem the flow of her enchanting song, his free hand traced the line of her ribs down to her narrow waist.

She shivered, her body trembling beneath his ministrations. Good. Let her know the overwhelming desire she'd inspired in him with just her music. Let her suffer the longing and unquenchable thirst. If he played his hand right, he could have his way with the sultry siren and still have enough time to complete his mission—killing the Obeah, Busara.

The thought of thrusting between the minx's legs made him hot all over. But to mount her too quickly would take away from his pleasure. He wanted her to lose all control to him. A slow, deliberate seduction was more to his liking. Apparently she didn't know of him or his curse or she'd have run screaming by now. Surely Busara sent her with enough knowledge to lure him away from Siren's Cove, but no information about his true nature. Now, he would lure her into trusting him and turn the tables on her. For he fully intended to kill Busara to break the ungodly spell.

Even with the limited light of the starry night, he could tell the siren's skin was darker than the fashionable pearly white of English ladies. The contrast to her spun-gold hair would surely be remarkable in the light of day and he found himself wanting to wake to the sunrise and her lying next to him. How beautiful would this woman be by daylight?

"If I remove my hand, do you promise you will not sing and bewitch me once again?" He lowered his hand enough for her to move her lips, his other hand skimming over the triangle of soft curls at the juncture of her thighs.

"I promise not to sing." Her voice was breathy, as though she didn't have full control over her words and thoughts.

He dropped his hand from her mouth, although she failed to promise not to bewitch. Her omission titillated his senses with the possibilities and his cock rose to nudge her rounded bottom. With both hands now free to roam, he splayed them across her belly and raised them until they rested beneath her plump breasts. "What is your name, witch?"

"Melodie." She sucked in a sharp breath, her ribs expanding against his palms. Did she feel the pull of attraction as strongly as he? He tweaked her nipple.

Melodie gasped.

"I am Rafe, the captain of the *Serpent's Curse*. Do I frighten you, Melodie?" He liked that her name fit her musical voice and the siren's song she'd used to lure him away from his destination.

"No." Her back stiffened and she leaned away from his chest. "I'm afraid of no man."

"Then why did you gasp when I touched you?" He lifted his hand, cupping one voluptuous mound. His thumb traced circles around the puckered nipple.

"I didn't gasp." When he rolled the tip between his thumb and forefinger, she sucked in another breath.

"Sounded suspiciously like a gasp to me."

"So I gasped." Her head lolled back until it rested against his chest. "That doesn't prove I'm afraid of you or any other man."

He tipped his head forward to capture one of her shell-like earlobes between his teeth, moving so close his cock wedged into the crack of her ass. Sandwiched between the firm cheeks, he hardened into steel. His tongue toyed with her ear before he blew a warm breath across the damp lobe and her neck.

She trembled, goose bumps rising to add to the delightful pucker of her aureoles. Her hips swayed, causing her bottom to rub against his prick.

His hands dove downward. One cupped her sex, a long, rough finger delving between the folds. "Do you fear yourself?"

Avoiding his question, she asked one of her own. "Why do you wish to kill Busara?"

His lips tightened and his cock almost wilted at his reasons, but for the silky smoothness of her skin rubbing against him. "That is my business."

"Well now it is mine as well. As you might have guessed, Busara sent me to stop you."

Rafe nodded. "I'd assumed as much. But you will not deter me for long. I will kill the hag and break the curse she set upon me."

"She cursed you?" Melodie stepped away from him. "You

must have done something extremely dreadful for her to curse you."

"I did nothing more than what was my right as governor of Mystique Island. I asked that she remove herself and her magic from Siren's Cove to open it for ships to enter." He stood straighter.

Melodie's eyes widened and her hand covered her lips. "You would take the cove away from us—uh, her?" From wide-eyed fear to fiery anger, she changed in the blink of an eye. "You can't, you thieving pirate!" She flew at him with the force of a fierce kitten, ready to claw his eyes out.

Rafe grabbed her wrists and held them high above her head.

Her breasts rose and fell with every raging breath she took. She stood close enough to him that he could capture one nipple between his teeth. The siren need not sing to capture his attention. Her womanly attributes had his full focus. "You're right. I cannot. Not with the curse she's placed on me. She's forced me into the life of a fugitive, a pirate."

"What's with you humans, anyway? Do you always take, take, take? Have you never thought to let the innocent be at peace?" She kicked out, landing her bare heel against his shins.

With a grunt, Rafe spun her, slamming her back against the boulder she'd been on when he found her. In another swift movement, he snatched her wrap from the sand and twisted her wrists in the garment. Then he snagged the garment over a protrusion of jagged rocks just above her head, effectively hanging her by her wrists, her feet barely touching the sand.

Melodie had to get free of this monster. He could easily leave her hanging on the rocks until someone found her. In the meantime, the menace could attack and kill Busara and steal the cove, killing the precious treasure within.

Yet staring at the broad shoulders, narrow waist, and straining cock of her captor, Melodie's desire reared its sultry head.

With her nakedness splayed against the rock, she was completely subjugated to his whim. The walls of her pussy dripped in anticipation of him forcing himself upon her, fucking her until she cried out for more.

What was she thinking? Had she lost her mind? "Let me down at once!" Melodie kicked at the air, twisting and turning in an attempt to free her hands.

"No. Not until you get a few facts straight." He stood back far enough to remain out of range of her flailing feet and knees.

The more she wiggled, the tighter her bindings twisted around her wrists. Finally, she quit fighting and rested against the rocks, her breaths coming in ragged gasps. "What facts?"

Rafe moved close, so close, she couldn't raise her legs to kick him. "Fact one: Busara is far from innocent." He leaned against Melodie and nipped at her breast.

The gentle pain reverberated through her body, sending shocking pulses to her cunt. "Don't . . ." When he nipped again, her back arched against the rock, pushing her breast more fully into his mouth. "Don't do that."

"Why not?" He laved the puckered peak with the tip of his tongue until she moaned. "Do you find pleasure in my tongue?"

"No," she lied, pressing closer despite her plea for him to stop.

He laved her other nipple, shoving his knee between her thighs.

How she wanted him to thrust into her warm wetness and take what she offered.

"I wish to know what you meant by 'you humans'? You are human." His softly spoken words tickled her moistened skin. "Or perhaps you are a witch like Busara."

Before Melodie could formulate an answer between the waves of passion threatening to swamp her defenses, Rafe's fingers found her folds, delving between her nether lips.

With a deftness that could only come from practice, he stroked a nub of flesh she'd never imagined to be so sensitive. Biting down hard on her tongue, she welcomed the pain, wishing it would drown out the pleasure of his fingers. "Of course I am human. Why would you think otherwise?" She gasped when he dipped into her pussy, swirling around the juices.

"Most human women do not respond with such abandon, or sing siren songs to lure poor sailors to their demise. Nor do they go around tossing their clothing on deserted beaches."

"Perhaps because human males have placed unnecessary constraints on their passion." Despite her determination to remain unmoved by his skilled hands, Melodie couldn't resist wrapping her thigh around his waist, bringing her pussy closer to his straining cock. She wondered how it would feel to have such a thick shaft plunged deep inside her. Would it hurt? Would she cry out? Would it make her long for more? Would she die before he filled her completely?

As Rafe's lips and teeth blazed a path of fire from her breasts downward, Melodie's body flamed to his touch. Hot searing passion flared within, making her pussy ache. Anticipation of Rafe's final conquest made her weep for fulfillment. "Please," she moaned.

"Please what?"

"Let me go." She longed to run her hands over the hard muscles of his chest, to delve her fingers into his wavy locks, drawing his mouth closer to hers, that she might seal his lips with a kiss.

No. She was there to stop the pirate from killing Busara, not to fuck him, as badly as she wanted to—as badly as she needed to. She'd never given herself to another—human or merman. She'd never felt so compelled to forge that bond to offer herself so brazenly, like any whore in a port tavern.

Busara needed her.

Melodie needed Rafe.

Confusion cleared when the man laying siege to her body dropped to his knees and spread her legs wide, resting one of her thighs over each of his broad shoulders.

Her eyes widened, tremors sweeping through her. "What are you doing?"

"What does it look like?" He smiled up at her, as his face drew closer to her aching core. "I will conquer you, witch, without lifting a sword."

"Surely you do not mean to—"

"Indeed, I do." He touched his tongue where his fingers had been, flicking at the swollen nub she'd only recently discovered as a point of extreme sensitivity.

Melodie's body exploded with a barrage of sensations.

Rafe's tongue disengaged and he glanced up at her, his brows raised, a superior quirk lifting the corners of his lips. "You will do anything I wish, won't you?"

Her body hummed and strained toward his magical mouth. "No."

He strummed her clit again, this time relishing every slow stroke as if tasting of an exquisite dish served on a golden platter.

Melodie cried out, her knees clamping tightly to his ears. "Please, oh please." Were those *her* weak cries? Had she sunk so far into lust she'd forgotten her purpose? "You can't . . . kill . . . Busara. Ohhhh, for all that is glorious and wonderful!"

Rafe chuckled, the sound rumbling in his chest, vibrations radiating upward from his shoulders into her thighs. Then he touched her again, lapping at her dripping cunt, swirling his tongue through her moistness, making her even wetter. His fingers parted the lobes of her ass and traced the tightly puckered ring around her anus, poking in and out. He tested and taunted her until she feared she would surely go insane before he finally plunged his swollen dagger deep inside her throbbing cunt.

As her body peaked and she thought she would shatter into stardust, Melodie was aware of Rafe's muscles bunching to rise.

Now he would come into her. Now he would make her one with his body. He slipped her legs from his shoulders to his waist, positioning his cock at her entrance. He leaned forward until his lips brushed the lobe of her ear. "Alas, you will know my mastery." Then in a short, hard thrust, he slid into her, filling her, stretching her until she thought she would explode, bursting past the thin barrier of her virginity in a single fateful stroke.

"What's this? A virgin siren?" He made to pull away from her, but Melodie clamped her legs around his waist, slamming him home again.

"Please, let my arms loose that I might touch your body as you have touched mine."

"You were a virgin?" He frowned, the expression ferocious and at the same time endearing.

"So, I'm not a very experienced siren." She rubbed his ass with her heels and wiggled her hips, loving the feel of him inside of her. "Please let me go."

As if in a trance, Rafe loosened the ties binding her wrists.

Her arms ached from being stretched for so long, but she wrapped them around his neck and held tight as he laid her in the sand and covered her with his body.

A delicious ache radiated from her core where he'd been and came again in a long sheathing movement.

She dug her heels in the warm sand and pushed up to meet him, thrust for thrust, the rhythm building to a thunderous crescendo. The alternating slapping and sucking sounds combined with low moans. Was it her or him? Melodie didn't care. She rode the wave of glory until she crashed into shore in a spectacular burst of pleasure.

Rafe drove into her one last time, burying himself deep inside her, holding tense but steady as his seed pulsed into her womb. When he collapsed in the sand next to her, he gathered her close. "Why?" He kissed her neck, her chin and the tip of her nose. "Why did you sacrifice your virginity?"

" 'Twas a small sacrifice to save the cove."

"You would whore yourself for a tract of land?" He shook

his head. "I will kill Busara for sending you to me. She had no right." He slid from inside her and stood. "I will kill her for sending an innocent to do her dirty work."

Melodie staggered to her wobbly legs and pressed a hand to Rafe's chest. "She did what she had to. The cove must be protected at all costs."

"Why? Just tell me why." He grasped her waist and held her in place.

"It's not my secret to tell, but it is important to protect it from human invasion. Whether it be you or the new governor, Lord Braithwaite."

Rafe's face suffused with deep red. "You would whore yourself to Braithwaite to protect the cove?"

Melodie hoped that day would never come. "I would whore myself to the devil himself to protect Siren's Cove."

"Then to hell with you and to hell with Busara. I will find the entrance to Siren's Cove and kill the Obeah woman if it's the last thing I do." He glanced up at the formidable barrier of the rocks and back to the sea.

The sun peeked over the horizon, spreading a fierce red light across the sparkling ocean.

"Too late." Melodie smiled at the beautiful sunrise. "When the sun is up, you cannot find the entrance to Siren's Cove. You will not kill Busara now."

"You witch!" He marched toward her, his hands out as if to strangle her.

Melodie dove into the sea and swam out a way, willing her body to make the change from woman to mermaid. As her feet merged and her tail formed, she treaded water for one last glimpse of the man who'd captured her soul that night.

"Come back here." He plowed into the water until he stood waist deep. "You may have fooled me once, but I will return tomorrow and nothing you can do will stop me."

3

_____

As Melodie dove beneath the surface, Rafe could feel the change come upon him. His legs became one long writhing tail and his lower body coated in the shiny silver scales of the mighty sea serpent. Sunlight penetrated the ocean's surface reflecting off those hated scales sending shiny spots of light in every direction with each movement. He swam out to where Melodie had been, searching and yet not finding her in the clear blue depths of the sea. How had she escaped him?

No matter how angry he was, he couldn't help worrying about her welfare. So many dangers lurked in the ocean's depths. Even among the coral reefs, sharks trolled the waters for an easy dinner. What had happened to her?

Until the sun was at its zenith, he searched for the beautiful Melodie, determined to find her and get her back to shore where she would be safe from creatures like him.

Was she safe in Siren's Cove? With Braithwaite determined to take the plot of land for his own, was Melodie safe hiding there with the witch Busara? And why were they so fierce in their protection of the cove that the Obeah woman would cast a curse upon him?

He'd never considered he might be wrong about the cove. Hell, he hadn't bothered to ask the old woman what was so important about the still waters that she felt it necessary to keep all humans out.

When he'd exhausted all hope of finding the elusive Melodie, he turned toward Newport. If he couldn't find the siren, he could at least check on Braithwaite's doings in the busy port.

Skimming the bottom of the bay, Rafe swam slowly toward one of the loading docks, careful not to leave a wake and thus give his position away. He surfaced in the murky shadows around the piers and stared up at the dock opposite his hiding place. The native Caribs carried boxes and barrels up the planks of a British warship. From what he could see, the supplies weren't provisions for a long journey but enough weaponry and gunpowder to wage a battle with any unsuspecting vessel.

"Hurry along, we don't have all day!" A burly man dressed in the uniform of the royal navy cracked a whip, the sound making the workers jump and cringe.

A man dressed in the pompous costume of a man of royal lineage joined the burly taskmaster. Rafe recognized him as Governor Lord Braithwaite, his successor. "How soon until the ship is ready?"

"By midday tomorrow, yer lordship."

"Good, we'll need the cover of night in order to find Siren's Cove." He tucked his hands behind his back and rocked on the heels of his shiny black boots.

Another man in the garb of the ship's captain joined the governor, a satisfied grin lifting his lips. "Are we waging war on the Spanish Main, yer lordship?"

Braithwaite frowned. "Don't be insolent, Captain Jensen."

Unaffected by the governor's ill temper, Captain Jensen's brows raised on his forehead a subtle challenge to Braithwaite's authority on the island. " 'Tis only the Obeah woman guarding the cove, is it not?"

"True, but we know not what manner of trickery she might engage in. I will have whatever treasure she's hiding in Siren's Cove. There is also the matter of the *Serpent's Curse.* Better to be prepared than not."

"Aye, sir."

"Move along! Hurry it up!" The taskmaster snapped his whip over the back of an old man laboring beneath the weight of a gunpowder barrel.

The man stumbled and dropped the barrel. The wooden sides split open, scattering the gray powder over the planks of the dock.

"Stupid fool!" Braithwaite grabbed the whip and lashed out at the dark-skinned Carib. The whip slashed the man's skin, leaving red welts and open wounds. Bright red blood stained the whip's length, the sun glinting off the moisture.

Rafe's own blood boiled.

The governor showed no signs of stopping his brutal rein of terror on the old man, his whip snaking out over and over until the man lay moaning.

Unable to stand by a moment longer, Rafe dove down and a moment later and surfaced beneath the dock.

With a mighty roar, he burst from the water, rising fast and sure, splintering the wooden planks of the dock. Sailors and natives scattered, screaming and racing for the shore. Some fell into the water, while others held on to the piers anchoring the dock to the land.

Lord Braithwaite dropped to his knees, whimpering like a child scared of the monster beneath his bed, only the monster was real and angry.

Captain Jensen regained his balance quickly and drew his cutlass, ready to do battle.

As quickly as he'd ascended, Rafe fell back into the water,

taking the old man with him. He held the man above the water, skimming the surface all the way back to where his ship hid among the lesser islands surrounding Mystique.

He roared with his approach and a rope ladder and spare rope dropped over the side of the sloop. Crew members climbed down the swaying ropes to the water, displaying only mild concern over the fearsome monster. Having dealt with Rafe for the past few months, they knew he posed no threat to them as long as they remained loyal to him and the rest of the crew of the *Serpent's Curse.*

One sailor reached out and snagged the limp man beneath his arm. "Let us 'ave 'em, yer lordship. We can take it from 'ere."

Rafe gave over his hold of the injured native and slipped back into the depths until he completed the transformation. Each time he sank deep into the ocean, his body shifted and shrank. Bones redeployed to different locations until his legs divided and his gills disappeared. Once the transformation was complete, he had only minutes to reach the surface and breathe.

When he breached, he swam to the rope ladder and hauled himself aboard.

"Good te see ya, Rafe." Murphy met him at the railing and pounded his back in a hearty greeting.

Seumus met him with a pair of trousers. "Thought ye might have run into a wee bit o' trouble in Siren's Cove."

"As a matter of fact, I did." *A siren by the name of Melodie.* Rafe slid damp legs into the trousers provided and then strode barefoot across the deck to the captain's quarters.

Murphy followed. "As ye showed up as a serpent, I assume you didn't kill the witch."

"No, I didn't kill the witch. Somehow she knew I was coming."

"Did she send an army of natives to stop you?"

"No. Only one."

"He must have been a big, brawny sort to put a halt to your

plan." Murphy circled him, inspecting his bared skin. "I see no battle wounds."

His skin heated, not so much from embarrassment over being bested by a female, but because of what had deterred him from his goal. Hot, passionate sex with a virgin sacrifice. "Not a man. A siren."

Murphy's eyes widened. "Bless my soul." Then he was pounding Rafe's back again, his face wreathed in grins. "And you lived to tell about it? You are one lucky man." He rocked back on his heels and smirked. "Perhaps I should attempt to find this Siren's Cove. To kill the Obeah woman, of course."

A flash of rage overcame Rafe so quickly, he grabbed Murphy by the throat and raised him from the wood flooring. "You will stay away from Siren's Cove, do you understand?"

Unable to speak with a fist wrapped around his vocal chords, all Murphy could manage was a slight nod.

"Let 'im go, Capt'n." Seumus laid a hand on Rafe's shoulder. "He was only temptin' yer ire."

For a moment longer, Rafe held Murphy until rational thought returned. Then he dropped his friend and shook out his hand.

Murphy rubbed at the marks on his neck. "A bit touchy, are we?"

"Don't." Seumus gave him a warning glare.

Rafe's eyes narrowed. What had come over him that he would attack a loyal friend over a taunt? Had it been the image of Melodie splayed naked against the rocks, her legs wide, her pussy wet with passion? Or the image of Murphy as the next man to partake of her sweet offering?

He shook his head to clear the wool gathering in his mind. Melodie was a distraction who'd set his mind adrift. He had bigger problems than protecting her from one of his own. "Braithwaite prepares to launch his own attack on Siren's Cove in two nights."

Seumus nodded. "I suspected as much. He wants whatever Busara is hiding in the cove. Must be fantastic treasure for him to want it so much. Did ye at least discover what that might be?"

"No." What had he accomplished by his night's sojourn? Nothing. He'd failed miserably. But he wouldn't let it happen again. "I'll go back tonight and find Busara and either she lifts my curse or she dies."

"Are you sure you don't need a little help?" Murphy asked.

Rafe's blood pounded in his ears and his hands clenched into tight fists, but he held his calm. "I'm quite certain."

Seumus nodded. "This time, plug yer ears with cotton or wax to avoid the lure of the siren's song."

"I will." He wasn't as concerned about the song luring him from his destination but the woman herself. Having tasted her honey he was drawn like a bee to return for another sip. Not tonight. He had to break free of the spell in order to fight Braithwaite on his own terms and free the island of his tyranny.

"Kanoni, I'm so glad you're here." Melodie hurried toward the Obeah woman's hut, her belly tied in knots, her body afire with memories of her pirate's tryst. "Where is Busara?"

"She's away tending to a sick man in the village." Kanoni rested her hand on Melodie's forehead. "Your face is flushed. Are you well?"

Melodie pushed her hand away. "No, I'm not well."

"Then sit. I'll gather mother's herbs."

"You can't cure me with herbs." She spun and walked a few steps away, wrapping her arms around her belly. "My stomach and chest hurt so bad I think I shall die."

"Did you eat something bad?"

"No." Tears welled in her eyes and she turned to her friend. "It's him!"

Kanoni's brows dipped into a fierce frown. "A man? Did he hurt you?"

"No. Yes. Oh, I don't know," she wailed.

Her friend propped her fists on her narrow hips. "If he hurt you, Kanoni will do terrible tings to him."

"No, no, he didn't do anything to me I didn't want him to." Melodie's cheeks flamed and she shied away from her friend's knowing look. "He touched me in the most glorious places." Her voice faded off as her mind recaptured the magic of his hands and tongue.

"Is that all?" Kanoni let out a relieved sigh. "For a moment you had dis girl worried."

"Is that all?" Melodie flung her arms wide. "He wants to kill your mother!"

The Obeah's daughter shrugged. "Dat will never happen. She has de magic about her."

"He is a very determined man, Kanoni."

"Determined to kill my mother, or to deflower virgin mermaids?" She smiled and wrapped her arm around Melodie's shoulder. "Come, girl, talk to Kanoni. What happened last night? Did the stars cast their spell on you? Did my mermaid friend fall in love?"

"No!" Melodie pulled away. "How could I fall in love? I've only known him for one night."

The dark-skinned young woman shook her head as if blessed with a maturity beyond her nineteen years "It only takes a moment for some."

"But that's impossible, I tell you." Melodie paced in front of the Obeah's cabin. "He held me captive and . . . and . . . did things to me." Her voice trailed off into a whisper.

"Ah."

Kanoni's lips tipped upward in a gentle smile. "He made love to my Melodie, did he not?"

"Yes." Melodie sank to the dirt and buried her face in her hands. "I thought I could lure him in and kill him. But once he came, he was so beautiful I couldn't kill him. I couldn't. He could just as easily have killed me."

"Der, der, my sweet." Kanoni sat on the hard-packed earth beside her and patted her back. "All is not lost."

"But it is!" Melodie looked up through tear-soaked eyes. "He'll be back to kill Busara and I won't be able to stop him."

"Are you afraid he will come back, or more afraid he will not?"

Melodie stared at her friend for a long moment and then dissolved into even more tears. She hadn't cried this much since her parents died. "How could this have happened? How could I?"

"How could you fall in love?" Busara's deeper voice sounded from behind the two younger women. "Why do you think I sent you to ward off Lord Rafe Herrington's attack?"

"To make me fall in love with him?" Melodie stared at the woman she'd come to for help.

"No, to make him fall in love with you."

"But he doesn't love me! He only . . ." Her chin dropped to her chest. "Made love to me."

The Obeah woman crossed her arms over her breasts. "He will be back."

"Only to kill you." Melodie leaped to her feet and grasped the older woman's hands. "I failed you."

"You did no such ting." The woman's boney fingers clutched hers. "I am still alive, am I not?"

"Yes, but—"

"No buts. 'Tis true. And he will be back, not because of me, but for you." She held her hand up to stem the flow of Melodie's denial. "Oh, he will tink he comes for himself, but he is only a man. They don't always know how to listen to de heart."

"What if he kills you?"

"He won't. 'Tis not in de bones." She tapped a finger to the sack tied to her waist containing her collection of bones. "He will come to know his love for you."

"But we are too different. He is a man. I'm half mermaid."

"You are alike in more ways dan you tink," Busara said. "You will have decisions to make."

"Decisions? Rafe Herrington is the former governor of the island. I could never fit in his world. I've already made my decision. I want to be a mermaid forever."

"You haven't changed your mind?" Busara asked.

"No."

The Obeah woman's eyes narrowed and she fixed a hard stare on Melodie. "Then tomorrow you will have your potion."

"I will?" Melodie's heart leaped. After years of being caught between two worlds, she was finally going to get her wish.

"Yes, now, go. I have much work to do. Play with de little ones in de cove. They love to swim wit' you."

Despite having her greatest wish within a day's wait of coming true, Melodie warred with uncertainty. She looked to Kanoni.

The younger woman grabbed her hands and squeezed. "Trust Mamma. All will be well."

What more could she do? Lord Rafe Herrington was a man. Melodie would soon be a mermaid forever. Their worlds were vastly different. Even if Melodie chose to be human, she'd never fit in his life. Not that he'd made any declarations of undying love. Nor would he.

Melodie left the small cottage and walked down to the cove, her heart heavy with thoughts of her future. She couldn't deny she wanted to see Rafe again. But what good would it do? And what if Busara was wrong? What if Rafe killed her?

4

As night neared, Rafe made his way toward Siren's Cove, promising himself he would complete his mission. If the Obeah woman wouldn't give him the potion to cure his curse, he'd kill her and hope that by killing the old woman, his curse would reverse.

Dusk had melted into the darkness of night as he neared the shore. To avoid Melodie's enticing music, he'd taken the precaution to plug his ears with candle wax before he set out. He moved in silence just beneath the surface until his serpent's belly scraped against the sandy bottom. Popping his head above the surface, he realized he'd unwittingly returned to the same rocky point where he'd made love to Melodie. He should have taken the more direct route, entering Siren's Cove under the cover of dark when the witch's magic couldn't hide the entrance.

The shoreline stood empty, the rocks casting dark shadows in the light from a million stars. He willed his change back to human form, his gaze rising to the boulder where he'd originally found Melodie.

From where he stood, waist deep in the surf, he couldn't see her. Why hadn't she come to lure him away again? Not that she could with the wax firmly in place inside his ears.

Despite his decision not to stop and dally with the beautiful siren, disappointment flared in Rafe's gut. Had their lovemaking been nothing more than a brief interlude free of emotion or longing for more?

Rafe realized he'd secretly hoped for another encounter with the amazing Melodie. He could almost see her as she'd been the night before, tied to the rocks, her dusky skin a smoky blue in the starlight. Her breasts . . . ah her breasts.

His cock grew long and hard and Rafe moaned.

An answering moan sounded from the top of the rock.

"Melodie?" Fear sliced through him as he scrambled up the monstrous boulder. Was she hurt or ill?

When he reached the summit, he discovered his fair maiden lying with her hand tucked beneath her cheek, her hair in a wild tangle around her.

Dropping to his haunches, he bent his head close, his lips hovering over hers until he could feel the warmth of her breath against his cheek. Not until then did he let loose the breath he'd been holding.

The temptress was sound asleep. He could have laughed at his own panicked reaction, but the fear for her life only made him more confused about his obsession with this woman.

She wore the same white wrap she'd worn the day before. In her sleep, the folds had parted, displaying a considerable amount of her thigh, one rounded hip and a hint of the soft curls at the juncture of her thighs.

Rafe drew in a deep breath and let it out. Breathing did not ease the strain on his cock. Only sliding it between the siren's legs would satisfy his need.

Before he could stop himself, his hand reached out and gently lifted the wrap, letting it fall to her side.

Now he could see the golden brown triangle of curls covering her mound.

Melodie rolled to her back, one knee falling to the side, opening her to Rafe's view.

That was all the invitation he needed. He had to have her, had to taste her, feel her and fuck her once more.

His fingers skimmed the silky skin of her inner thigh, running from her knee upward until he brushed against her sex.

Her own hand lifted, fluttered and fell to her belly, inching downward to delve into her mound and find that hard little nub at the center of her pleasure.

Careful not to fully awaken her, Rafe dropped to his belly between her legs and parted her folds, kissing her fingertips aside.

"Ummmm . . ." Her ass wiggled against the cool stone surface, her pussy rising toward his mouth.

He accepted her slumberous offer, intent on bringing her fully awake and aroused at the same time. Slowly, so as not to startle her, he dipped his tongue into her pussy, licking the entrance in a sensuous circle and then tracing a pathway in an upward glide to her clit. He stroked her once, leaned back and blew a warm stream of air over her moistness.

"Oh please," she moaned, her knees drawing up, her heels pressing against the hard surface of the boulder. She raised her ass up moving her pussy closer to his mouth. Her fingers combed through her curls, one hand dipping low to press into her center. "More."

When Melodie touched herself there, heat exploded in Rafe's groin. He should be entering Siren's Cove and locating the Obeah woman. But not until he'd fucked this beguiling siren long and hard. He couldn't get himself off that rock in the state he was in, much less walk.

More determined than ever to have his way with her, he flicked her fingers with his tongue, urging them away from her cunt so that he could replace them and bring her to the edge of insanity.

Her hands moved to her folds, parting them that he might touch her clit.

Rafe slid his hands under her ass, lifted her to his mouth and drank of her pussy, sucking and licking with a ferocity matching his passion.

She dug her fingers into his hair and pulled him closer. "Rafe, tell me this is a dream, that I might never awaken," she gasped.

To Rafe, her words were but a whisper of muffled sound. But he understood and lifted his mouth from her long enough to answer. " 'Tis no dream." Then he reached out with his tongue, teased and toyed with that swollen nub he knew would bring her the greatest pleasure.

Her ass clenched in his hands and she pressed upward, a cry rising from her lips. A cry he could hear even through the wax still in his ears. "Rafe!"

While she still rode the wave of her passion, Rafe climbed up her body and fit his cock between her legs, pressing the aching tip to her hot and moist cunt. "Sing now, sweet siren." Then he plunged into her, ramming his cock in until his balls slapped against her buttocks.

She wrapped her legs around his waist, her heels digging into his ass.

Staring down into her now opened eyes, Rafe rocked into her again and again, reveling in her slick, tight pussy. He'd never known a woman so fiery in her passion, so wanton in her abandonment. The more he had of her, the more he wanted.

With each thrust, she moaned, urging him on, demanding his passion and ultimately his release. He peaked in an explosion of sensations, shooting his seed into her womb in a long shuddering thrust. When the tremors subsided, he collapsed over her, exhausted.

Her wrap had fallen away, leaving no barrier between them.

Rafe took pleasure in the silkiness of her breasts pressed against his chest.

"I didn't think you would come." Her breath stirred the hairs beside his ear.

"Even without your song, I could not stay away." He pulled the candle wax from his ears and tossed it into the sea. Easing over, he rolled her to her side and lay next to her, without breaking their intimate connection.

She hooked her leg over his hip anchoring herself more firmly on his cock while her fingers trailed across his chest to pinch a nipple. "Is it always so volatile . . . making love?"

"I find you inspire such recklessness." He bent to flick his tongue over a turgid nipple.

Melodie's back arched, pressing her breast closer for him to take full into his mouth. Her body shifted and wiggled, as if she wanted to get closer than skin against skin. Her warmth burned against him, making him hard again.

When he'd has his fill of one luscious orb, he moved to the next, lavishing his attention on it with equal diligence. "I believe it will always be volatile when I make love to you."

One moment she swayed and moved to his hands and lips, the next she pushed against him, pulling free of his strengthening desire.

"What is it?" His gaze darted around for the source of her withdrawal.

"I have to go." She stood, wringing her hands, a frown pressing her brows together. And were those tears shimmering in her eyes?

Rafe climbed to his feet and grasped her shoulders, forcing her to look at him. "What did I say?"

"Nothing." Her voice choked on the word and she stared at his chest, not into his eyes. "I have to go."

"No. Not until you explain."

"Please." She jerked out of his grip and clambered down from the rocks. "Just leave me alone."

Before Rafe could leap to the ground, Melodie dove into the sea.

He watched the waves, waiting for her to surface to know which way she'd gone, but she never did.

Damn. He stared up at the stars. What had he done to disturb her so?

Rafe dove into the sea, knowing he had no chance to find her after his last attempt had failed. How she swam so fast, he couldn't begin to understand. Perhaps he'd been right in assuming she was a witch, and she just disappeared.

He wanted to find her and wring the answers out of her, but dawn would soon be there and he still had a mission to fulfill. Transforming to his serpent form, he swam along the coastline using the starlight to guide him. The entrance to Siren's Cove could only be seen at night from the sea. When he'd about given up hope, the shoreline disappeared and an opening appeared leading into a spacious, protected cove.

He'd found it.

Far from the elation he should have felt, all he could muster was quiet determination. He had to make Busara understand how important it was for him to be human and resume governorship of the island. If she didn't, he had no recourse but to kill her in order to break the spell. If Braithwaite continued on his course of destruction, Busara would lose her cove and the Carib peoples their freedom and lives.

As he entered the warm waters of Siren's Cove, he dug deep within himself to change back into a man so that he could complete his task. Not always did his concentration affect the change. To his relief, it worked this time.

As his tail disappeared and legs took their place, swimming became more difficult. He surfaced to breathe and tread water.

Ahead a figure emerged onto the shore. By her supple shape and movement it had to be Melodie.

When he opened his mouth to call out to her, something feathery brushed against his legs. He jerked to the side and stared into the inky waters. Then something grabbed his big toe and yanked down.

Unprepared for the sharp tug, Rafe went under, water filling his nostrils.

He surfaced, coughing and sputtering.

Was that a child's laughter he heard? Without waiting to find out, Rafe struck out for shore. As he swam he felt as if tiny little fingers were pinching, poking and pulling at him.

What was the Obeah woman hiding in Siren's Cove? A new kind of miniature monster she planned to use to infect the sea?

He swam faster until his feet hit bottom and he ran the rest of the way up the shore onto dry land. The tinkling sound of giggles followed. He didn't have time to explore the source because several yards ahead of him, Melodie entered the edge of the forest.

If he wanted to catch her, he must hurry. On bare feet, he raced across the sugary sand, closing the distance before she disappeared down the twisted trail. He was upon her before she heard him and, to keep her from sounding the alarm, he clamped a hand over her mouth and one around her waist.

She jabbed her elbow into his gut, but he held on. He carried her kicking and squealing down the path, eventually emerging in front of a ramshackle hut he recognized as Busara's.

The old woman stepped through the door carrying a small, glass vial in her hand. "I expected you sooner."

He set Melodie on her feet, removing his hand from her mouth, but not the one from around her waist. "Then you know why I've come."

Melodie twisted in his arms and beat against his chest, tears streaming down her cheeks. "You can't kill Busara, I won't let you."

Rafe clasped both her hands and held them. "That's completely up to the old woman."

Busara sighed. "Killing me will not be necessary. I have what you came for." She held out a dark brown vial. "Take dis and leave Siren's Cove. When you return to your ship, swallow all of what's inside. But you can not return to de sea before dawn of de second day, or de potion will not work and you will forever be what you are today." When Rafe took the bottle from her, the old woman waved her hands. "Now leave."

"What is it?" Melodie grasped Rafe's hand.

Instead of answering Melodie, Rafe focused a steely-eyed stare on Busara. "If this is a trick, I will return and then I *will* kill you."

"No tricks. You have proven your worth to de island. Perhaps I was not fair wit' de young governor. Take de potion and be gone." She spun on her heel and disappeared into the darkened doorway.

Rafe didn't trust her. Not after what she'd done to him. If he had any other choice he'd have taken it, but with Braithwaite poised to claim the cove the following evening, he had to trust that the old woman wasn't lying.

He turned to the beauty standing beside him.

She stood proud and naked, unconcerned by her nudity. Her light mocha skin glowed in the light from the torch burning at the edge of the hut. Her luminous brown eyes glistened with moisture and her lips quivered.

He ran his free hand through her silky golden hair and captured the back of her head, drawing her close. With his lips hovering over hers, he promised, "I'll be back for you." Then he touched his mouth to hers, his lips claiming hers, his tongue delving in to taste tangy sweetness.

She pressed against him, her nipples tangling in his chest hairs, her hips grinding against his.

His cock filled and swelled, pressing against her belly, eager to take up where they'd left off back at the boulder.

"I want to come with you," she said against his mouth.

Her words brought back all the reasons he'd sought out the crafty, old Obeah woman to begin with. "No." He broke the kiss and held her away from him, drinking in her beauty one last time. If the potion didn't work, he couldn't come back for her. He couldn't make her wait for him to return. He left her standing by the old hut and strode down the path to the cove, his pace quickening the farther away he moved from the sweet siren. Before long he was running, his lungs near bursting by the time he dove into the cove's warm waters. As fast as he could, he swam toward the sea, his body changing into the monster Melodie could never see. With luck, he'd return as a man.

5

After being threatened once, Melodie didn't dare disturb the old woman until she emerged from her hut. With the sun high in the sky and half the day gone, she'd paced the path between the cove and the hut at least a hundred times. She'd gone for a swim and rested her eyes for all of half an hour, and still the old woman remained in her hut. How long would Busara sleep?

When the Obeah woman finally surfaced, Melodie all but pounced on her. "What did you give him? What was in the potion?"

"Dat is between me and de young lord."

"It won't kill him, will it?" Melodie had never known the woman to use her magic to kill another living thing, but the precious secret of Siren's Cove was sufficient reason to consider poisoning anyone who might destroy it.

Busara frowned at her. "He will get what he deserves when he chooses his fate."

Melodie flung a hand in the air, all patience for Busara's riddles gone with the long sleepless night. "What is that supposed to mean?"

Busara's lips lifted in a secretive smile. "All will reveal in time."

"By Poseidon!" Melodie spun and walked away.

"Where you be goin'?" Busara called out to her.

"Somewhere away from here, where people don't talk in riddles," she flung over her shoulder. Her feet carried her toward the cove, the last place she'd seen Rafe. Before he'd disappeared into the water.

"I have need of your assistance," Busara called out.

"Kanoni can help. I'm leaving."

"Aw, then you do not wish me to make your potion?"

Melodie was halfway into the woods when she ground to a halt. She made a slow turn. "You wouldn't tease me, now would you?"

The old woman laughed. "Busara never teases."

She took a step toward her. "You're truly going to begin preparation to make me a mermaid forever?"

The old woman's gray head dipped in a regal nod. "Dat I am."

After wishing all her life to be a mermaid forever, now that the time had come, why was she so hesitant? Melodie trudged back to the hut and stood in front of Busara. "You have my attention. What do you need me to do?"

Busara reached inside the doorway and hauled out a heavy iron kettle. "Carry dis down by de cove and build a fire beneath it."

For the next four hours, Melodie fetched, carried, gathered, chopped and mixed some of the most vile-smelling ingredients she'd ever dealt with in her entire life. She tied a piece of cloth over her nose, wondering how in the world she'd manage to swallow the concoction once it was complete.

When sun spilled into the sea on the horizon, Busara stood beside the fire and held her hand over the kettle. "De last ingredient is a scale from Poseidon's tail. De only one I've ever found." She dropped the scale into the pot and stirred it one last time. " 'Tis done."

Melodie untied the cloth from beneath her nose and used it to wipe away the beads of perspiration on her forehead. A sense of reckoning settled over her, or was it dread? Either way, she gazed down at the soupy brown fluid in the cauldron. "I guess this is it." She glanced up at Busara. "What do I do now?"

"You must drink a cup of de magic before de sun sinks all de way into de ocean. So if you want to change forever, drink up."

Melodie glanced toward the orb of orange mixing bright colors into the placid sea. With only a few minutes before the sun disappeared, she scooped a ladle full of the foul brew and lifted it to her lips, staring at the liquid. "Are you sure it will work?"

The old woman glared at her. "You doubt the Obeah?"

"No. Of course not." But she hesitated, her mouth dry at the thought of swallowing the nasty mixture. This was what she wanted, what she'd asked of Busara for the past few weeks. If she drank this potion she'd never know the torment of being a freak. She'd blend in with one race, not be caught between two worlds, alone and afraid.

On the other hand, she'd never be human again, never walk on the land, and never make love with a man. She'd be forever a child of the sea. Although she could visit Siren's Cove, she could never come ashore. Her hand trembled and her heart raced, her breathing coming in tiny gasps. She could do this and live the rest of her life in the sea she loved so dearly. *Do it!*

"Mamma!" Kanoni's frightened voice rose about the humming in Melodie's ears. "Mamma, where are you?"

"By the cove," she answered.

Kanoni staggered through the trees onto the sandy beach, her breath coming in ragged gasps, her dress damp and torn. A bright red slash marred her right cheek, blood still oozing from it.

Melodie dropped the untouched liquid, ladle and all, back into the kettle and raced to her friend. "Kanoni, what happened?" She gathered the girl in her arms and held her shaking body.

"De governor caught me spying by de docks and beat me wit' his whip." She buried her face against Melodie's chest and cried.

When Busara moved up beside them, Kanoni fell into her mother's arms. "Mamma, oh Mamma." Sobs wracked her slender shoulders. "I only managed to escape by falling into de water and pretending to drown. I almost did, but for de kindness of our people."

Busara gathered herbs and made a poultice, applying it to the angry cut on Kanoni's face. "What was so important de governor would tink you be spying?"

Kanoni grabbed her mother's wrist and choked back her next sob. "He prepares a ship. Tomorrow he will sail into Siren's Cove and kill you. You must leave."

The old woman patted her daughter's back. "Don't you worry about dis ol' woman. I can take care of meself."

"But he's bringing a warship, Mamma." Kanoni pressed her mother's hand to her cheek. "Even you cannot fight cannons wit magik. You need help. You need someone like Lord Herrington to help protect de cove from Braithwaite's warship."

"Do not worry yourself. Do not worry."

"I have to worry, Mamma. I love you. We must send word to Lord Herrington at once. De governor is preparing as we speak."

"Does anyone know where to find Lord Herrington?" Melodie asked.

Busara stared into the distance, her gaze unfocused in that uncanny way she had of seeing what was not there. "He has gone ashore at Devil's Island."

"The pirate's port?" Melodie had heard of it and avoided it like the plague. Only wanton women and wicked men dared wander into the port. Many men met their deaths by the fearless cutthroats roaming the tawdry streets.

"He went ashore to speak to Glory Hogan."

"The one-eyed pirate who skinned his first mate alive for stealing a woman from him?" Melodie's breath caught in her throat. Rafe was in over his head in the midst of murdering marauders, and Busara refused to evacuate the cove in the face of certain death to herself and the treasure hidden in the cove's waters. Melodie had to get to Rafe and warn him of the danger to the cove and beg for his help. Dare she go ashore on such a disreputable island?

The old woman glanced at the sun fading into the water and turned to Melodie. "You only have a moment to take your potion. Hurry before the last of the sun disappears."

Melodie took the ladle from Busara. If she drank the potion, she couldn't go ashore and find Rafe. She handed the ladle back to the old woman. "I can't."

"This is your only chance to be a mermaid forever. I cannot recreate de mixture without another scale from Poseidon's tail and this is only good for a couple hours."

She'd wanted this for so long, but now, her own needs were secondary to protecting Siren's Cove and Busara from Braithwaite's destruction. "So be it." She untied her wrap and walked into the cove.

"Melodie? Where are you going?" Kanoni called out to her.

"Hush, child. She knows where. 'Tis all dat matter."

Rafe sat with his back to the wall in the Gold Doubloon Tavern on Devil's Island, his hand resting on the heel of his cutlass. He'd come with Seumus to recruit cutthroats and mercenaries to fight against Braithwaite's army of British sailors due to attack Siren's Cove on the morrow. A part of him resisted the idea of opposing his own countrymen. From what the Carib peoples reported, Braithwaite had replaced those against his "methods" with less conscientious rogues, easing the burden of guilt from Rafe's mind.

Thus far, they'd secured the services of twenty men of questionable background, with one thing in common. They'd all been thwarted by the new governor in one manner or another.

Seumus had stepped out to talk particulars with another potential crew member, leaving Rafe tapping the edge of his heavy pewter stein against the stained wooden table. He sat with muscles tensed, ready at a moment's notice to quit the foul-smelling establishment.

A buxom tavern wench sashayed in front of him and deposited a pint of ale, displaying a pendulous pair of breasts large enough to smother a careless man. "Care fer more ale or anything else yer heart desires?" She sidled up to him and ran her fingers through his hair. "I could do a bit more than serve yer drinkin' needs, if ye get me drift." She reeked of stale alcohol and smoke and her hair lay in greasy curls around her head like a pile of soiled rags.

Much control went into suppressing his revulsion. "No, thank you. I've business to conduct."

"I could be a little business fer ye." She pulled the front of her chemise down exposing a rounded nipple large enough to suckle a bull calf.

"His business is with me, so leave." The familiar, feminine voice spoke from behind the rounded bar maid.

When the tavern wench turned, she revealed the woman standing behind her. Flaxen hair and mocha skin stood out in the course establishment, garnering the attention of all the other men. Dressed in a similar style as the dirty tavern wench, she looked amazing and tempting all at once.

Rafe couldn't decide whether he should throttle her or hug her. His cock pushed for the hug—anything to get close to the temptress of his thoughts.

The tavern wench planted her fists on her hips. "Ye think ye can make me leave?"

Men turned at the sound of her raised voice, their leering grins giving Rafe an uneasy feeling and a distinct twinge of something very like jealousy.

"No," Melodie replied in a low, calm, yet firm voice. "I would hope you'd have the decency to step aside and let me conduct my business with the gentleman."

A smile tugged at Rafe's lips as he crossed his arms over his chest. How would she squirm her way out of this confrontation? She deserved a little shaking up for taking the risk of coming to Devil's Island on her own.

"I say he's mine." The wench planted her heavy hands on Melodie's shoulders and shoved her hard enough to send her reeling into a toothless pirate's lap.

Rafe leaped to his feet.

"Now, I see's ye be wantin' some of what I 'ave to offer." The barmaid stuck out her over-large breasts, blocking Rafe's path to Melodie.

He grabbed her shoulders and smiled down at her. "I said no thank you." Then he set her to the side and strode across the floor.

Trapped by the filthy hands of a drunken ruffian, Melodie fought and kicked. "Let me go, you dirty pirate!"

His hands groped the front of her dress, ripping the bodice down, exposing her lovely breasts to the cheers of the crowd.

White-hot rage roared through Rafe's veins and he jerked the pirate up by his matted hair.

The pirate screamed like a woman and dropped his hold on Melodie.

She tumbled into a heap at his feet and scrambled away, pulling the tattered remains of her dress over herself.

Rafe held the man up by the hair with one hand, while clutching his throat with the other. "Do not ever lay your hands on this woman again, or I'll slit your neck from ear to ear and toss you to the sharks."

The man gurgled; his lips moved but no words made it past his vocal chords. When his face turned an alarming shade of blue, Rafe shoved him over the table into another man's chest. Men scrambled to get out of the way of the angry lord, leaving Melodie standing alone.

Rafe grabbed her by the hand and jerked her against his chest. "You're coming with me." Without pause, he tossed her over his shoulder and strode out of the tavern to the cheers of the men left behind.

"Put me down!" Melodie gasped. Between having her stomach smashed against Rafe's brawny shoulder and being bounced through the busy port at Devil's Island, she could barely breathe.

A man with steely gray hair and a shaggy beard joined them and ran to keep pace with her captor.

"I can walk by myself." When he didn't respond, she pounded Rafe's back. "Put me down, at once."

He smacked a large palm against her bottom. "Keep quiet, woman."

"I'll take 'er when yer done with the bonny lass," a man with only two teeth shouted from the entrance to an even more disagreeable tavern than the Golden Doubloon.

Melodie trembled, fighting the nausea rising up her throat. She'd never seen Rafe in such a state, rage burning in the dark red color of his face. What did he hope to accomplish by carrying her through the streets like a common trollop?

Her own anger built. When they reached the docks and Rafe set her on her feet, she flew at him with both fists clenched. "How dare you treat me like a child or worse, a whore?"

"Be quiet and get in the boat." Before she could formulate a sharp retort, he picked her up and tossed her into the dingy tied to the dock. He turned to the man who'd followed them. "The men?"

"Already aboard the *Serpent's Curse,* Capt'n." He waved his hand toward the rocking boat where Melodie stood, ready to climb back out. "After ye, sir."

"I'm not going anywhere with you." Melodie reached up to grasp the pier and pull herself out of the swaying dingy.

"You will sit and hold your tongue, woman." Rafe dropped into the boat, took his seat and pulled her onto his lap. "Let's be off, Seumus before someone decides to challenge us for her. I may be tempted to let them have her."

"Aye, Capt'n." He untied the rope from the pier and stepped into the skiff. Applying his back to the oars, he struck out across the bay to a lone sloop resting in deeper waters.

"And to think I came out here to ask for your help. I'll be boiled in oil before I ask for anything from you." She wiggled in an attempt to shake free of his stranglehold on her body. The movement made her aware of her affect on his desires. A hard ridge pressed against her bottom, reminding her of the things he'd done to her on the seashore, of his cock sliding in and out of her pussy.

Just as quickly as it had built, her anger shifted into an equally fiery passion. She rationalized to herself that Rafe had rescued her from a ruffian. That should count for something. So, he'd been a bit abrupt in his method of removing her from danger, but he'd gotten her out relatively unscathed. She squirmed against his cock.

A low moan sounded in her ear. "Be still, wench," he whispered so low that the other man would not hear.

If not for the man facing them in the tiny boat, she'd have been tempted to shuck her clothing and attack Rafe in an entirely different manner.

Instead, she attempted to revive her anger, reminding herself she'd been treated poorly. She had yet to tell him of Braithwaite's pending attack on Siren's Cove and she still needed his help. "I can sit on the seat next to you, you know."

His hands tightened on her waist. "I like you just where you are."

"Can no argue wit the Capt'n. Yer a bonny lass." Seumus's gaze drifted to the ample amount of skin exposed by the tear in the dress she'd stolen from a laundry line on Devil's Island.

She gathered the edges, pushing them higher, while glaring at the man's leering gaze.

"Tell me, Melodie, why were you on Devil's Island?" Rafe turned her enough to stare at her eye-to-eye.

She swallowed her anger and anything else she'd been feeling. "Siren's Cove is in danger. Lord Braithwaite's preparing an attack as we speak. He plans to invade the cove tomorrow night. We need your help to stop him."

"And why should we stop him?" Rafe's brows rose. "You've yet to tell me why the cove is so precious."

Melodie bit hard on her lower lip and shot a glance at Seumus. "I can't tell you."

"Then I can't help you."

"Oh, you!" She raised a hand to slap his face. But he caught it in his own.

"Are you ready to talk?"

"I told you," she said through gritted teeth, "I can't."

"Guess you'll be my permanent guest until after Braithwaite does his deed."

"If you won't help me, then at least let me go so that I might help them myself."

"No." His answer was flat and final.

She bucked against him, kicking and biting, but no amount of effort broke his grip. When she finally realized the futility of her fight, they'd reached the ship.

"Toss down a rope," he called up to the tall redhead leaning over the rail.

"Aye, Capt'n."

A length of rope fell into the boat and a rope ladder snaked down the side of the sloop.

Rafe bound her hands.

Even if she wanted to leap from the skiff into the sea, she'd be weighed down by clothing and her hands would be useless. She'd drown before she could make the change into her mer-form. "You're a monster!"

He stared into her eyes—his own were black, shining orbs, completely unreadable and dangerous. "Aye, I am a monster, in more ways than you know."

Once again, he tossed her over his shoulder and carried her up the rope ladder to deposit her on her ass on the deck. "Take her to my cabin."

"Aye, Capt'n." The tall redheaded sailor grinned and lifted her as if she weighed nothing, carrying her more like a child than a sack of meal. At least he had more sense than his captain. When he set her down on the floor of the captain's cabin, she turned and pleaded, "Please, you must let me go. Braithwaite will attack Siren's Cove on the morrow and I must be there to help defend it."

"My apologies, my lady. Until the captain says so, I can't let you go." He backed out of the cabin, his departure followed by the soft click of the lock being turned.

With her hands tied behind her back, Melodie had little hope of breaking out of the cabin. She searched the room for a knife, sword, or anything sharp to scrape against her bonds, finally settling on the rusty hinge of a trunk. Dropping to her knees she scooted her back to the trunk and scraped the rope against the hinge. A strand broke and she could move her wrists a little better, but she had a way to go before she could free her hands.

Digging against the hinge, she worked at the rope, scraping the skin off her wrist in the process. Another strand broke. She jerked and tugged her wrists until the rope burned her skin and finally, she managed to free her hands at last.

As she stood, shaking the feeling back into her fingers, the door opened.

Melodie shoved her hands behind her back.

Rafe strode in and kicked the door shut behind him. "Now that we're alone, you'll tell me what the witch is protecting in Siren's Cove."

"No, I won't."

A frown settled between his brows and he marched across to her, grabbing her shoulders. "You will tell me, now."

"I will not." She jerked her hands up through the middle of his, knocking his hands free of her shoulders. While she had him off guard and off balance, she shoved him hard.

The back of his legs caught the edge of a trunk and he fell backward.

Melodie raced for the door, throwing it open.

Before she reached the top of the gangway, a hand caught her thigh.

"Stop, woman!" Rafe bellowed.

She grabbed the handrail and kicked out at her tormentor, landing a heel on his chin.

He grunted, but maintained his grip on her leg, dragging her backward until he held her in the vicelike grip of his arms.

"Let me go. I have to help Busara."

Rafe carried her back into his cabin, kicked the door shut and turned to lock it. After dropping the key into a drawer in a built-in cabinet, he turned her to face him.

Locking her arms against her sides with one of his arms, he brushed a loose strand of hair from her forehead.

A pang of guilt burned in her gut at the angry red mark marring his chin where she'd kicked him.

"You will tell me what secret the Obeah woman keeps in the cove before the night is over."

6

His jaw hurt and he'd tired of fighting her, but he'd keep up the pace all night if that's what it took to take his pretty siren. More than anything, he wanted to recapture the magic they'd shared on the seashore. The ride out in the skiff had him half-crippled with desire. So much so, he could scarcely climb the rope ladder onto the sloop, his trousers were so tight.

After he'd secured his course and set sail out of the harbor, he'd returned to his cabin, visions of lusty lovemaking hurrying his steps.

Being attacked and knocked off his feet hadn't been part of his plan. Being called a monster only brought home to him the need to stay clear of the water in order for the potion to work. Soon he'd be free of the serpent, never to live as a monster in the sea. He could go back to his life as governor of Mystique Island.

For tonight, he'd stay dry in his cabin, with the lovely Melodie to keep him company. Though it would appear he must woo her once again to gain her favor. He tucked a strand of her spun-gold hair behind her ear. Following his fingers with a kiss, he sucked her earlobe between his teeth and nibbled until she moaned, her body melting against his.

"Did you miss me?" he whispered into her ear.

Her back stiffened. "No."

His fingers slipped over the curve of her naked shoulder, sliding down her arm, carrying the torn dress with him. A faded green overdress lay in his way of claiming her easily. "I liked the white wrap you wore on the beach much better."

"Take me back to the cove and I'll wear it for you." She leaned into him, her lips brushing against his neck.

"Not until you tell me what you're protecting?"

For a moment, her body grew rigid. As quickly as she stiffened, her body relaxed and she pushed the shirt from his shoulders, sliding it down to his waist where it hung from the waistband of his trousers.

"Take me back and I won't wear a thing." Melodie stood on her toes and pressed her lips to his, her hand gliding behind his neck to press him closer. Her breasts, free of the torn dress, rubbed against his chest, gently pulling at the smattering of hairs.

"Why wait? I can have you naked here." Rafe took what was offered and gave back, his tongue swept between her teeth to twist and tangle with hers. Locating the laces of her bodice, he loosened them and slid the garment down over her rounded hips. The baggy dress beneath followed until Melodie stood naked before him, candlelight making her soft mocha skin glow.

Placing tiny kisses along his jawline, she worked her way to his neck and lower. "Are you certain you won't reconsider helping Busara?"

"Why should I help her when she cursed me?" He grasped her hands and pulled her toward the bed in the corner of the wood paneled cabin.

Melodie didn't put up much of a fight. "She had good reason."

The warmth of her hand in his and the promise of what they might do in the sheets versus a hard boulder made him anxious to climb between her legs. "I lost everything because of Busara."

"What did you lose? A governorship? A beautiful mansion to live in?" She stopped in the middle of the room, bringing him to a halt too. "You still have your life."

"Is that it?" He stared down at her. "Is she protecting her own life by living next to Siren's Cove? Can she live no other place?"

Melodie emitted a not-so-ladylike snort. "Busara is not concerned with her own life. She takes care of others in need of her protection. That is her way and the way of her mother and her mother's mother. They have always lived by Siren's Cove and always will." Her fingers found and loosened the string holding his trousers up. With a few deft tugs, she had his trousers down to his boot tops.

He sat on the bed and pulled off his boots and trousers. The white shirt followed, falling like a cloud to the floor.

Now as naked as she was he couldn't disguise how much he wanted her. His cock rose rigid and hard.

Melodie's gaze settled on it, a soft gasp escaping her lips. "You are a magnificent man, Lord Herrington."

Part of him reveled in her assessment, the other part stood reminded of his half-state in life. "I will be soon." He sat on the bed and drew her between his knees.

She rested her hands on his shoulders, her thighs touching his cock. "What did you mean by your words, 'I am a monster, in more ways than you know?' "

Rafe's breath stopped in his chest and for a moment, he couldn't think past the breasts dangling within reach of his lips. Did he tell her he was a monster and watch her run screaming from his cabin? Or should he wait until he'd been cured and tell her then? He chose the latter, pulling her close to capture a nipple between his teeth. "The day after tomorrow it won't matter." For on that day the cure would be complete. All he had to do was stay free of the sea until dawn of the day after next.

Lacing her fingers into his shoulder-length black hair, she tugged hard enough to tip his head back, breaking his hold on her breast. "I wish to know now."

"As soon as you tell me what Busara holds dear in Siren's Cove, I'll tell you about the monster."

She chewed on her bottom lip, a frown creasing her brow. "My dear pirate, you have me at a loss."

"At least I have you." He lay back on the bed, dragging her over him. "That is all I care about at the moment."

"Do you only live in the moment?" Her legs parted and she straddled him, rising to her knees. With her pussy poised over the tip of his cock, she had him wishing she'd continue on her downward movement. Yet, she held off, awaiting his answer.

"When it's with you, I live in the moment." He didn't dare live for a future. Not until his state of being was settled one way or the other. Preferably as a human. Until he'd met Melodie, he'd only focused on one thing and one thing only. Returning to his human life as the governor of Mystique Island.

Since he'd met her, he'd realized how much more there was to life than governing an island. Despite his frustration, he admired her dogged loyalty to guarding the secret of Siren's Cove. Although by stubbornly withholding the information, she'd made him all the more curious and determined to learn the truth.

"You know I must go to help Busara before tomorrow." She leaned over him and pressed her lips to his.

In a sudden move, Rafe flipped her over and pinned her to the sheets. "You fail to remember, I have captured you. You are my prisoner."

The corners of her mouth lifted in a sad smile. "You cannot capture a siren. She will always escape you."

"Not this one." He held her arms over her head with one hand while he pushed a strand of her hair from her face. "I will hold you forever."

She chuckled. "Silly man. The only way to hold a woman forever is to set her free. If it is her choice to be with you, she will be with you forever. If you force her to stay, she will never be yours."

"Then I'll make you want to stay." He nudged her knees apart and lay between her open legs, his cock pressing against her moist heat.

"Pray tell, how will you accomplish such a feat when I am bound and determined to go?" Her words spread over him like heated oil, filling every pore of his skin. Her ass rose from the bed, making his cock dip into her wetness.

Titillated by the promise of more, his cock strained closer, jerking in anticipation of being cloaked by her smooth, wet channel.

Rafe moaned and pressed deeper, his moan growing in intensity along with the sensations spreading throughout his body. If he wanted to make her stay, he had to satisfy her needs before his own. With all the control he could muster, he slid free of her.

She blinked up at him a frown forming on her brow. "What? Don't you want me?"

"Is it not evident?" He straightened on his knees and cast a glance at his shining cock, coated in her juices.

She sat up and grasped him in her hands. "Then why the hesitation?"

"I will woo you into staying with me with a little magic of my own."

Her brows rose on her forehead, a smile teasing the edges of her lips. "Ah, the man can be taught."

Though his cock hurt with the need to be inside her, Rafe bent to take one of her breasts into his mouth, laving and nipping until she squirmed beneath him.

When he moved to the other nipple, she gasped, "You do have a bit of magic in you."

"I haven't even begun."

As if to prove his words, Rafe blazed a trail of kisses down the length of her torso, dipping his tongue into her belly button.

Melodie's pussy ached, her knees falling wide to allow him greater access to all of her. When his fingers found the mound of curly hair, she almost cried out. Gently, he parted her folds, strumming her nub with the tip of his finger, drawing juices up from her pussy to coat her highly sensitized clitoris.

When his mouth replaced his fingers, he hit her nirvana.

A cry escaped her lips and she rose to meet his tongue, threading her fingers through his hair to bring him even closer. How one man could create such a firestorm of sensations inside her, she didn't know, nor did she care, as long as he continued what he was doing.

Her head tossed from side to side, her fingers kneading the back of his head.

Rafe's thumbs delved into her pussy, circling her entrance and dipping into the rich cream. He dragged the moisture lower to the tight lips of her anus. Round and round the entrance he layered the moisture, the entire time his tongue flicked against her clit.

Bombarded by sensation, Melodie lost all grasp on time or place, all of her energy and focus on the rising passion and overpowering release sure to come. Soon . . . very soon.

Another flick and she rocketed to the peak of the stormy precipice, teetering on the edge, her breath lodged in her chest. It couldn't get any better than this. She couldn't feel any more intense.

Then he pushed his finger into her ass at the same time as he slid his entire hand into her pussy. The pressure on her clit, the powerful thrust of his hand in her cunt and the titillating pressure against her anus sent her spiraling past the boundaries of reality and magic. Her body convulsed with her release, her feet pushing against the bed to sustain the pressure. Every muscle strained to milk her release for every second it would last.

Finally, she fell back against the bed, dragging air into her lungs. "By Poseidon, I've never felt like that before." Her voice was ragged, as if she'd swum across the sea at top speed.

Rafe smiled up at her, his lips shining with the juices of her womb. He scaled her body until he leaned over her and pressed a kiss to her lips. "I told you I knew a bit of magic."

"Aye, Capt'n, you do." She opened her legs wide, grasped his ass and pulled him to her wet center.

The stiff evidence of his own desire pressed against her, reviving her flagging strength. She planted her heels in the sheets and lifted up, driving his cock into her pussy. "Come to me, lover. Make me want to stay."

Moving in and out, he settled into a sensual rhythm similar to the steady rocking of the ship on the waves. As tension built, his muscles tightened beneath her fingers.

His movements progressed quickly from the gentle swells of the open sea to the violent pounding of the waves against the shore.

Melodie's fingernails dug into his ass, dragging him closer, her breathing coming in ragged gasps.

When she thought she might explode, Rafe slammed against her one last time, spilling into her in a rush of hot liquid, filling her with his essence.

She never knew how beautiful fucking a pirate could be. Had she known . . . well . . . she couldn't imagine it being better with another. Rafe had captured her heart as well as her body.

When he collapsed onto her, pushing the air from her lungs, she knew she could die happy right then.

But there were others depending on her and Busara. Others who could not defend themselves.

Rafe fell to the bed beside her, taking her with him without breaking the connection of his still-hard cock in her pussy. He pushed a hand through her hair, smoothing it away from her face. "You're beautiful, you know."

"Am I?" Would he think so when she turned into a mermaid with her tail and all the shiny scales? Her heart stuttered and a deep ache spread throughout her chest. She had no business staying with him. He was a man, she was only half a woman. He deserved a real woman who could be with him always, not just part of the time.

Her hands threaded in his hair, tugging him closer so that she could kiss his lips. One long, heartfelt kiss to last her the rest of her days. Since she'd given up her chance at being a mermaid, she'd have to continue in her dual life, living on land and in the sea. Her life was one she wouldn't wish on another, especially on one she loved.

A warm callused hand smoothed over her shoulder and down to her hip. "I could stay like this forever." His words faded and his eyelids closed as he dropped into a deep sleep.

His cock slipped from inside her, leaving her feeling empty and strangely lonely.

She lay for a long time listening to the sound of his breathing, touching his face and arms, gathering memories for the long days to come. Of course, she'd have to leave Mystique Island. Now that she knew there was nothing else the Obeah woman could do to change her, she had no business staying. And to see Rafe, knowing he would never be hers, would kill her.

Yes, she'd best leave before her heart broke completely.

Late in the night, when Rafe slept the deepest, Melodie slipped from the bed.

She dug in the drawer where he'd deposited the key and unlocked the cabin door. With no need for clothing, she didn't waste time dressing. All she had to do was get past the men and over the rail to be on her way.

Careful, so as not to wake Rafe, she turned the key in the look. It clicked open, the noise like a cannon blast to her ears.

A quick glance back at the captain reassured her he slept on. Holding the door in one hand, she gazed at him in the last flickers of the few remaining candles. He was beautiful, his naked body flung out across the sheets, his dark hair tousled and his full luscious lips curved in a dreamy smile.

Melodie almost closed the door and returned to the bed. But if she didn't get back to the sea soon, she'd change into a mermaid when her body demanded it. Wouldn't Rafe be surprised to wake to a fish in his bed?

No, she'd be better off leaving him while he had fond memories rather than when he turned away from her in disgust.

The dark corridor led to the stairs that would take her to the deck. She shivered, dreading walking up the steps and risking being seen naked by Rafe's crew. As a mermaid, her nudity didn't bother her. As a woman, her human modesty demanded she be covered in the presence of men. All but one. And he was asleep. If she wanted to get away, she must hurry before someone sounded the alarm.

At the top of the steps, she peeked out on deck. A solitary man stood at the ship's wheel, staring off into the distance. No one else stirred in the dim light from the fingernail moon.

Keeping to the shadows, Melodie worked her way around the railing to where the skiff was tied to the side of the sloop. She didn't want Rafe to know about her ability to transform into a mermaid. Taking the tiny boat would throw him off.

He'd never suspect he'd slept with a creature from the deep. His memories of her would be of a woman, not a fish.

Careful so as not to make a lot of noise, she threw all her weight into the ropes and hoisted the skiff into the water. It hit the surface with a splash.

"What? Who goes there?" A shout rose up behind her, not five feet away.

Without pausing to think or see who was there, Melodie dove over the rail. As her hands hit the water, a cry rose in the night, "Man overboard! No, it be a woman!"

Swimming beside the skiff, she pushed it clear of the sloop, all the while her feet transformed into a tail. When she'd made the change, she was able to move much faster, putting distance between her and Rafe. Now, it was up to her to save Siren's Cove. Once she'd done that, she could leave Mystique Island, never to return.

7

Rafe leaped from his bed at the shouts from up on deck. He knew before his feet hit the ground, Melodie had gone. He didn't have to look at the empty bed or the door standing ajar. Deep inside he felt the emptiness of the cabin.

Without regard to his state of undress, he raced through the cabin and up on deck.

"She dropped the skiff into the water and jumped over the side, Capt'n." Seumus stood by the rail, peering into the dark, swirling water of the Caribbean.

Rafe grabbed his boatswain by the shirt and held him up. "Why didn't you stop her?"

"She was over before I knew what she was about."

He knew it, even as he dropped Seumus on his feet. "Where is she now?" Melodie had proved she could swim when he'd first seen her by Siren's Cove. But could she manage a skiff long enough for them to find her? Could she row long enough to get to shore? They were quite a way out. Only the strongest rowers could make it back. Fear pinched his chest.

"I got to the side as soon as I saw she was goin' over. I only saw the skiff for a moment, then 'twas gone. She's gone, Capt'n."

"No, she can't be." He turned to Seumus. "Bring out the other skiff. I'm going after her."

"Wouldn't it be faster if you were, you know, in your other form?"

The thought of Melodie drowning before she could get to shore, coursed through Rafe's mind, followed by the knowledge his cure would be undone if he chose to dive in and save the siren. She had taken the skiff. Melodie had shown remarkable resilience and an aptitude for getting where she wanted to go. And Rafe knew exactly where she'd go.

"Set sail for Siren's Cove."

"Aye Capt'n, but remember the sun will rise soon. We willna see the entrance." Seumus climbed the steps to the ship's wheel.

"Then we'll drop anchor in the cove to the south until sunset." He leaned against the rails, staring into the dark waters as the gray light of dawn edged up over the horizon.

"What's the stir, Capt'n?" Murphy crossed the deck from the door leading to the crew's quarters.

"I set a heading for Siren's Cove. I'll be getting off there."

"Going after the girl?"

"Yes, and to warn the Obeah to get out before Braithwaite's attack. I want you to prepare the crew. We'll intercept Braithwaite tonight when he makes a run for the cove."

"Aye, Capt'n."

In the meantime, Rafe dressed and paced the length of the sloop until they neared their destination. He might not be able to get to Busara through the cove, but surely he could cross over land and find her. If he had to hack his way through the junglelike vegetation until he did, so be it.

Melodie swam straight for Siren's Cove, arriving as the sun rose, spilling bright pink and orange rays onto the still water.

Little hands tugged at her as she moved through the cove. She didn't have time to stop and play, she had to get to Busara. The old woman would have a plan for defeating Braithwaite's attempt to take over the hidden bay.

"Busara!" Melodie lay on the shore until her tail changed back to legs, then she ran up the path to the Obeah woman's hut.

"Melodie, where have you been? I looked for you last night." Kanoni paused in the doorway of Busara's hut before she ran out and hugged her friend. "Were you out swimming all night?"

Melodie's face burned. "Not quite."

Kanoni's brows rose. "You were with de pretty pirate?"

"Yes."

"Did you enlist his help?"

"No." Melodie's shoulders slumped. Despite her attempts to secure his promise to help, alas, she had failed.

"Why did you not stay until you did?"

"I didn't want him to see me as a mermaid." She hung her head. "He wouldn't understand."

"How do you know?"

"He was governor before he was a pirate. He would expect a woman to be . . . well . . . a woman. I need to see Busara. Where is she?"

"She will be back in a moment. She left early this morning to help a woman with her sick baby. I expected her back by now."

Melodie touched a hand to Kanoni's arm. "She didn't go near Newport, did she?"

"Don't worry, Mamma's careful." The dark-skinned young woman smiled. "She knows how to slip in and out without being caught."

"I know she's a very intelligent woman, however, with Braithwaite intent on taking over the cove, she should be over cautious. He might decide to surprise her outside of the cove's protection." Melodie glanced around the hut. "How long did you say she's been gone?"

"Since before sunrise."

"Perhaps we should go after her."

"No need, my children, I am here." Busara stepped through the trees into the clearing surrounding her hut. "What's this? You're worried about me?"

"Yes, Busara." Melodie rushed to the woman and took the heavy bag she carried. "Since Lord Braithwaite's planning his attack for tonight, I would not be surprised if he tried to capture you before he even enters the cove."

"As you can see, I am fine."

Melodie sighed. "Yes, but for how long? I wasn't able to convince Lord Herrington to come to your assistance."

"He may come around, yet, given time."

"But we don't have time. Something must be done before the sun sets. Braithwaite will be here with his warship and the cove and all its inhabitants will be in danger."

"You worry too much for one your age." Busara retrieved the bag from Melodie and entered the dark doorway of her hut.

Melodie waited for her outside, not having been invited to follow.

The old woman surfaced a few minutes later with an empty bucket. "Kanoni, I have need of water from de stream."

"Yes, Mamma." She took the wooden bucket and disappeared into the vegetation.

"Busara, the cove will be unsafe if Braithwaite showers it with cannon balls. Should we not move the others?"

The Obeah shook her graying head. "No. We will all remain here. All will be as the bones revealed."

Frustration welled inside her, but Melodie didn't voice it. She couldn't just wait for someone to attack and kill the precious inhabitants of Siren's Cove. Doing nothing, wasn't in her nature. If Busara wasn't going to do anything about Braithwaite, Melodie was.

She spun on her naked heel.

"Where are you going?" Busara called after her.

"I have to go back. Lord Herrington has to see reason."

"Be careful, Melodie," Kanoni cried as Melodie passed her on the trail.

Melodie didn't stop and turn around. Instead she broke into a run tossing over her shoulder, "I can't stand by and let Braithwaite destroy you, your mother, and the cove."

She transformed into her mermaid form and swam out to sea, headed for where she'd left the *Serpent's Curse*.

When she arrived, the ship was gone. Fear struck her. Where would he have gone? He wasn't near Siren's Cove. Maybe he went back to Devil's Island. She hurried to that scandalous locale.

The *Serpent's Curse* rested in the busy smuggler's port off Devil's Island as it had the day before.

Melodie swam ashore, trading her tail for legs. What were the chances of finding another dress hanging out to dry? From one shanty to the next she stole toward the Golden Doubloon until she found a drunken pirate passed out behind a building.

After nudging him with her foot several times, Melodie was certain he wouldn't wake. She tugged and pulled until she'd removed his garments. The smell of ale and sweat permeated the clothing and the fabric was itchy, but she didn't have time to look for others, she had to get to Rafe soon and convince him to help the Obeah woman in her fight to protect Siren's Cove.

Swallowing her revulsion, Melodie slipped into the shirt and trousers. She used a scrap of rope to tie the gargantuan pants around her waist, rolling up the bottoms of the legs so as not to trip over them. Then she tied her hair up in a scrap torn from the tail of the shirt. When she was satisfied she was decently covered she hurried on bare feet to the Golden Doubloon.

Inside the smoky interior, she searched for Lord Herrington.

He was nowhere to be seen. Men sat in small groups around

the stained and dirty tables. The man whose lap she'd fallen into the night before spotted her.

Melodie's cheeks heated. Surely he couldn't see in her filthy pirate's clothes the same woman she'd been the night before. A glance down at the white shirt confirmed her fear. Her breasts had puckered, the dark tips pressed against the flimsy fabric of the shirt. She crossed her arms over the evidence and shot a glance back at her tormentor from the night before.

His eyes had narrowed and he pushed to his feet. "There, girl."

Melodie's heart slammed against her chest and she spun on her bare heel.

"Stop, wench!" The man pushed aside chairs in an effort to reach her.

Melodie raced out of the tavern, crashing into a huge wall of male flesh. The man's partner blocked her path, his massive, hairy arms wrapping around her in a shacklelike grip.

"Let me go!" Melodie kicked his shins and attempted to raise her knee to aim at his groin.

With a quick yank, he'd jerked the scarf from her hair.

The thin man emerged, his lips twisting into a smirk. "Look what we've caught." His gaze ran the length of her from her tiny feet to the dark circles of her nipples showing through the thin white fabric of her shirt.

"Let me go!"

"You're the woman Lord Harrington carried out of here last night."

"I don't know what you're talking about. I've never been here before," she lied, though she knew it was useless. The man recognized her. And after his sound defeat the previous evening, he wasn't letting her get away.

Melodie cast a desperate glance around. Where was her knight in shining armor when she needed him?

"I want a turn at her." The giant oaf dropped a hand to her breast and squeezed hard.

Melodie cried out and stomped the top of his booted foot. "No one is having a turn with me."

"Seems you're not in a position to choose." The thin man glanced around the busy streets. "I know someone who will pay for this one."

"You mean we can't have her?" The big man's voice whined and he hugged his arms around her middle lifting her off her feet.

"Let me go or I'll scream."

The thin man laughed out loud. "Won't nobody care."

Melodie screamed a short burst, before a meaty palm clamped over her lips and nose shutting off the noise and her air. She fought like a wild cat desperate to breathe, but the arm around her was like an iron band. Before long her vision blurred around the edges. No. She couldn't faint. She had to stay awake and get to Rafe. The inhabitants of Siren's Cove depended on her to find Rafe and his men.

Darkness edged in until she knew no more.

"Capt'n!" The old Carib Rafe had rescued from Lord Braithwaite's whip hurried as fast as his rickety legs could carry him through the streets of the port on Devil's Island. When he stopped in front of Rafe, he doubled over, gasping for breath, his lungs wheezing with the effort. "Capt'n."

Rafe set his pint of ale on the table he occupied with Seumus and studied the man's progress up the street until he staggered to a halt in front of him. "Yes, Kamau, what is it that has you dying for breath?"

His words tumbled out. "Lord Braithwaite's spies have her."

Rafe's chest tightened, even as he asked, "Have who?"

"Miss Melodie. They have Miss Melodie." He collapsed to his knees, clasping Rafe's hand. "You must help de poor girl."

Rafe shot to his feet. "They have Melodie? Where? When did this happen?"

"At de Golden Doubloon, only a short while ago. I ran as fast as dese ol' feet would go."

"Did you see where they were taking her?"

"They carried her toward de docks."

Rafe leaped to his feet; the chair he'd been sitting in toppled to the ground. "Come on Seumus, we're leaving."

"What about the other men we be needin'?"

"We're done here." He didn't wait for Seumus, but raced through the streets toward the dock.

Why had Melodie risked coming back to Devil's Island and the Golden Doubloon? Was she insane? When he got his hands on her, he'd shake sense into her stubborn head.

If he got his hands on her. A cold knife stabbed at Rafe's gut. Images of what a man could do to her raced through his head making him ill. His pace quickened.

When he reached the docks, he glanced out at a sloop, its sails unfurling in the light breeze, headed out of the bay. As sure as he breathed, he knew Melodie was on that ship.

A toothless old drunk lying on the wooden planks grasped at his leg. "Are you Lord Herrington?"

Rafe didn't have time to stop and talk; he was intent on reaching the skiff and rowing out to the *Serpent's Curse.*

"I'm s'posed to tell yer."

"Tell me what, old man?"

The man's head lolled backward. "Now what twas it? Can't think without another drink."

Rafe lifted the man by the collar. "What were you supposed to tell me, fool?"

"Now, I really can't think. My mouth is vera dry. If'n I was to have a drink, I might remember."

Rafe pulled a gold coin from the pouch at his waist and pressed it into the man's grubby hand. "Tell me."

The old man clutched the coin in his palm, and licked his lips. "That'll buy a pint or two. Yes, indeed."

Rafe slammed the man against a pier. "What did they tell you!"

The old man frowned. "I was gettin' to it. Let me go and I'll tell you."

Rafe dropped the man and waited, his back teeth grinding against each other.

The drunk straightened his ragged clothing and looked at Rafe down his dirty nose. "If you want the girl alive, you have to help Lord Braithwaite. Meet him on the leeward side of Mystique Island at dusk, or he'll kill her."

Rafe's heart sank. Braithwaite had her. "Damnation!"

"What is it, Capt'n?" Seumus finally caught up to him, breathing hard.

"Come on, we have to find Braithwaite."

"We don't have enough men to fight him, Capt'n."

"It will have to be enough." He climbed into the skiff and took up the oars. Seumus untied the moorings and scrambled into the skiff as Rafe pushed off.

Even before he'd climbed the rope ladder into the *Serpent's Curse,* Rafe shouted orders to the crew to set sail.

The other sloop had a lead on him and he couldn't hope to catch it. With only an hour to dusk, he'd just have enough time to get there.

Manning the ship's wheel himself, Rafe let the sea breeze blow the cobwebs from his head. Why was he so worried about one girl? So what if they killed her. She meant nothing to him. She'd left the ship. Stolen into the night without a word. Then why was he so intent on finding her and seeing that she was safe?

Somewhere in the past few days, she'd not only stolen into his life, she'd stolen into his heart. Her fierce determination to save the cove matched his own determination to save the island from Braithwaite's clutches. How could he do it? His sloop was built light for speed. He didn't stand a chance against a heavily armed warship. If he pitted his ship against Braithwaite, it was certain death to himself, his ship and his crew.

What other choice did he have?

The closer they moved toward the final confrontation, the clearer his direction became.

He brought the ship to a halt before they came into sight of the warship.

"Why are we stopping here, Capt'n?" Murphy climbed to the bridge, his hand on the hilt of his cutlass. "The men are ready to fight."

"They will be slaughtered if we go against a warship. I can't do that to them."

"Then what's your plan? Are you giving in to Braithwaite?"

"No." Rafe stripped his shirt from his back and untied his trousers. "I'm going in first. Give me half an hour and follow."

"But, Lord Herrington—Rafe." Murphy laid a hand on his shoulder when he moved toward the steps leading down to the quarterdeck. "You can't go into the sea until tomorrow morning or the witch's potion will not work."

"Do you think I don't know that?" Rafe's voice was harsh, his jaw set. "I've made my decision. Lord Braithwaite cannot be allowed to continue his reign of terror on Mystique Island and especially not Siren's Cove."

"What about you? This was your only chance to return to normal. Would you give it all up?"

An image of Melodie standing on the shore of Mystique Island, her head thrown back, her skin glistening in the moonlight, her eyes filled with a determined gleam. "Yes, I would give it up." To save her and protect her precious cove.

When he reached the railing, he turned and smiled at his first mate. "Do not worry, friend. I find that I can do more good for Mystique Island as a pirate than I ever did as a governor. Perhaps you will be the next governor." He slapped the man's back and laughed, suddenly feeling better about his choice. "Braithwaite will get a surprise he didn't expect."

Now, if he could get to Melodie before they killed her. Once he saw her safely to shore, he'd have to disappear out of her life as well. A sea serpent had no chance at a life with a human. She deserved a real man, one who could give her happiness and children. Not a murdering pirate who wasn't always a pirate, but something much worse. Melodie deserved better.

Rafe dove over the rail into the water. The familiar sensation of his transformation overcame him and he sank deep into the sea. His body lengthened, the bones expanding until he was larger than his ship. Staying deep in the water, he swam toward Siren's Cove and his destiny.

Lord Braithwaite had bound Melodie's hands and set her out on the end of a plank jutting over the deep ocean. They were far enough away from the island, a normal woman couldn't reach shore before drowning. What they didn't know was that she could easily swim to shore, or anywhere else she wanted to go as a mermaid. But for one problem. Braithwaite had dumped a dead pig in the water below the plank. Sharks from all around smelled the blood and converged on the carcass. The resulting feeding frenzy turned Melodie's stomach and struck fear in her heart. With her hands tied and her legs encased in trousers, she'd struggle to transform. And making the change amidst a feeding frenzy would alert the sharks to her as a potential food choice.

Melodie lost her balance on the plank as a wave rocked the warship. She dropped to her knees and struggled to keep from toppling off.

"Where's yer man when ye need him, wench? If'n he does not come soon, ye'll be feedin' the sharks, ye will." The thin man instrumental in capturing her laughed.

Melodie wiped the fear from her face and sat, her feet dangling over the wooden plank. "I do not need to be saved. It is you who will need saving. Mark my words, pirate. You think Braithwaite will keep you alive once he has no further use of you?" She laughed.

The man's leering grin faded and he shook the end of the plank. "Shut up, woman."

Melodie struggled not to fall. The sharks below had the water stirred up to a milky pink, their razor-sharp teeth gnashing at the carcass of the dead animal. How would it feel for those teeth to rip into her flesh? A shiver shook her.

"Leave her be. I won't have my bait eaten before I catch the serpent."

What did he mean by catch the serpent? "Lord Braithwaite, you are sorely mistaken if you think Lord Herrington will come to my rescue. I'm merely a tavern wench. He will not be interested in what becomes of a lowly wench, I assure you."

Braithwaite's brows climbed up his forehead. "My spy assures me, Herrington fought hard to save your lowly arse in a barroom. That's enough for me. However, if he doesn't come for you, then you will become shark food." He turned to the captain, dismissing Melodie. "Keep a sharp eye out for the serpent. Any disturbance in the water, you let me know. I'll be in my cabin."

"Aye, gov'nor." The captain crossed to the rail, stared out across the ocean and then glanced up at the crow's nest. "Anything, Hawk?"

"Nothin', Capt'n."

Before the captain could turn to stare back out at the water, the ship lurched and rose from the sea as if a giant hand lifted it and tossed it to the side.

Melodie slid from the plank and fell into the water near the dead pig, her shoulder brushing against the shredded carcass.

Her heart pounded in her chest and she jerked around, fully expecting the next bite to be taken out of her own hide.

The sharks scattered in all directions as if afraid of something more deadly than themselves.

Weighed down by her clothing, Melodie sank deeper, farther away from the school of sharks. She struggled to shed her trousers to allow her tail to transform. With her hands tied behind her back, she could do little to assist. She drifted through the red tinged swirling waters to the floor of the ocean, her bones stretching and converging. Anxious to complete the transformation, she welcomed the aching pain of her conversion. As soon as her tail began the change, the scales ripped through the fabric of the trousers and the garment fell away. Once her tail was free, she swam to the nearest coral and rubbed the rope across the sharp edges. One by one, the strands broke, all the while Melodie kept watch for the marauding sharks.

They circled above, the pig once again reengaging their interest.

Something long and monstrous swirled around the bow of the ship, shading the sunlight down to where Melodie rested near the bottom.

At least the sharks hadn't found her yet, but what was that up above? When the last strand broke, Melodie swam far enough away from the sharks and yet close enough to study the creature coiling around the ship.

With a mighty surge of monster and water, the ship rose ten feet into the air. Men leaped over the side into the water. With another source of food at their disposal, the sharks set upon them and ripped them apart. Men screamed as the ship flew through the air and crashed against the ocean surface, tossed like a child's toy.

Melodie had never seen such a fearsome creature, but rather

than swim to safety, she watched in morbid fascination as it swam after Braithwaite's warship. Again, it lifted the ship. This time Melodie noted it used its tail to toss the ship in the air. When the warship hit the water, the timbers shuddered and split, the ship breaking apart into a million splintered boards. Braithwaite and the captain were among the many men lost in the debris, the sharks consuming all they came across.

Then the serpent turned and headed in her direction.

For a moment, Melodie's fear held her rigid in the water, afraid to move lest the monster see her. Then she turned and swam as fast as her tail could take her. Her first instinct was to head for Siren's Cove. The thought of the inhabitants kept her from going there. She headed out to sea, as far away from the cove as she could get. If the monster chose to follow her and eat her, at least he would be well away from the cove. With Braithwaite no longer a threat, Melodie could rest assured Siren's Cove would remain protected by the daylight invisibility spell Busara had placed on the cove's entrance.

Now all Melodie had to do was save herself. Before she'd gone far, the *Serpent's Curse* sailed into view.

No, she had to save Rafe from the monster in the water. If the creature saw the ship, surely it would attack and kill all aboard.

Melodie glanced over her shoulder at the monster gaining on her. She had to hurry or she'd be eaten and no one could lure it away from Rafe's ship.

Before she'd gone another knot, something snagged her tail and brought her to a halt in the water. She fought, wiggling and thrashing until she tired and surfaced.

"Damn and blast! Be still, woman!" Two strong arms wrapped around her middle, holding her steady in the water.

"Rafe?" Relief was quickly followed by fear for him. "Rafe, look out! There's a monster in the sea."

"No there's only me."

She turned in his arms, determined to make him see sense

and get back on his ship. Not until she faced him did it dawn on her that he was the only other thing moving in the water.

"Where did it go?" She tried to dive down to search, but Rafe held her above the water.

"Right here, Melodie." He grasped her shoulders and stared into her face, sadness in the depths of his expression. "I'm the monster."

Melodie shook her head. "I don't understand."

"Busara cursed me to the sea. Half the time I'm a man, the other half, I live in the sea." He turned his head enough that she could see the gills behind his ears.

"You're the serpent?" She reached out and ran her fingers over the gills as if touching made it more real. "You destroyed Braithwaite's ship?" Her eyes widened and she glanced down into the water where silver scales reflected the moonlight streaming down upon them.

"You see, I'm not always a man."

A smile lit her face and Melodie laughed out loud.

Rafe's brows drew together. "I fail to see the humor."

"All this time, I thought I had no chance of fitting into your world, or you in mine." She laughed again and flipped her tail out of the water. "Don't you see? We're two of a kind."

"That reminds me. We need to get a few things straight before we commit to anything."

All the humor fled and Melodie's heart hammered in her chest just as fast as when she'd been chased by what she thought was a monster. "Commit?"

"Why didn't you tell me?" He stared down at her shiny rainbow colored scales.

"I didn't think any man could love a fish."

He shook his head, a smile tugging his lips. "But you, my dear, are priceless. Promise me . . . no more secrets."

"And the same goes for you. Busara's curse was quite brilliant, was it not?"

"Aye." His lips twisted into a wry grin. "Now I see why she was so adamant about protecting the cove, I can hardly blame her. She was protecting you."

"And the potion was to change you back to human?" She smoothed a lock of his hair from his forehead. "You gave it all up to save the cove?"

"And you." He grabbed her hand and kissed her fingertips. "Because somewhere along the way, a siren's song lured me to my destiny."

"Am I your destiny?" Her swiftly beating heart took wing and soared.

"Yes." His long serpent's tail wrapped around her mermaid tail. "Ummmm . . . I think I could like this. But if we're to spend a lifetime together, we can not have secrets between us."

"Who said anything about a lifetime together?" Melodie's hands wrapped around Rafe's neck and she pulled his head down until her lips hovered against his. "Do you love me, serpent?"

"It's insane. I've only known you a few days, yet I can't seem to get you out of my thoughts and I only want you in my bed."

"Only in the bed?" She rubbed her bare breasts against his equally bare chest.

A hand moved between them, cupping one of the rounded mounds. "I've never considered making love in the water, but I'm willing to try."

While they'd been talking, the *Serpent's Curse* sailed closer. Seumus's head appeared over the side of the railing. "Me pardon, sir."

Rafe pulled Melodie against him to hide her naked breasts.

Smothering a giggle against his neck, she nibbled on one of his earlobes, happiness building in her like a storm of bubbles.

"Stop that, wench," he muttered.

"Capt'n, what happened with Braithwaite?" Murphy asked.

Rafe's gaze never left Melodie's. "Taken care of."

"Did you leave anything for us?" his first mate persisted, brandishing his cutlass.

"Salvage what you can, pick up any survivors, leave the rest for the sharks and leave me the hell alone." He dragged his gaze from Melodie and shot a glare at his ship. "Go."

The burly Scotsman, Seumus, chuckled. "Aye, sir. Ye wouldna be needin' help with the merlady, now would ye?"

"I think I can handle the situation on my own, Seumus."

"Don't count on it," Melodie whispered against his ear. Then she licked his earlobe.

"Capt'n?" Seumus peered over the railing.

Melodie ducked below the surface.

"I'll catch up to you later." Rafe followed her, chasing through the ocean after her.

She stayed just a little ahead until she entered the blue grotto, illuminated by the reflection of the moon on the water. Inside, she waited for her love.

As Rafe gathered her in his arms, his phallus grew and lengthened into a slick, straight shaft. "Ah, so there is a chance for satisfaction beneath the sea."

Melodie smiled and wrapped her hands around his length.

He halted her hands. "Before we go further, what treasure is kept in Siren's Cove?"

Melodie continued her slide down his length, a secret smile gracing her beautiful face. "Babies, dear pirate. Hundreds of little merguppies. Now can you pay attention?" Her lips slid down his length where her hands had been.

Rafe forgot all else as he sank beneath the ocean's surface in his lover's arms.

Ghostly Legacy

Layla Chase

1

Southern Norway, 1625

Garet the Protector glanced sideways at the beautiful woman kneeling beside him, her fair head bowed as she listened to the bishop's intonations. Long had he waited for this day to come. Three protracted years had been lived since he first spotted Reidun of the Dale at the Harvest Festival and known she would one day be his.

The day of their union in marriage had finally arrived.

The trembling of the wildflower bouquet reminded him of her youth . . . and her obvious uncertainty about the wedding night to come.

That was probably the cause of the uneasiness he'd felt since awakening. He forced those worries aside. Surely, her mother and sisters would have explained her wifely duties. As a couple, they would work out the rest. From this night forward, he would no longer achieve his release in hurried interludes with tavern girls, exchanges that never left him satisfied.

The bishop swept his hands upward, encouraging them to rise.

Relief surged deep inside—the marriage was a fact. Garet held out his arm, his gaze lingering on her delicate features.

Reidun glanced up, crystal blue eyes rounding then quickly looking away, and gently rested her soft hand on his arm.

His skin warmed under her touch, and he couldn't stop the quickening in his groin. Hours remained between now and the time they would ascend the stone stairway to the master chamber and the enjoyment he intended to share in the marriage bed. His body rebelled at enduring the wait. To avoid embarrassing himself with his evident readiness, he would have to keep his distance during the coming feasting and toasting of their ceremony.

They turned and stepped away from the altar, the good wishes of his knights and Wybjorn Castle servants washing over them in a buzz of words.

Garet released Reidun's hand and watched as his young wife blushed and accepted wreaths of flowers from her maiden friends.

"Ja, Garet, you did it. I can't believe the stag of Glomma Fjord has succumbed." Halvor, captain of his knights, clapped him on the shoulder. "Many a maiden at Delling's tavern will be saddened without the chance to vie for your affections."

"You jest, my friend." Garet tore his gaze from Reidun and grinned at Halvor, a friend who had joined him in many nights of drinking and wenching.

"Nay, on our last visit, I overheard wagering on which you would bed first."

Pride ran through him and he crossed his arms over his chest. Garet shook his head. "Your time is coming, my friend. I've seen the way you look at Iduna. Your wedding will not be far behind mine."

A grin spreading his thin lips, Halvor's gaze flicked across the room. "I'm too young."

Garet elbowed his friend. "Twenty-six is not too young and I'm only a year older." He glanced over the heads of the crowd to catch sight of Reidun's golden hair. Just seeing her, knowing they were finally pledged one to the other, kept his blood racing.

"Closer to—" Halvor stilled, his gaze narrowing then shifting to the corner of the room.

Catching sight of his friend's hand tightening on his sword hilt, Garet turned, senses alert. An invader? An enemy among the crowd?

Thirty feet away, Reidun bent her head close to a small man with pointy chin whiskers, her slender hand outstretched.

The air around the man shimmered.

A troll! The hairs on the back of Garet's neck prickled. All motion slowed and his chest constricted. With a hand gripping the familiar rough haft of his knife, he stepped forward. "Rei—" He swallowed hard, his throat suddenly dry. "Reidun, no." He pushed forward, needing to stop her from touching what the troll offered. As he drew close, he heard the little man say, "In your beloved's hand, may your love prosper as far as your lands' outer reaches."

Nothing to worry about in those well wishes. He let out a breath and slipped an arm through his wife's, ignoring the stiffening of her posture.

Three hours later, Garet paced along the stone hallway outside the master chambers, his jaw clenching when each step jarred his aching groin. From downstairs came the off-key singing of those still imbibing in the abundance of ale and wine. On many an occasion he'd been the one to stay until the gray light of predawn, serenading the prosperity of the new marriage.

Not tonight. This was—

The iron latch rattled.

Garet spun toward the sound.

The heavy wooden door eased open, and a dark-haired maid stepped into the hall and then glanced in both directions. "She awaits within, sire."

With long strides, Garet closed the distance. "At last." He brushed past the young girl, only vaguely aware she whispered a few words.

Once inside, he shed his belt and knife and cast them onto a nearby bench. All his attention was on Reidun who stood near the stone fireplace. His wife. Her blond hair shone in waves around her shoulders, hanging almost to her waist. Lit by the glowing flames, the thin fabric of her nightclothes hid nothing of the slim figure beneath. Intent on filling his hand with her golden hair and stroking her soft skin, he strode across the chamber.

At his approach, her gaze widened then flitted to the side and her hands clasped together in front of her breasts.

Clenching his jaw in frustration at the display of her nervousness, he stopped several feet away. He would have to slow his actions. "Wife, undress me."

"Ja, I can do that." A hesitant smile touched her lips and she moved forward with gliding movements. "Of course." Slim fingers pushed bone buttons through holes in his linen shirt, occasionally brushing his chest with their warmth.

Unable to resist, he raised a hand to her hair, sliding the silkiness between his fingers. He leaned close and sniffed the sweetness of honeysuckle, his cock twitching at her nearness.

Task done, she glanced up and then dropped her chin, her hands loose at her sides.

"Take off my shirt." He watched her face, sensing her hesitancy. "And then my breeches and hose."

A gasp escaped her pink lips. "All your clothes? On the first night?"

"We are retiring for the night. Naked is how I sleep."

Brows pinched together, she bit her lower lip and nodded.

When her hands were too slow in their rise toward his shirt, he yanked it over his head and tossed it aside. He had heard men boasting of hesitant brides soon won over by joy at the hands of their husbands. Reidun might be one who is shy about her body. He reached out a hand and cupped her chin, waiting until her gaze rose to meet his. "We are husband and wife. Nothing is shameful about being naked before one another."

A quick nod made her hair swing to curtain her face. "I have been told the instructions."

Instructions? That sounded ominous. "Good, then turn down the bedclothes and climb inside. For tonight, I will grant you privacy in undressing." He turned and sat on a bench at the foot of the bed, tugging off each tall leather boot in turn and dropping them to the floor. Seconds crept by as he listened to the rustling of clothes and the straw mattress, waiting until he heard the bed ropes creak before standing and shucking his breeches and hose. His cock bounced at being released and his nipples drew tight in anticipation of the mating to come.

He rounded to Reidun's side of the bed and slid in close to her side, a hand covering the warm skin of her stomach.

She sucked in a shaky breath and her body stilled.

Something in that involuntary sound set his blood pounding, the steady thrum echoing in his ears. The chase was on. His fingers tangled in the curls over her mons and he nibbled kisses down her neck. After he'd tasted every inch of delectable skin on her neck, shoulder and jaw, he eased back, intent on seeing her eyes. "You like this?"

Reidun looked up, her blue eyes wide and watchful. Like a golden waterfall, her wavy blond hair spread over the pillow top. "I like your kisses." Her quick nod moved the waves and they seemed to ripple.

The beautiful sight before him was one he'd only dreamt about. His breath caught in his chest, and his cock pulsed against her bare hip. The friction of skin on skin sparked jolts of pleasure. "Touch me."

At the feel of hesitant fingertips tracing the contours of his body, he couldn't stop from taking a deep breath to expand his chest. A small sense of victory entered his thoughts. Soft touches trailed down his torso and back up, running along the hard ridges of his belly.

"Get to know me, my body." The smoothness of creamy skin under his hand as he traced her slender curves brought a groan to his throat. His kisses trailed down from her shoulder to her chest, his tongue making lazy circles over the swell of her breast. Stretching forward, he laved long strokes toward the end, swirling around the tip of her nipple.

With a low moan, she arched, pushing her body closer.

Unable to resist her offer, he closed his mouth over her tightening nipple and suckled hard. Each movement of his jaw pressed the tight bud against the roof of his mouth, pleased at the natural reaction of her body to his touch. Between thumb and finger, he rolled her other nipple, feeling her press against his hand.

A moan sounded and she wiggled under his hand, her lips tentatively brushing against his neck.

"That's right, Reidun." Her gesture broadcast her acceptance and his body pulsed with the need for release. He ground his groin against her hip and she pressed back.

Levering himself onto his elbows, he wedged a knee between hers and captured her mouth in a devouring kiss. His mouth slanted over her lips, tasting her sweetness. He pressed her legs apart and poised the head of his cock at the warm embrace to her womanly charms.

Soft hands grabbed at his shoulders and she pulled him closer.

Finally, a response. His large hands cradled her face, thumbs rubbing along her temples, caressing her soft skin. But he wanted more. His tongue traced her lips and coaxed her tongue into following his.

The tip of her tongue met his and circled, and her legs fell open.

Her acceptance heated his blood. He tilted his hips and the head of his cock was surrounded by the tight warm channel of her pussy. Delicious, enticing. His tongue plunged deep and retreated—foreshadowing his body's other impending movements. The moment he'd waited for so long was here. He could finally claim her as his own.

A flex of his hips and his cock moved deeper, seeking her maidenly prize. He stroked, hating the momentary pain he'd soon cause his innocent bride but knowing it had to be.

Under his mouth, her lips stiffened and her palms moved to his chest.

Garet reveled in the feeling of her body moving against his and surged deep, swallowing her surprised cry. He held his hips perfectly still and brushed kisses over her eyes, her brows and her cheeks. "Sorry. Be still a moment, the pain will fade."

"Ja," she whispered. "I understand." Her quick breaths puffed on his cheek and her hands dropped to the mattress. "Best to finish."

In his aroused state, all that registered in his fevered mind was the last word. He flexed his hips into a primal rhythm, stroking into her warm honeyed channel that held him tight then pulling back only to plunge inside again.

Reidun's high-pitched cries sounded in his ear.

He cupped a plump breast, his thumb flicking across the pearled bud. At the point he was inside as deep as he could get, his heart felt at peace. When he drew out, the connection with her ebbed, but the urge to be one again rose high. The heat in his groin flared and he pumped faster, one hand clamped tight to her hip, the other braced high on the mattress.

Hushed panting cries emitted through her lips. Her blond hair moved from side to side on the pillow.

Blood pounded in his ears and through his body, and his breath huffed from deep in his chest. He circled his hips and plunged his cock into her dewy pussy once more, pumping the release of his hot seed deep inside.

Home, he'd come home. He'd waited so long for this union, to be with his beloved as a man and woman were meant to be together. A feeling of lassitude washed over him and he sagged to the mattress, draping an arm across Reidun's warm body. "Ah, my sweet." When he raised a heavy hand to caress her cheek, his fingers slid on tears slipping down her face.

With a rustling of sheets, she turned on her side facing the far wall. The sounds of her hiccupping sobs rang in his ears and echoed through the bridal chamber. A sad sound that tore at his heart.

2

Present day

Truda Borg pulled on the emergency brake and exited from the Volvo, drawing in a breath of the late spring air. With hands braced on the top of the open door, she rolled the stiffness from her shoulders and feasted her eyes on the landscape. Before her stood Wybjorn Castle, the latest addition to Norway's Historic Trust. Set at the foot of a craggy hillside, the castle's stone walls displayed aging typical of more than four hundred years of exposure to the elements.

In her eyes, the castle was beautiful.

Two years of negotiations with lawyers, estate agents, and accountants had gone into its acquisition. As each month passed, she'd felt a stronger urgency to achieve this final result. Now, her task was to examine and inventory the castle's contents. And she could hardly wait. She leaned into the car, grabbed her briefcase and purse, and strode across the crumbling parking lot toward the entrance.

Each step brought her closer to the fulfillment of a personal wish—to walk the halls of a place where her legendary ancestor had once lived.

As she pulled open the heavy door, her hand registered the unusual coldness of the metal handle. Just inside the door, she paused and closed her eyes, the lack of visuals allowing her to sense the air. She let her "sight" reach around her body, hoping to receive a sense of the warrior ghost who reportedly roamed Wybjorn's interior.

"God dag. May I help you, miss?"

Truda opened her eyes and looked straight ahead, only to see a framed painting across the entry. She tilted her head down and spotted a very short, gray-haired man, dressed in padded doublet, breeches, and hose. The pointy toes on his leather boots turned up at the end, adding to his elfin image. Hmm, nothing in her reports stated the private museum had docents dressed in costume.

"God morgen. My name is Truda Borg, and I believe you're expecting me." She paused, watching his face for a response. When none came, she continued, "I'm here representing the Nordic National Historic Trust."

"Oh. An inspection? I was not notified." The little man sniffed and straightened, his whiskered chin jutting out.

"A bit more than that. I'm here to perform an inventory." Just saying the words gave her a thrill.

"I must examine your credentials. Follow me." He spun on the heel of his boot and stomped toward an open doorway, his strident steps ringing out against the flagstones.

Her own steps were slow, her gaze scanning the entry and the various arched doorways leading deeper into the castle. Excitement at finally being in control of this structure raced through her thoughts. No areas would be cordoned off from her inspection. She would walk in the exact rooms where Reidun of the Dale had lived.

At that thought, she raised her gaze to the balconied hall overlooking the entry. Years of study had imprinted the floor plan of the castle in her mind. The living quarters would be just on the other side of that hall. For just a moment, the air at the edge of the wall shimmered, making the gray stones waver.

Her breath caught in her throat. Could this be a sighting? So soon? Hoping for a stronger connection, she let her eyelids drift shut.

"Miss? Are you coming?"

The curator's impatient words broke into her thoughts. When she opened her eyes, she looked again at the corner of the stone wall. No distortion. Just solid gray stone. With a frustrated sigh, she turned. "Yes, I'm right behind you." Get the business details worked out first. Then she'd let the genealogist in her loose to search out verification of her family's lore.

What had once been an anteroom was now being used as an office. A very tidy office. The man sat in an ornately carved chair, his small form dwarfed by the breadth and width of a mahogany desk.

Truda itched to study the carvings on the chair back, anxious to learn if they held clues for whom it had been originally made. Later, she'd have plenty of time.

The curator waved a hand at a chair, less ornate and shorter, positioned opposite him.

After sitting, she opened her briefcase, retrieving the folder with the required documents. One glance at the nameplate on the desk told her what she needed. "Mr. Vegard, here is my letter of introduction from the Trust." She extended a sealed envelope and waited until he leaned forward and took it. "And here is my resume." That paper she placed on his desk. "I want you to be assured of my experience working with relics and antique artifacts."

With slow movements, he picked up a pair of wire-rimmed

glasses from his desk and perched them on the end of his large nose. A letter opener flashed in his hand, and he ripped open the envelope.

From behind her, a puff of cool air touched the skin above her jacket collar. A moment later, the skin on the back of her hand tingled.

An involuntary shiver ran over her skin, and she sucked in a breath and waited. Unable to do as she wished and close her eyes to center herself, she did the next best thing. A quick glance verified Mr. Vegard's attention remained on her papers, so she slipped off her jacket and laid it across her lap.

Her thoughts centered on the entity she suspected had just entered the office. This presence had shown itself earlier than the others she'd experienced. For now, she wanted as much skin as possible exposed. To encourage another contact.

Legend held that the ghost of Garet the Protector roamed within Wybjorn's walls, unwilling to go to his final rest in Valhalla until he learned his answer. Journals from his descendants who lived in the castle attested to occasional sightings during the past four centuries.

Ever since she was a little girl, she'd heard this story of thwarted love, of a groom on a quest to find his bride gone astray. Nana Arnora even claimed a matrilineal connection to Reidun's lineage. Truda's own experiences with love were pale and shallow in comparison to such a legendary love. Against the odds of long-lasting connections in the modern world, she still held onto the hope of finding one.

In waves, her body flushed with the pull of sensual awareness. Her gaze darted around the room, excitement building at the fact she was finally inside the castle. And at the thought of a ghost sighting.

"Do you have additional credentials?" Mr. Vegard appraised her, an eyebrow arched over his half glasses.

"More?" His insolent pose fired her anger and she clenched

her fists in her lap. "Sir, you hold a letter from this country's most honored establishment for the preservation of antiquities."

A screech sounded as his chair lurched to the side. Mr. Vegard grabbed for the edge of the desk and looked over his shoulder, eyes wide. With visible effort, he turned back toward her and cleared his throat. "I did recognize the letterhead. As someone who has served the Wybjorn for many years, I have a concern about the interests of others."

The way he said 'others' made her believe he meant 'outsiders.' Might as well get all the business aired. "About that service." She leaned forward, trying to appear conversational, not combative. What was happening here? "I have to admit, sir, I haven't located documentation of the exact year you were granted this post."

A hand waved. "Don't bother with that." He leaned forward to pick up the other paper and the chair tipped. Hands braced on the blotter, he slid from the chair and moved around the desk, lips tight and eyes narrowed. "Shall we get started?" He approached her side and grasped her elbow. "Which part of the collection may I show you?"

Startled at his erratic behavior, she scrambled to her feet and let him lead her. Finally, her mission could begin. "Whatever is the closest exhibit."

"The armaments or the scullery or the Great Hall." Mr. Vegard walked with purpose through the doorway and turned left.

A tickle ran across her shoulders and she shivered. "Doesn't really matter where we start. I'm here to go over the inventory before signing the authentication report."

His steps slowed. "The inventory of the public displays?"

"You've misunderstood, sir. I thought the original notification had already been sent from the lawyer's office." She hesitated, unsure of how to proceed in this awkward situation.

"I'm sorry to be the one to inform you, Mr. Vegard, but your services will soon be terminated. Wybjorn Castle has been assigned a manager who is a current Trust staff member. Mr. Kirby Alviss will be installed following my authentication."

The little man stilled, squaring his shoulders. "I feared as much."

Empathy for his obvious disappointment softened her words. "I'll be glad for your assistance throughout the authentication process. Your knowledge is valuable to the Trust."

Mr. Vegard raised his head and his gaze touched on the items in the hallway, his narrowed eyes shiny. With head held high, he marched into his office like a wind-up tin soldier.

Probably gone to retrieve a set of keys. Wanting to give the man a few moments to compose himself, she walked to the closest display case and looked at a brass helmet and pitted sword. The fact she'd reviewed the photos of a particular museum's holdings never prepared her for the heady experience of gazing at the real artifacts. A totally different experience.

On her circuit of the entry, she felt faint brushes against her lower back. Her nipples tightened with a delicious jolt. How strange. A reaction to the closeness of the presence or of the cool air inside the stone walls, she couldn't say which. She wanted to wrap her arms around her middle and concentrate on the entity that shared this space. But this was not the time.

Time. With a start, she realized Mr. Vegard had been gone entirely too long.

"Mr. Vegard?" She turned and walked toward the archway, a slight pressure on her elbow as if she were being escorted. That odd thought somehow comforted her. "May I assist you in any way?"

When she rounded the corner, she gasped. The previously neat and tidy office looked like it had been ransacked. Drawers hung open, the contents inside jumbled. On the desktop, a haphazard pile of heaped files slid off one another. But no curator in sight.

Uncertainty filled Truda. Was he that despondent over the turn of events? "Mr. Vegard?" She came around and peeked under the desk, wondering if the short man had retreated there. Not knowing what to expect, she walked to the window overlooking the front garden and the parking lot. Hers was the only vehicle in the lot. She searched her memory. Had another vehicle been parked there when she arrived?

Would the man have left in a snit? Professionally offended at being replaced?

No, another explanation must exist. She thought of the floor plans to the castle and tried to remember another way out from this room. This castle had hidden passages so common for the times as a backup defense. She just hadn't thought she'd have to know all their locations on the first day.

A natural organizer, she itched to set the desk to rights and tuck the folders into the proper hanging files. But she hesitated over causing further offence. Her curiosity rose at the absence of the little man. Where could he have gone?

Cool air whooshed past her face, and she instinctively edged back until her rear bumped the desk. Bracing her hands near her hips, she closed her eyes, waiting for the presence to move again. When she felt nothing else, she spoke, "I know someone is here. I can sense you."

For the count of ten slow breaths, she waited. A faint sound like a masculine snort sounded off to her left, and she restrained herself from opening her eyes. He was playing with her. A smile pulled at her lips. "Okay, remain hidden for now but know this, Garet the Protector, I'll find you sooner or later."

After opening her eyes, she again spotted a shimmer at the edge of an opening. This time, moving near the archway back into the foyer. She straightened and followed, a strong pull tugging her in that direction. Her feet moved almost as if on their own into the middle of the foyer and stopped. Having experienced similar situations in the past, Truda knew to allow the presence to set the pace and let herself be led.

"Garet, thank you for welcoming me. I do feel your presence and you're not going to scare me away." She spread out her arms and slowly turned in a circle, waiting for an indication of which direction she should take.

The hair on her forehead lifted as a cool breeze tickled her face. As eerie as the sensation was, she knew not to show an adverse reaction. "Ah, that's nice, refreshing. I wish you'd show—"

The door behind her clattered and voices sounded. "Come along, Skipp and Disa, this will be our last stop."

Truda whirled and dropped her arms to her sides. "Oh, hello. Um, welcome to Wybjorn Castle." Truda stumbled over the introduction and scanned the immediate area for a brochure to hand these visitors. While skilled at the technical end of curatorship, she'd not worked with the public since early in her college years.

A tall man escorted in his wife and two school-age children. "Afternoon. Are we too late for a tour?"

"Normally the tours are self-guided." Truda crossed to the wall where a rack held papers and grabbed a handful of brochures. "Here are diagrams of the various public displays." As she handed out the brochures, an idea formed. "Why don't I tag along in case you have questions?" Might as well satisfy her rampant curiosity and get her own tour at the same time. "My name is Truda."

"We're the Ingmars. Any suggestions of where to start?"

A gangly boy stepped forward. "I want to see suits of armor and swords."

"We saw those first last time." A shorter, blond girl squared off. "I want to see the weaving looms."

Truda's mind raced over the available public inventory. "I believe everyone will be happy with what they see here. Shall we begin?" She hesitated over making a suggestion. Which was closer—the armament display or the room with household items? A tingle ran along her arm, and her hand was lifted to point toward the east hallway. "Uh, this way, please."

The group turned and walked in that direction, the children continuing their argument.

Out of the corner of her mouth, Truda whispered, "Really. I can make some decisions myself." Her wrist tingled from the contact and her blood thrummed.

The family moved more quickly than she liked, and soon they were out of hearing.

The scenes in the wall hangings captured her attention and her steps slowed. Each tapestry recounted an important event in the life of one of the castle inhabitants, and she loved studying their details. Most of these were of coarser fabric and cruder stitching—maybe created by those new to the craft.

"Miss? Um, Miss Truda?"

The young girl's voice drew her back and she hurried down the hallway. As she rounded the corner and entered the Great Hall, her steps slowed. The family stood before a huge tapestry depicting a large gathering of people. Obviously, an important ceremony of some type.

Her attention was captured by the event on the wall, and she fought to turn her head to the family. "Did you have a question?"

"Disa asked about this weaving." The woman flipped the pages of her brochure. "Where is this one listed in the brochure? I'm curious about the year and whose wedding this depicts?"

Wedding? The sound of the family's questions warbled in her ears and Truda felt herself sway. She locked her knees and turned to face the tapestry. As her gaze scanned the figures and the elements, she had a sense of dèjá vù. The story she'd heard so many times was now before her in muted color and with fine details.

The wedding of Garet the Protector and Reidun of the Dale.

"On that day, she was mine." A masculine voice rumbled nearby. "Truly mine."

Finally, confirmation—the entity was definitely Garet. Air tickled her ear and whooshed at the tendrils escaping her up-swept braid. Pressing her arms along the side of her breasts to mask her body's instinctive reaction, Truda blinked and stepped closer to the family. "Excuse me? Did you say something?"

Mrs. Ingmar frowned and shook her head. "Just the question about the wedding."

"Oh, of course." She turned to face the tapestry, wishing for undisturbed time to study each and every detail. "This is the wedding of a knight named Garet the Protector and the maiden, Reidun of the Dale. The ceremony took place in 1625."

The girl giggled. "Why didn't they have regular last names?"

An area where she had firm footing. "In the time they lived, people were known by the place where they were born or by a skill they had. Garet proved himself strong in battle and earned that title."

The young girl bounced on her feet. "And Reidun was from a valley?"

"Correct." She nodded and felt cool air on her left cheek.

"Protector? My title was a lie."

At the brusque statement, gooseflesh ran over Truda's body. For some wild reason, he was communicating with her.

"So these people lived here for a long, long time?" The woman leaned close, her stomach brushing the guard ropes.

"Less than half a year."

His statement was curt and Truda shook her head, confused at keeping the dual conversations straight. The voice in her ear sounded so resigned, but she couldn't give her full concentration to the meaning behind his words. Not yet.

"Sadly, the castle ledgers don't have an entry for Reidun past the first year of their marriage. A notation states a small company of servants from her parents' holdings retrieved her to tend an ailing mother. No entry exists stating her return." Her heart tugged as she recounted the story. "On a trip to bring her back, Garet was mortally injured in a raid by Swedes."

"Raid, ha! More like an ambush. I was betrayed, I know it."

A shimmer moved along the stones of the west wall.

Truda watched the texture of the stones ripple and wave in succession, and then return to solid lines. As if the ghost paced the floor. Excitement welled in her body. Her other experiences with spectrals had been fleeting. With this one, more of her senses became involved with each encounter. His voice, although raspy, was as solid as those of the family not ten feet away.

"So when that happens and there are no heirs, who inherits the castle?" Mr. Ingmar tapped a finger on his chin as he studied the scene.

"Interlopers, that's who." A shadow passed in front of the tapestry. A split-second image of a tall muscular man in tunic and breeches, hair the color of summer wheat down to his shoulders.

Had she really seen that? Truda gasped, her hand coming up to cover her mouth. Excitement raced through her body, making her womb clench. Was that Garet, the warrior of her nana's stories, the one she'd always imagined as her knight in shining armor?

"Miss, are you all right?" Concern drew down Mrs. Ingmar's brows.

Pull yourself together. Be a professional here. "I'm fine, I just remembered a forgotten appointment. You were saying—

oh yes, about the heir. In this case, the castle was granted to another knight, Ragnor the Fighter."

"Stolen! Stolen by the jackal Ragnor. Thor's blood, woman, tell the tale right." The hem of the tapestry rippled from the ferocity of the warrior's pacing.

Truda's heartbeat thudded in her ears and her breath caught in her throat. Stolen? How? She hadn't known that fact. The ghost was feeding her new details.

"Oh, I see the listing here," Mr. Ingmar read. "A brave fighter who ruled in Glomma Fjord for twenty-five years."

"Mama, I want to see the swords."

"Wait just a few minutes, Skipp, I'm almost done."

Truda scanned the area in front of the tapestry but noticed no additional movement. She watched the faces of the Ingmar family but none seemed aware of anything unusual. As unobtrusively as possible, she edged to the east wall and leaned a shoulder against it.

The events of the past few minutes were unsteadying. The rumored entity existed and, in fact, was present here in the castle. Not only did she sense a presence, but she could feel his touch. When he grew angry enough, he materialized and with quite an impudent attitude.

No question remained in her mind, the entity was Garet. A warrior—a very striking figure of a man—who had lived almost four hundred years ago was communicating with her. Nothing in the household accounts ever hinted at betrayal involved in the raiding party. So she couldn't have known that from another source.

This was new information, received directly from the source. Her head spun with this exciting interaction.

A historian's dream come true.

A roar and a crash sounded from the entry. Truda jerked and opened her eyes to scan the room. The young boy was missing from the gathering.

"Mama!"

3

"Skipp?" Mrs. Ingmar dashed past her, face contorted in fear.

Truda followed, her mind scrambling for excuses for his mishap. When she reached the entry, she held back a groan. Why didn't people keep better control of their children?

Skipp huddled about midway up the stone stairway. Scattered along the steps were various pieces of a suit of armor. A suit that had been previously positioned on the stair landing. On the step above him lay a sword.

Truda unclipped the security rope and let the anxious mother rush past. "How is he, Mrs. Ingmar?"

Murmurs sounded as she checked him over for injuries. "He must have fallen on the stairs."

Truda looked closer at the boy who sat still, almost too still, his eyes widened with fright, his gaze darted all around him. Uh-oh. "I hope he's not injured, ma'am. This area is not part of the public tour." She climbed the stairs and stepped around the mother fretting over her boy.

"He must have tried to lift this sword. The weight was too much, so he stumbled and toppled the armor." Truda looked around, her gaze narrowed at what she thought really happened.

"I didn't stumble," the boy whimpered, "I was pushed!"

"The lad touched what he should not have."

Truda forced herself not to laugh at Garet's self-righteous tone and bent to slip a hand under Skipp's elbow. "I'm sure heavy armor falling on you felt like you were being pushed. Those pieces are made from iron."

"Ah, the lady has a quick tongue. I like that."

At this very moment, she didn't care much about what the ghost liked. "Can you imagine the men who wore those into battle? They must have been very strong to walk around wearing metal plates." She needed to escort these people gracefully from the castle and close the doors to the public. Although she wasn't sure how she felt about being locked inside with a ghost, until she figured out what these interactions with Garet meant, she couldn't risk any more accidents.

"Very strong, indeed. Want to feel my muscles?" Garet's raspy voice sounded near her ear.

His cool breath tickled her neck. In reaction, her breasts grew heavy and her nipples tightened inside her bra. Just what she didn't need right now.

Hunching her shoulders to disguise the obvious points on her blouse, she helped the boy down the steps, aware his mother fluttered at his other side. "Mr. Ingmar, could you bring your car close to the front door please? You'll want to get Skipp into the car as quickly as possible."

Within the span of five minutes, the sightseeing family loaded into their car and it sped away. The swirling dust from their hasty retreat was just now settling. Truda raised a hand to shade her eyes and looked at the green grounds surrounding Wybjorn Castle.

Animal pens dotted the hillside a few hundred feet to the

south with sheep and goats munching on grass. The corner of a vegetable garden could be seen at the edge of the corral. A calm, pastoral sight that was nothing like the atmosphere inside the walls. She made a mental note to check if this site was one established to depict routine castle life. If so, where were all the docents?

For now, she had more immediate problems. Like a ghost who didn't like intruders or having the relics touched. Well, he'd met his match because that's exactly what she intended to do. With one last look around the area, she took a deep breath of crisp air and reentered the castle.

Pulling the door closed, she studied the antiquated locking mechanism then pushed a small knob sideways and heard the reassuring click as a bar slid into place.

No more unexpected interruptions. Now, the task of setting the armor back to rights. Without a photograph or a sketch, she wasn't sure how she'd accomplish that. At least now that she and Garet were alone, she had no worry about appearing to talk to herself.

"That wasn't nice, Garet." She started across the foyer. "That child could have been hurt. Then even more people would have entered your domain."

"Give my actions more credence, Truda."

The sound of his deep voice saying her name went straight to her heart—and her pussy. She whirled toward the voice that came from near the office archway, her gaze searching the wall for evidence of his presence. Nothing. "Meaning?"

"The youth was in no danger."

The low rumble of his voice tickled her senses, making her wish to hear more. "Really? I saw the mess. Didn't you notice how close the sword came?" As a pretense of how she should be feeling, she forced her expression into a scowl. Instead, their argument was turning her on.

"Did you see? The pieces stopped halfway down the steps. I kept the armor from hitting the little brat!" Garet's shadowy outline materialized against the gray wall, muscled arms crossed over his chest. A band of hammered silver encircled one wrist.

Anger brought him forth. Truda thought back to the other incident. The angrier he had gotten, the more substantial he'd become. If she kept him revved up, maybe he'd share other bits of information. "Well, there were other ways. You didn't have to scare a child. Now, I have to set this back—" She flung out a hand and turned, her words dying on her lips.

The reconstructed suit stood in the corner of the landing, sword in place at the knight's right side. He'd fixed it. That was a nice gesture on his part.

No! She couldn't go soft. If she did, he'd disappear. The man intrigued her and she wanted to see all of him. And find out what he meant by asking her if she wanted to feel his muscles. A trembling went through her insides. Could that be possible?

"Garet the Protector, you are given fair warning." She jammed her hands on her hips. "I'm here at Wybjorn to discover its secrets. I'll be digging into all the corners and opening every drawer."

Cool air blasted her left side and ruffled her hair.

"You're one of those secrets." She followed the path of rippling tapestries down the hall. "I've come to learn all there is to know about the life here at Wybjorn. Especially I've come to learn about Reidun."

"Do not speak her name."

A shadow moved at her left side. At the vehemence in his tone, she hesitated, then moved forward as she caught sight of powerful thighs clad in breeches matching her stride. "I must. The mystery will be solved." She'd reached the Great Hall and approached the tapestry, her gaze drawn to the tall figure in the center of the detailed weaving. Had the weaver been skilled enough to accurately capture his features? "I want to discover why a bride left and was never heard of again."

Air buffeted her face and she sensed him storming past her in a frenzy of pacing. Revealing her family connection to his lost bride didn't seem wise. She gazed around this end of the hall but couldn't catch a shimmer against the wall or see the tapestry move. "Why was a strong fighter like yourself lost in a border raid?"

Suddenly, all around her the air was still. Too still. The silence unnerved her. Where had he gone? Had she stepped over an unknown boundary and sent him away?

"Do you not listen, woman? I suspected a traitor in my company," he bellowed. The shadowy outline of his tall form stalked toward her, blue eyes blazing.

A thrill at seeing more details of the Norse warrior sent shivers over her skin. His forehead was broad, his nose aquiline and his whiskered jaw strong. Telling herself she couldn't show weakness, she lifted her chin and waited. "But you'd survived so many other attacks."

"You have come to taunt me with my shame?"

The words were spoken in a voice as dry and brittle as old parchment. As his words faded, so did his image. She spun in a slow circle, her gaze searching for him in every corner of the hall. When she closed her eyes and quieted her thoughts, she could tell he'd left. Her heartbeat returned to normal. A wave of loneliness washed through her and she wrapped her arms around her stomach.

Garet moved through the now-quiet halls of his home, his castle. His prison. Probably sulky to have withdrawn, but his routine had been disrupted. The languid snoozing he normally enjoyed fit his mood better than having to confront a nosy, opinionated woman who trespassed in his castle.

The same woman he could not clear from his thoughts. Her first challenge of the little troll who kept watch inside Wybjorn brought him to awareness and then piqued his interest. Closer inspection displayed a handsome woman in drab modern clothing. Normally, the display of creamy skin exposed by short skirts and absent sleeves caused no reaction. But combine that with the fire in this woman's green eyes and her willingness to confront him, and he was intrigued.

Intrigue bled into interest and now he prowled the hallways, looking for where she'd gone. The strange conveyance of shiny metal remained in what had once been the courtyard.

He wandered from room to room, curiosity driving his feet forward. After looking in all the common rooms, he ascended the stairs to the private ones, and eliminated all but the master chamber. With a rueful shake of his head, he slipped through the door left slightly ajar. How dare the invader choose his private quarters as the place to settle! He crossed his arms and glared at the intruder but she gave no reaction.

She lay across the mattress of the canopy bed, and her shapely chest rose and fell in steady rhythm. A shaft of moonlight slanted through the open fenestral window. The muted light made her skin glow and ripples of her blond hair covering the pillow shone like spun gold.

At the realization she slept, he allowed his gaze to take in the changes her presence brought to his room. A strange case lay open on the chest at the foot of the bed, clothing folded inside. Perched on a stool near the bureau sat a smaller case. He had no reference of usage for numerous small vials and bottles or their colorful contents.

After several minutes of struggling to remain indignant, he shrugged and approached the side of the bed. The rasp of another's breathing within these four walls was strange. Her quiet, whispery sounds rolled around his ears. With a shake of his head, he couldn't deny he'd missed that sweet sound.

His gaze moved slowly over her body, and he wished that his hand could replicate the movement. Ah, to feel the rounded curves of a woman's body, to smell the herbs used in the toilette, to taste the tang of ripening arousal. All these were denied him and had been for so long, that an almost forgotten part deep inside ached with regret.

Unable to resist, he slid a knee onto the mattress, watching her face for any sign of disturbance. Only the slightest rustle of the straw filling sounded. When she didn't move, he stretched out full-length, leaving a hand's span distance between their bodies. As the minutes passed, he studied her profile, how her nose tipped up at the very end, how her eyelashes cast shadows on her cheeks, and how her lips pursed a bit when she breathed out.

Unable to resist, he stretched out a shadowy hand and held it over her open mouth, hoping to feel the movement of her breath. Nothing.

Damn, I wanted to feel that.

Truda rolled toward the middle of the bed and mumbled, "Mmm, to feel that."

Surprise shot through Garet and he studied her face to see if her eyes were open. No, still closed. Although he knew the outcome, he lifted a hand and with a forefinger, outlined her perfectly shaped eyebrow and caressed the fullness of her cheek. He watched his hand touch her face, yet he felt nothing. No sensations registered on his skin.

Her hand rose to brush her cheek and she shifted on the bed. "Garet?"

He jerked at the sound of his name coming from her lips. Why would she speak his name? Was he in her dreams?

Her head moved on the pillow, and the sheets rustled. She

raised an arm over her head, and the front of her night rail gaped, exposing the shadowy hint of a rounded breast. Rounder than he'd expected for a woman with little extra flesh on her frame. The sight made him yearn for what he could not have. For what he did not deserve. A man too rough with an inexperienced young bride wasn't granted wishes, or second chances.

From deep in his chest came the urge to see her nipple. To see the pink tip of her creamy breast. He'd always enjoyed the texturing as the nipple tightened into a bud under the attention of his fingers or his tongue.

She stirred and her hand lowered to the buttons and one, two, three, her night rail was open almost to the waist.

Why had she done that? Could she be hearing his thoughts while she slept?

In amazement, he watched while she eased the fabric to one side and exposed a breast to the moonlight. His mouth went dry.

Perfection. If ever a perfect breast existed, this was it. Plump enough to fill a man's hand but not overly so. Tipped with a pink aureole that reminded him of a berry perched on top. He wanted to cup her breast and stroke a thumb from the outside toward the darker flesh, approaching but stopping just shy of the tip. To make her squirm with wanting until he did caress the sensitive end.

Truda's hands lifted to her breasts and mimicked the actions of his thoughts. Both thumbs slid along her skin, rubbing in slow strokes, but no further than the aureole. "Mmm." Her legs shifted on the mattress, turning first toward her right side then toward her left.

Unable to believe what he was seeing, Garet could not resist pushing for more. He thought of the next step, of how he'd roll the tips between a thumb and forefinger. And then watch as the pink tip lengthened and puckered tight into a hard bud.

Supple hands shifted and moved to the tips of her nipples, slender fingers rolling the pearled tips. A moan built from low in her throat and escaped. Her legs pressed together, capturing the lightweight fabric between clenched muscles.

A faint ache throbbed through him. The sight of a woman pleasuring herself was one he'd thought not to see again. Did he dare? Although he did not understand how, Garet could only conclude the woman acted as if directed by his thoughts.

He was a warrior. He didn't quail at obstacles but met them head-on. Again, he let his gaze take in the length of her slender body. Gauzy nightclothes shrouded her curves and lay partially opened, exposing her taut belly and full breasts.

The thought that he wanted to possess her flashed through his mind—that he wanted to caress every inch of her body. To learn every curve and indentation, every freckle and every scar so that he might think that he knew this woman Truda.

As soon as his thought ended, he saw her hands run over her own body, pausing over a jagged scar on her elbow and a row of raised freckles on her shoulder blade.

Wrong as his actions may have been, Garet was not able to stop himself. Too many decades, centuries even, had passed since his thoughts were other than what to do next to bother the little troll of a man who'd most recently been guarding his possessions. In this woman, he sensed one who was interested in knowing of his life, his past.

From what she'd told Vegard, she intended to search through the castle holdings. The idea of sharing the castle caused him no alarm. A task that would involve several days of work to complete. And several nights.

With growing awareness, he watched her hands smooth over the skin on her breasts, caressing.

Show me your muff, Truda. Let me see your womanly treasures.

A little smile touched her lips. "My treasures." She wiggled her hips and shoved at the fabric, displaying short brown curls at the juncture of her slim thighs.

A cropped thatch, ja? Easier to spot the little nubbin of delight. Curiosity at seeing her female petals overtook his enjoyment of her breasts, and he slid off the bed and walked around to the footboard. *Now, spread your legs and touch your folds. Slide a finger inside and drag it out across your clitty.* He watched as first one and then two fingers disappeared inside, reappeared and plunged back inside. Her pussy glistened with dewy juices and the moonlight caught the reddening of her folds.

Truda's breath gasped in and her other hand tweaked her nipple. "Ah, ah . . ."

Garet loved that sound, the one when a woman's excitement was climbing, and her body's natural reactions were taking over. He watched her head toss back and forth on the pillow and her toes curled as if she fought the sensations building in her body. With one last glance at her hand working her silky petals, he climbed onto the mattress, hearing the straw crinkle beneath his weight.

Lying beside her, he urged, *Relax and let your body take over. Let your fingers touch you in places I wish I could but don't dare. You are beautiful and enchanting and full of life. Take this enjoyment. Relish this act. Feel the life force well from deep within.*

He stiffened and jumped to the floor. Why had those thoughts flowed into his mind? An honorable man would not presume to invade her privacy.

A connection with this woman would serve no purpose. She had entered the castle through the front door and, when her duties were completed, would leave the same way. A feat even a strong warrior like himself had not accomplished in several centuries—no matter which avenue he'd chosen.

She moaned and the mattress crinkled from her frenzied movements.

With a last glance over his shoulder, one final lingering look at the woman caught in a silvery beam, he clenched his jaw and strode through the doorway. The raw cry of his name stilled his movement—but only for a second. Fists clenched at his sides, he took two more long strides and turned a corner, leaving behind an empty hallway.

The rumblings of his deep voice stopped. No more praise to bolster her ego and encourage her brazen acts. Truda listened for a repeat of the words that set her heart singing and her body aflame. "Garet?"

No deep voice answered her call, but she couldn't ignore the rhythms racing through her body. Her nipples tingled and her womb clenched. The pressure in her pussy spiraled higher and she pressed her thighs together, trapping her hand. Positioning a hand over her mons, she captured her clit between two fingers and massaged, alternately squeezing and releasing the tight bud.

Rubbing harder, her hand circled over her pussy, dipping her middle finger into her moist channel, wishing the finger was broader and rougher and belonged to the warrior knight she'd spotted in the Great Hall earlier that day. Just the memory of that man stalking across the room, his blue-eyed gaze capturing hers, bulging muscles tensing and releasing with each step, sent her over the edge. She arched off the mattress, her climax coming with hard pulses. "Ah, ah, ahh!"

Her cry of release brought her to wakefulness and she dragged open her eyes. Quick glances toward all four corners of the room confirmed what her heart already knew—she was alone. Fast, panting breaths provided essential oxygen, and the pulses in her pussy simmered to an occasional jolt.

Blood still raced through her system, echoing in her ears and making her skin tingle. Achieving pleasure without her sex toys hadn't been necessary for a long time. As her body relaxed and her breathing slowed, she registered another emotion—the ache deep inside from his absence.

Had her excitement summoned him to her side?

She remembered his encouraging tone, but not the exact words he'd spoken. Had he been the one to plant the idea for the carnal escapade?

4

The next morning, Truda stood in front of the mirror and brushed her hair, still damp from her morning bath. She finger parted it into three sections, ready to braid it.

Leave it down.

Goose bumps ran along her shoulders at the voice rumbling in her head. The same one that had encouraged her wanton behavior during the night, the one that told her she was beautiful. She ran her gaze around the space behind her but could detect no evidence of his presence. No shimmering lines or shadowy figures.

A wave of disappointment ran through her. Since wakening, she'd hoped for a glimpse of the man responsible for her sexual satiation. A feeling so rare in her current life.

"Maybe I'll leave it down." She gave her head a shake, feeling the waves bounce around her neck. "No stuffed shirts to impress, no serious image to maintain." This was definitely a different look—softer, more romantic.

"Good enough for a shopping trip to the village." To test if she could force Garet to show himself, she ran hands down her hips and turned one way, then the other to check the fit of her slacks over her ass.

A strained groan sounded then was quickly muffled.

Triumph shot through her. This was looking to be a fine day for research. She grabbed her purse and strode from the room, curious if Garet would follow or show himself before she left on her excursion to town. Since Wybjorn would be her home base for a while, she needed to stock food.

As she descended the stairs, she gazed around the entry, ending with the sturdy castle door. The door that she'd locked from the inside. Irritation crossed her thoughts, and her feet scraped to a stop. "Damn, I can't leave. There's no key."

A detour to the office brought her into the disarray left behind from Mr. Vegard's hasty retreat. Yesterday, she'd only had time to sort through about half of the files before tiredness overtook her, and she'd climbed the stairs in search of a comfortable bed. From that quick perusal, she'd learned the man had been thorough in cross-referencing data.

"Garet, are you here?" She shifted her attention to the large desk, muttering, "Where did someone as logical as the curator keep the main key to the castle?" After an exhaustive search, she wandered over to the chair in front of the computer and jiggled the mouse. Maybe a list was stored here. A screen popped up that asked for the password. Hmm, this could take a while.

From an outside pocket of her purse, she pulled a sack of trail mix and plopped into the chair. Vegard obviously doted on the castle, its inhabitants and its possessions. "What would he have chosen for a password?" She flexed her fingers in the air over the keyboard, then typed in several variations of names of rulers, lords, years of famous battles or events. As she worked, she scribbled a list of attempted combinations on a scratch pad beside the mouse.

Her stomach rumbled and she glanced at the clock on the wall. No wonder. Two hours had passed. The list had grown to two pages. Enough guessing for now. She stood and swayed, raising a hand to her forehead. "I've got to get protein. And soon."

Throwing out an arm for balance, she teetered. A pressure along her right side steadied her until she clamped a hand onto the back of the chair. "Thanks, Garet. I knew you were here. What I really need is help in finding a key to the front door. I don't want to be a rude guest and leave the door unlocked when I leave for supplies." She waited to the count of twenty, hoping for his cooperation. Deep down, she knew she looked for a sign he accepted her presence.

When no helpful clues crossed her mind, she lifted her purse onto her shoulder and headed deep into the castle. "Okay, I'll just have to use a back exit. But I am leaving." She breezed through the doorway and disappeared.

Garet clenched his jaw and planted his feet to keep from following her. He would not expend effort to help her leave the castle. Abandoning him was her choice.

Earlier this morning, waiting outside his chamber for her to emerge had been trying enough. The sounds of running water and the soft splashes of a person bathing had tested his resolve to grant her privacy.

Who would have known if he'd slipped into the room and watched her bathe? He would have. Or possibly she would have. She'd heard his comment about her hair, he was sure of it—and his reaction to her posturing in front of the mirror. What vigorous man wouldn't react to tight cloth wrapped around slim female hips? Following last night's invasion of her sleep, he'd debated his actions. Although he felt a growing connection to this woman, he'd vowed to honor her privacy.

A vow that didn't stop him from moving to the top floor and standing on the walk along the battlement. Overlooking the courtyard, he watched as she ambled into view from the west side of the castle and climbed into the metal box on strange black wheels. A dull roar sounded and the thing he knew was called an automobile moved down the road. Strong alchemy was connected to a contraption that moved without the aid of oxen or horses, but she controlled the machine well.

What a damn fool. Hadn't he learned his lesson centuries ago about a woman turning away and leaving? Nothing to be gained by watching the contraption disappear. His thoughts raced for something better to occupy his time. He vowed to return to his quarters and reclaim his space. Let her find another room in which to spread out her strange clothes and the multi-colored bottles.

With determined steps, he headed toward his room. By the time he'd entered and was surrounded by her things, his resolve wavered. This woman might be an ally. She had stated agreement that his defeat in the border skirmish had been at the hand of a traitor.

Inside, he battled between anger at this person who disrupted his routine and curiosity over what else she would say. The fact she hadn't gone screaming out of the castle at his antics with the gatekeeper, or at his first touch, proved she was used to his type of energy. A couple hundred years had passed since he'd received such positive recognition. Admittedly, the link with the living world was tenuous, but he clung tight.

The sun rode low on the horizon when Truda drove the car around to the back side of Wybjorn Castle and eased it under the overhang of a small shed. She filled her hands with several flower bundles she'd been unable to resist and grabbed a couple bags of groceries.

"Hello?" Entering directly into the kitchen, she called out, "I'm back, in case you were worried. I enjoyed a delicious brunch at the Bergen Café and then bought myself some food." After speaking, she waited for a change in the air around her or a sound to indicate Garet was near. When she couldn't discern his presence, she blew out a disappointed breath.

Taking only a few minutes, she'd stored the food in a cupboard and the small refrigerator hidden behind a heavy wooden pantry door. "I wanted to bring some color indoors." Two glass vases sat on the counter, and she tore the paper from around the flower bundles. With no answering sound, she assumed she was alone.

Why had he deserted her? His refusal to help find the key and his continued silence made her think she'd done something to offend him. Maybe her nighttime experience had just been a dream, her wishful thinking that the powerful warrior she'd glimpsed yesterday would slip into her bedroom. Her male colleagues were the type who played tennis or racquetball to keep in shape. The sight of a muscular man with a broad chest under his tunic and hard thighs straining his breeches had set her heart racing.

The fact that he had a sexy mouth, ice-blue eyes and tousled wheat-colored hair hadn't hurt either. What got to her most was his voice—deep, rough, and scratchy—like it was out of practice.

Probably Garet was still mad over her intrusion into his private home. In that case, he was probably even madder that she'd chosen what must have been the master suite for her own sleeping place.

She couldn't help herself. Ever since she was a small girl, she'd wished for the opportunity to be the star in her own fairy tale. How better to be like a princess than to sleep in a bed with a canopy above and blankets to pull around the sides?

On purpose, she'd left the linen-covered lattice window slightly ajar because all good fairy tales showed a starlit sky through an open window. How else could she wish for her prince to come? As silly as that might sound for an adult, once in a while, she did indulge the young dreamer deep in her soul.

"Don't you agree these will look lovely in the entry?" She circled an arm around each vase and carried them toward the front of the castle, her shoes clicking along the tiled floors. Maybe the flowers with their colorful blooms and sweet fragrance would appeal to his other senses and she'd get a response.

After setting the vases on tables where they couldn't be missed, she threw out her arms and spun in a circle until she faced the office. "Enjoy what you can from these. I'm going back to work. Time to tackle that password again."

Truda passed through the door and immediately noticed a disturbance in the room's air. He'd been here recently. The specifics of what she sensed were hard to pinpoint. Different from the prickly sensations along her neck of being watched, but the feeling was more than a scent. Whatever was in the air when Garet was near made her blood pump and her nipples harden.

Ever so much better.

Fighting back a smile, she scooted the chair closer to the computer table and clicked the mouse. When the screen refreshed, she spotted that the password box had been filled in. GandR1625. Of course. Garet and Reidun, with the year of their wedding. With a trembling hand, she scooted the cursor arrow to the OKAY button and clicked.

The wallpaper with the crest for Wybjorn Castle dissolved and desktop icons appeared. A double click on the word processing program revealed dual columns of folders. The titles assured her they contained all the information she could ever want. From husbandry purchases to breeding counts to crop yields to household accounts. Her fingers tapped the keys in excitement, debating over which file to open first.

Access had been granted with Garet's help. No other explanation existed. The gesture was sweet and thoughtful, and her heart warmed. She looked over her shoulder, her gaze scanning the perimeter of the room again, and grinned. "Thanks for the secret word. This saved me lots of time."

Still, he kept himself hidden. With a sigh, she turned back to the monitor, eager to discover a hidden treasure. To combat the overbearing quiet of the old chilly structure, she clicked open a folder and read aloud from the scanned pages from a book of household accounts. Deciphering the Old Norse might have taken another curator some time but she'd had lots of practice. Part of this was her family history.

Plus, she knew the exact year she wanted to study.

Garet drifted, letting her voice relating the details of daily castle life surround his senses. Her tone changed, softened with concern, at the mention of the spread of an illness or the birth of a crofter's babe.

"See here? Right here, the document says, 'A party of ten led by our protector beat back fifteen raiders. They'd broached the eastern boundary and were caught in the clearing by the old growth forest.'"

He jerked alert and watched her fingertip trace across the luminous surface of the square box and listened to her words. He remembered that skirmish—the fog that enshrouded the group, the fighters who rode with him, even the name of their mounts.

"So, what I want to know is . . ." She arched her back and rubbed a hand over her neck. "Oww." With a groan, she stood and rolled her shoulders backward as she glanced around the room. "I'm so tired I can't even tell if you're still here or not."

His fingers itched to massage away the stiffness that must reside in her unused muscles. The ability to sit for long spells in front of that small box, attention on nothing but the images before her eyes, was unknown. In his time, people performed active, physical tasks.

She leaned over the chair, clicked a small rounded disk and the images changed. "How was that raid different than the fateful one?" Her lips rounded and a yawn escaped, a hand rising to hastily cover it. "Sorry."

The box went dark and she straightened, pulling out a silver apparatus from the side and slipping it into her pocket. Then she turned and walked slowly across the office floor. "Was your group larger than usual? Had your preparations for battle been better?"

At her insinuation, he moved from his spot in the window alcove, ready to confront her.

"I'm going to bed." She shuffled out through the doorway and then stuck her head back in. "Isn't the victor determined mostly by luck?"

Garet stiffened. Hours had passed since he'd spoken, but he would not let this question go unanswered. Again, she insulted his abilities. Again, she spoke of what she did not know. With long strides, he stormed across the entry and bounded up the stairway to the landing then turned to confront her ascent. "Luck is only a small part of going to battle."

For only a second, her steps hesitated and then she continued trudging up the stairs, her curtain of hair hiding her face.

"I know you heard me."

"Is this the pattern now?" Her gaze moved around the area, brows drawn low.

He paced the landing, unsure of the reason for his turmoil. Why did he care that she knew he was a trained soldier? That a multitude of preparation went into each surveillance of the estate?

Truda stopped and jammed a hand on her hip. "You talk only when I disparage your abilities? Not exactly the communication I'd hoped for. Don't you understand?" Her stance softened and she held out her hands in appeal. "I want to help you." With a shake of her head, she rushed up the steps.

How could he explain that strategy drove each raid? Frustration tightened his muscles and he whirled—

They collided and sudden warmth hit his body. She was there, inside him. For one glorious moment, he was filled with a sweet rush of vitality. Then the sensation faded, and he was left almost as empty and cold as always. He staggered backward, struggling to pull in air.

Truda grabbed the polished wood banister and crumpled to the stone step. "Oh, Garet." Surprise widened her eyes as she looked directly at him. "Is that how you always feel? So cold?"

She saw him? Right now, when he wasn't angry? Slowly, his body registered uncomfortable points of contact with the stone wall at his back. He spread his fingers and ran them over the rough stones, feeling a hint of every scrape. Slowly, he raised a leaden arm and, for the first time in centuries, saw his hand with enough detail to spot the nicks and scars of battle. The shape was definitely there but through it he could see the gray steps below.

"What just happened?" she whispered, her voice shaky.

His gaze cut to her pale face and her stare remained fixed on him. "I know not." But he could hazard a guess and deep inside, he knew he wanted more.

"I'm so very tired." She braced a hand on the step, struggled, and slumped back. "I'm not sure I can stand."

"Let me help." He stepped to her aid and felt like chain mail dragged at his limbs, slowing his actions. Reaching her side, he cupped her elbow with one hand and wrapped the other around her waist.

She stood, leaning against his side. "I like this."

First, a spicy scent teased his nose. In both places where he touched her, his body registered the contact as light brushes of two objects. Confusion warred with the unusual physical awareness. "Walk slowly until your strength returns." Slowly, so he had a reason to keep touching her.

"I can feel your hands, Garet. The touch is light but it's keeping me upright." Her head shook. "How is that possible?"

They reached the top of the stairs and he turned them down the hallway. All Garet wanted was to savor the soft woman in his arms.

"Did I wish you into being?"

Rather than start a discussion over how to qualify his current state, for once he held back his words. He hesitated before crossing into the master chamber, debating the wisdom of entering the room together. A room that held the memories of the previous night. Carnal memories that he'd spent most of the day fighting. "I am not certain."

His grip loosened and he guided her through the doorway, urging her forward and holding contact until she walked out of his grasp. "Will you be all right now?"

"What?" Her body stiff, she turned and her gaze gauged the distance between them. "Why are you out there?" With arms outstretched, she stepped toward the doorway. "I've just found you. Don't leave me."

His heart beat faster, the sound rumbling in his ears. Did he dare? One look into her imploring green eyes and he wavered in his decision.

"I want you to stay. Please."

5

With breath caught in her tight throat, Truda watched Garet's indecision. She'd already asked him to stay. Twice actually. And she wouldn't speak again, but she would hope. If she were facing the other direction, she might even wish on a favorite star.

Narrowed blue eyes searched her face, deep furrows in his forehead.

Chin lifted, she met his hard gaze and pressed her lips tight to prevent herself from asking again. Even if every bit of her woman's nature screamed not to let him leave tonight. Her breasts were weighted with awareness and her nipples pressed tight against her bra. This surprising turn of events would enhance what she'd felt last night. She let her gaze sweep his big, muscular body. Many times enhanced.

"You have had quite an experience."

Could he read her mind, too? She shook away that thought and lowered her gaze. "True." Did she really look so much like a porcelain doll?

"I do not wish to intrude—"

With a deliberate move, she lifted her hands to the top button of her blouse and pushed it through the buttonhole. Her fingers inched down the fabric.

"Uh, to intrude on your . . ."

She unfastened another button and glanced up, hoping she infused her expression with the right touch of regret. "I understand."

A third button popped free. She turned toward the bathroom and took a couple steps, being sure to put a swing in her step, before looking over her shoulder. "Thanks for your help." Who she saw was the warrior of centuries ago. Every magnificent muscle in his powerful body was tensed and primed for action, his fists clenched at his sides.

Before she stepped over the threshold into the tiled bathroom, she opened the front of her blouse and let it fall over her shoulders and down her arms to the floor. Pretending she didn't care if he followed or not, she lit several candles on shelves around the room. Then she flipped the handle to seat the plug and twisted the taps of the bathtub. With a flick of her thumb, she popped open a canister of bath salts and sprinkled the water's surface. The headiness of lavender mixed with the rising steam.

Despite the turmoil rumbling in her stomach, she moved slowly, wanting to appear as if she hadn't a care in the world. That she was just doing what she normally did. She unzipped her slacks, let them pool at her feet, and then kicked them to the side.

"I don't understand what has happened any more than you do."

He'd stayed. Hope flickered inside her chest. Wearing only a lacy red bra and bikini panties, she turned to face him. All her brazenness evaporated, and she worried over what he'd think of her body. Until she looked into his concerned expression, brows lowered and eyes haunted. "That's all right. We can figure it out together."

He leaned in the doorway, arms crossed over his chest. His hungry gaze roamed her body and rested on her breasts, a muscle at the side of his left eye twitched.

In immediate reaction, her nipples budded and scraped against the lace, sending tingles straight to her pussy. For an instant, she considered removing all her clothes, but something held her back. She needed a gesture from him first. An indication of what he wanted.

"Better check the water."

Life intruded at the worst times. She broke her gaze from his and moved to the tub, twisting off the handles. Realization that she'd heard and watched him speak those four words hit. Oh damn. When she turned, she gasped in surprise.

He'd moved to the foot of the tub, his gaze hard on the rippling surface of the water. With closed eyes, he inhaled, his chest rising. "Were the crystals lavender scented?"

"Yes. You smell them?" A thrill went through her. Maybe she really had wished him into existence. As illogical as that sounded, she didn't care. He was within arm's reach and they were communicating like normal people.

The expression of wonder he turned on her warmed her heart.

His chin dropped in an abrupt nod. "When you were in my arms, I thought I'd imagined your spicy scent. It was one I could not name. But lavender I recognize."

Her mind raced at which scented lotion she'd applied that morning but she couldn't remember. Too many exciting things had happened since then. She waited for him to speak.

"Truda, I must—"

She shook her head, searching his expression for any sign of what he would say. The strangeness of seeing both the shadow of his expression and what was behind him was beginning to wear off. "No musts or shoulds, speak of what you want."

"The bath looks inviting."

Disappointment weighed heavy at the sight of his closed expression, and her shoulders sagged.

"Think it will hold us both?"

Her head jerked up and a grin spread across her mouth. A practice she'd learned about in her research popped into her head. She wanted to show him the respect due a man of his station during his time. "Only if you go first, and allow me the privilege of bathing you."

Blue eyes looked into hers. "Ja, for the beginning." Then his gaze went back to her breasts and down to the scrap of red silk covering her mons.

Excitement filled her, making her body tingle, and she felt her nipples tightening into hard buds, aching for his touch. Her entire body yearned for his touch but that would have to wait.

"I do not know what to expect. But I am willing to explore." His hands rose to the ties at the neck of his tunic and he loosened them then pulled the garment over his head.

Truda held her breath, wondering in how much detail his body would be revealed. By the time the tunic landed on the floor in a heap, she had her answer. Enough detail to see the man was in top physical shape—chest and shoulders defined by smooth, hard muscles, arms that bunched and flexed as he moved, and a stomach that resembled a carefully laid rock wall.

Garet fingered the ties at the side of his breeches, yanked them open and then bent to shove them down his legs. When he straightened, he looked at her and then the tub.

Although she tried to let her gaze scan his entire lower body, she couldn't help staring at the length and girth of his cock emerging from a thatch of brown curls and lying along his upper thigh. At the sight, her pussy clenched and she felt dewy excitement moisten her feminine curls. "Please get in the water. I'll bring some towels."

She turned toward the wooden cupboard and worried her

lower lip with her teeth, nervousness settling in her stomach. Almost a year had passed since her last sexual encounter. Nils, the swimmer, had not been built anything like Garet, the warrior.

A quiet splash sounded behind her followed by a long, low sigh. A sound of such contentment that cut straight to her heart.

She turned and approached the clawfoot tub, a stack of fluffy towels piled in her arms. Tossing one down near the side of the tub, she dropped the others on the lid of the commode. Now that the time to bathe him had arrived, she was unsure how to proceed. She glanced at him only to find his gaze watching her. "How's the water temperature? Too hot?"

"I can barely feel it. My senses are . . ." His brows lowered in a frown and he shook his head. "I know not how to describe what I feel."

The confusion in his expression was heartbreaking. From a nearby shelf she grabbed a washcloth and a bottle of her favorite silky body wash. Onto the wet cloth, she squeezed a mound of liquid and rubbed the cloth until soapy foam appeared. "Are you wet all over?"

His hands grasped the edge of the tub, his knees rose out of the water and he leaned forward to splash water over his head and back.

While he was underwater, she studied his closest hand, noting the crisscrossing of faint scars. The memory of a deep voice saying, "to learn every curve and indentation, every freckle and every scar" entered her thoughts. Garet's words. She reached out a tentative finger to trace a long scar and the very tip of her finger instantly cooled and then disappeared, swallowed by his body.

Garet jerked out of the water, shaking his head and flinging water everywhere. "Thor's blood, woman."

"I'm sorry." She jerked back her hand. "Did I hurt you?"

A sharp laugh sounded. "A slip of a thing like you hurting me? Surprised me is all."

Hoping to get back his easygoing manner, she focused on her task. "Lean forward and I'll let the water dribble over you." Maybe then she could see the outlines of his body and know how hard to touch him. This opportunity was too precious to screw up.

He complied with her instructions, rounding his shoulders and dropping his head between them.

From behind, she squeezed the washcloth and let the foamy bubbles land at the base of his neck and watched them slide over the ridges and hollows of his back. She lowered the washcloth to his neck and gently followed the trail of foam, making slow, caressing circles down the right side of his back until she reached the waterline.

"That is nice."

Under her hand, she felt the hard contours of his body that she couldn't touch with the pressure she would have liked. The result being the perception of a strong man instead of the reality of one. She couldn't repress her historian nature. "What do you feel? Can you describe the sensation?"

He raised his head and looked over his shoulder, blue eyes intent. "I feel featherlight strokes of warmth sliding over my back, as if being touched by a butterfly's wing."

His words, spoken in a husky, sad voice, brought a lump to her throat and she could only nod.

"I appreciate you are making this effort. That counts almost as much as experiencing the actual sensation." His gaze dropped to her breasts and then he turned away.

Each time he glanced at her body, she felt his gaze like a caress and her desire kicked up a notch. Biting back a moan, she pressed her thighs together and pushed her thoughts away from her pulsing labia. This bath was to comfort Garet.

Yeah, right.

With gentle moves echoing what she'd already done, she soaped the rest of his back and then scooted her kneeling towel to the side of the tub. "Lift this arm, please."

He complied, his stare intent on her hands as they moved. "The act of watching you bathe me strengthens the sensation." He flexed his hand and his bicep jumped. "I wonder if you would feel my kiss."

She sucked in a breath and swabbed the length of his arm. Her thoughts raced as to what type of kiss he meant, but she forced her words to be calm as she answered. "I felt your hands supporting me on the stairs. I believe I would feel a kiss." Sudden shyness hit and she couldn't meet his gaze. Had that sounded too needy?

She dipped the cloth into the water and poured on more body wash then lowered the cloth toward his chest. She watched almost in awe as her hand moved over the contours of his well-defined muscles. Under her palm, she felt the nubbin of a male nipple and moved lower, over the bumps of his rippled abdomen. Restraint at not pressing as hard as she'd have liked, to savor the texture and tone of his body, kept her muscles clenched.

Down into the soapy water, she moved her hand and ran the cloth along the top of his thigh. With slow moves, she turned her hand and pressed along the inside of his thigh, inching trembling hands toward his groin.

Drips plopped into the water, and she felt waves of her hair move against her left cheek.

His body shifted, bent knees rising out of the water.

She'd never bathed a man before and her mouth went dry at the thought of making the next bold move. Again, she hesitated, her uncertainty evident in her shaky hands.

"Truda, look at me."

She braced her hands on the tub and raised her gaze. In this position, the white porcelain of the tub provided a solid background and his body was easy to see.

A smile spread his mouth and his eyes held a blue glint. "I would prefer your hands on me . . . there."

Her gaze captured by his, she swallowed hard and the cloth fell from her lax hands. "Okay."

"You have used these letters before. What do they mean?"

She blinked, trying to follow his conversation. Her thoughts were on the request to bathe his cock and balls with her bare hands. "O-k-a-y means the same as all right, a word of agreement."

"Ah." He nodded, tendrils of damp brown hair falling alongside his face. "You may finish now."

To reach him, she rose on her knees and leaned her ribs on the top rim of the tub. Her hands slid up his legs, palms faintly tickled by the brush of bristly hair. The body wash made the water murky and kept her from seeing his manly armaments. When she reached his groin, she gently brought her hands together to rest on the thatch of coarse hairs and to encircle the base of his cock.

Oh, my. During the bath, its girth had grown even bigger. With slow strokes, she ran first one thumb and then the other along the curve of his balls, the skin rough against her movements.

A quick inhalation of breath sounded.

Careful not to squeeze hard, she alternated caressing strokes from the base to the head of his thick cock. One hand always in contact, to keep the sensations moving along his pulsing shaft. The moving water supplied about the same level of sensation as touching his body—she was stimulated but not to the same degree as if they touched.

Frustration settled just under her skin but she pushed it back. Her focus was Garet's enjoyment, not hers.

"Still your hands."

She stopped, her gaze shooting to his face.

He flexed his hips and pressed his cock along her grasp. Eyes closed, he reclined, forehead wrinkled as if in deep concentration.

"Tell me what you need, Garet. I want to help you."

He shook his head, his jaw clenched tight.

Maybe warriors didn't speak of needs. His expertise was action, not words.

But her experience the previous night proved that statement wrong. He had been eloquent with words, the words she'd heard in her sleep, the words that created that glorious orgasm. Maybe if she reciprocated. "Garet, I feel your strength, I feel your cock that pulses with life in my hands."

His eyes shot open and his body jerked, starting waves along the water's surface. "What?"

"I wish my touch was stronger on your body. I wish you felt each and every inch of my skin as I stroke your big, broad cock."

Eyes lit with understanding, he grinned. His hand rose, droplets rolling off his arm and plopping back into the water, and a finger traced the swell of her breast. "And I wish for you to join me in the tub. But only if you remove this binding garment and release your bountiful tits."

His use of a term she normally considered vulgar made her hot. Forget the centuries of behavioral conventions separating them, she wanted him. Bracing a hand on the edge of the tub, she leaned toward the other end and lowered the silver lever. As the water drained, she turned away to undo the clasp of her bra and let the straps slide down her arms. With her thumbs, she hooked the elastic of her panties and pulled them down her legs.

Then shyness took over and she was unsure of how he would regard her body. Slowly leaning over the tub, she flipped up the drain lever and twisted the handles to start fresh water running. All the while, she fought the urge to grab a towel to cover herself.

"Truda, the sight of your ass is enjoyable. Now display the rest of your female charms."

Finally, she turned and stepped into the clear, swirling water. The moment she met his gaze, she felt her nervousness disappear into the rising steam.

The heated gaze he ran over her body lingered on every detail. Almost as if his hand followed his gaze, her skin tingled in a path from her shins up her thighs to her crotch, circling over her belly and flicking between her breasts. Her womb clenched and her breasts grew heavy, nipples tightening into pearly buds and pointing in his direction.

With a twist, she reached behind her body and grabbed the handheld nozzle. A flip of the switch diverted the water into a showerhead she could direct as she wished. And she knew just how she wanted to use it. "Stand and I'll rinse you."

Brows drawn tight as he looked at her hand, he slowly stood. "Let me clean off the soap." She inched forward and raised her arm to direct the spray in a downward line from his chest to his knees. Water rolled in rivulets down his legs and glinted in the candlelight. She leaned to one side and reached the nozzle around his waist to get his back. Her movement scraped her breasts across his stomach and she gasped at the contact.

Garet's gaze narrowed on the spot where she'd touched him and his muscles tightened in response.

He'd felt her touch more definitely than before. She knew by his response that he had. Unable to resist, she quickly flicked off the water and knelt in front of his magnificent cock. With shaking hands, she cradled it in her palms and leaned forward to surround the tip with her lips. A faint movement tickled her tongue and she tentatively licked at the shaft.

He hissed and his hands cradled the sides of her head. "Stay still, and let me move."

Wishing she could grab hold of his strong thighs as an anchor, instead she braced her hands on the porcelain. She held herself still and waited.

A light brush against her mouth marked his thrust and then his slow retreat. The movement was repeated several times, each time the sensation moved farther along the roof of her mouth. But she wanted to feel more. The sensation was no stronger than the glide of fabric over her skin.

"I can't!" His hands at her temples urged her backward and his cock popped from her lips.

Pressure at her shoulders encouraged her to stand, but she resisted, unwilling to let him put distance between them.

She leaned her head back and looked up, past his rock-hard abdomen, past his chest with protruding nipples, to the anguished look in his eyes. "Let me help you. I know I can do this."

His head shook but he didn't voice his reservations.

This would have to be fast. She moved her hands from the tub and ran them up and down the backs of his legs. Her lips enveloped his cock and she bobbed her head along its length, closing her mouth to create a tight channel.

His response was instant. He thrust deep, his legs rigid.

She leaned forward just a bit more. Deep cold enveloped her from her mouth to her breasts and her hands. Every place where her skin touched his chilled body. At the same moment, she felt spurts of warm liquid at the back of her throat and heard Garet's roar of satisfaction.

Then she fell back into the water, shivering.

6

_____

Still gasping for breath, Garet knelt close to Truda and reached out a hand to stroke her shivering cheek. With surprise, he saw tan flesh where before only a shadowy outline had been. Her generous sharing of her energy had somehow made him more substantial. "Are you hurt?"

"No, j-just very cold." Teeth chattering, her gaze rose to his and her eyes widened, her awed green gaze running over his face and body. "Garet, I can't see through you."

Unable to answer her unspoken question, he did what he could to help. He stepped from the tub and reached for a towel. "Climb out. You need to get dry." He extended a hand, marveling again at seeing his real body after so long, and watched as her hand moved toward his, waiting to feel her touch.

Shivering, she rested her hand on top of his and pressed as she stepped out. With her other arm clasped around her stomach, she hunched her shoulders forward and stood.

The weight of her hand on his was stronger than earlier, when she'd caressed his body. The process of how this was happening was unfathomable, but he could not deny the evidence—he was becoming more real. He placed the towel over her back and moved it across her shoulders. The fabric bunched and rubbed on his hands and he felt its nubby texture.

"Go and climb in bed." He waited until she moved away then grabbed another towel and dashed it across his chest. The tickle on his body was a pleasant surprise and he bit back a laugh. With quick movements, he wiped droplets of water from the rest of his skin and looped the towel around his neck. His skin. He had trouble grasping this phenomenon but relished the return of his tactile senses.

He strode into the bedroom and approached the bed, feeling the bang of his balls against his thighs and the gentle bounce of his cock as he moved. Feelings that made him want to shout for joy at the wondrous gift he'd been given.

Truda lay curled into a small mound, the quilt pulled up to her chin. Her avid gaze centered on his lower body then slowly traveled to his face. She gave a wan smile and lifted up the quilt in invitation.

Garet dropped the towel onto the floor and slid onto the mattress, hearing the straw crunch as he stretched out. With care, he slipped an arm under her head and cupped her shoulder.

She squirmed closer, settling her chilled body against his. "Aww, you're warm."

Guilt flashed through him at the realization of the cost of her generous act. He should have been stronger and not given in to his selfish need. "I am grateful for your actions." He cleared his throat, unsure of what else to say.

Her small hand rested on his chest, fingers rubbing through his chest hairs. "Garet, in my time, men more freely express what they are feeling. In fact, in a relationship between a woman and a man, this sharing is expected."

"You should not put yourself at risk." His other hand moved in circles across her belly, urging warmth into her skin.

"Oo, this time the weight of your hand is pressing on my skin. That feels so good." She rolled onto her back, dragging a hand across his nipples. "Touch me, Garet. I want your touch everywhere on my body."

The jolt from her touch went straight to his groin, sweetening the tension he already felt just from being this close to Truda. Scooting onto his side, he propped himself up on an elbow, letting his shoulder make a tent of the quilt over her body. From the cold, her nipples were already drawn into buds. He couldn't resist the temptation of circling the rosy ring of her aureole with a finger, making his circles smaller until he reached the tip.

Emitting a low moan, she wiggled her shoulders, setting her tits into an enticing jiggle.

Blood racing through his body, Garet lowered his head and inhaled the lavender scent that clung to her skin. He stretched out his tongue and dragged it from the bottom of her tit to the tip, and then breathed a puff of air onto her wet nipple.

Her head moved from side to side and her hips ground into the mattress. "More . . . harder."

With an open mouth, he covered her nipple and sucked it deep inside. His hand cupped her other generous mound and squeezed, then tweaked her nipple with his thumb and a finger. The sensation of the small bud tightening beneath his fingers validated her body registered his motions, that his touches gave pleasure.

"Garet, I won't break. Don't be so gentle."

He had made a vow and he wouldn't renege. After scaring away one woman by indulging his true desire, he'd promised himself he would never do that again. The pain of having this special woman turn away would be too great. "Ah, honnig, you know not what you demand."

Rising on his elbows, he stretched over her torso, moving his chest against the tips of her tits. He caught a glimpse of her warm green eyes before her eyelids drooped and then he pressed a kiss to her lips. Sweet plump lips. He traced her lips with a questing tongue.

She responded with a tentative jab and then a full sweep of her agile tongue. A moan escaped and she blew warm air in his mouth. Soft hands cupped his jaw, holding his head in place, and her thumbs rubbed along his jawline.

Sparks of awareness ran along the bottom half of his face, and traveled down his throat to his chest. His skin heated, and became more sensitive. Thor's blood, she was giving too much again. He shoved off the mattress and rose above her body, breaking her hold and glared down into her startled gaze. "Stop that! I will not have you putting yourself in peril."

A whimper escaped her swollen lips and she sucked in her lower lip, nibbling. "I can't help myself."

His gaze went straight to her mouth, wishing for the ability to devour her lips. "You must." He jumped from the bed and paced, oblivious to the sight he made. "Or I will leave." A quick glance around the floor reminded him that his clothes were in the chamber for bathing. Intent on retrieving them, he turned.

"Wait, Garet. Please."

The plaintive tone in her voice stopped his movements and he looked over his shoulder, conflict over how to act heavy in his chest.

A slender arm extended from the mattress and she pointed toward the bureau. "Bring my nylons."

He glanced between her finger waving in the air and the square case that stored clothes, lying open on the bench across the room. "What is a ny-lon?"

A frown appeared between her eyebrows. "Nylons are stockings, um, like hose. Only you've never seen hose this thin, like a spider's web."

Confusion over her request occupied his thoughts, but this

was a simple task. One he could do without bringing harm. With three long strides, he was across the room and shuffling through her belongings. That strange spicy scent rose from her clothes, the scent that was Truda, and he inhaled deeply. He meant to ask her about the origin of that scent. In a side pocket topped with a strange chain of metal, he saw something that resembled the finely woven hose she'd described. Pinching it between his fingers, he lifted it and held it out for her inspection. "Is this what you want?"

"Yes, bring both pair."

As he walked back to the bed, he slid the silky fabric between his fingers. Strange. "All right." He extended his hand toward her. "Here."

Brows wrinkled over her eyes, her gaze met his and then skittered away. "Because you requested I not put myself at risk I thought this could be a way to keep my hands away . . . I mean out of the way."

Wonder filled his thoughts. Garet stared at her face, glanced at the long, skinny length in his hand, at her luscious tits with the rosy nipples peeking over the bedclothes, and then looked back at her flushed face. "You want me to tie your hands?" His blood sped through him and tension grabbed low in his groin.

An adventuress?

One interested in exploring a playful aspect of fucking?

"Well, maybe I'm presuming too . . ." Pearly teeth nibbling her lower lip, she reached a shaking hand for the quilt.

His curiosity won out. "No presumption." He leaned a knee on the mattress and reached for both her hands. With a few wraps and twists, her arms were held over her head by the strange stretchy hose. The pose arched her back and hitched up her tits. "This is a good solution."

He traced a finger down one smooth arm, passed through an armpit strangely devoid of hair, and down over her chest. As he touched her, he switched his attention between the skin he touched and her hooded gaze. As her passion grew, her green eyes deepened in color. He splayed his fingers to circle a thumb and pinky around her nipples until they pointed straight up. An invitation for a kiss if ever one existed.

Bracing his hands opposite her shoulders, he leaned over and barely touched her nipples with the end of his tongue, then circled the entire tip.

"More." She moaned and arched to press closer.

With careful moves, he ran the edge of his teeth up and down her peaked nipples then pulled back to blow on the wet tips. At the touch of his breaths, the nubs puckered tighter and he flicked one with his finger. "I like this."

She squirmed under his touch, and a long sigh escaped from her pursed lips. "As do I." Her legs shifted restlessly, a knee tilting toward the other, then switching after a few seconds.

With special attention paid along each and every bone, he covered her ribs in a line of kisses. He moved slowly inward from her sides, inching his mouth lower on her soft belly.

Short breaths sounded above his head, and he grinned at her reaction to his kisses. When he reached her navel, he plunged his tongue deep inside and swirled. At the base of his throat, he could feel the prickly hairs covering her mons and had to restrain his natural impulse to move immediately to her sweet treasures. He continued his slow descent, kissing and licking every bit of smooth skin he could reach. Smoothing a hand down her thighs, he urged her legs apart.

Into the crease of her inner thigh, he delved his tongue then scooted his body lower on the mattress, positioning himself between her spread legs. Open to his gaze, her petals glistened with dewy moisture. He inhaled and caught a faint whiff of the tangy scent of a woman's arousal. Delicious.

"What a pretty pink quim." He bent his head and ran his tongue along one long, slick fold, circled the tight clit and ran his tongue along the other fold. Her honeyed channel beckoned and he jabbed his tongue inside, feeling the walls press against his broad tongue.

He'd always enjoyed this intimacy, gaining as much pleasure from performing his actions as his partner did receiving them. Heaviness filled his groin and he rocked his hips, pressing his lengthening cock against the mattress.

Against his mouth, she pushed her moist heat and circled her hips as she tried to position herself to the best advantage. Sweet moans accompanied her movements.

His fingers spread her feminine lips, so he could probe with his tongue, thrusting into her heat and swirling deep inside. With flat strokes, he lapped at her folds, starting low and ending at her clitty with extra pressure. But he couldn't resist stretching his tongue and flicking that button with just the tip.

Her moans encouraged him on. He centered his mouth over her clit and sucked, giving her a long intimate kiss. Working his thumb along her folds, he rolled the bud with the pad and then thrust his tongue into her channel.

"Ah." Her legs shifted, one foot rising to her hip so she could press against his ministrations. "Oh God, Garet, I'm close."

He pulled back his head and his gaze traveled up her body, past her moist pink quim, her trimmed muff, her slender belly, and her generous tits. His gaze rested on her open mouth with the tip of a pink tongue wetting her lips and her glazed emerald eyes. A truly beautiful woman. "Tell me what you like." He glanced at the bindings on her wrists but he saw no reddening of the skin surrounding them to indicate they were too tight. "I want to give you pleasure."

The skin around her eyes crinkled as she smiled. "I know, and I'm enjoying everything you're doing. But there's just not enough pressure."

He scooted up the mattress and ran a hand between her nipples, rubbing them erect again. "What can I do different?"

"Sometimes I use a toy." Her mouth pinched tight, but her gaze held his.

Disbelief shot through him and he straightened his arms to better see her face. "You use a plaything of a child?"

A smile crossed her mouth and her eyes twinkled. "In my time, adults have toys, too. Lots of them, in fact."

"Where do I find this . . . toy?" He slid off the bed, an arm extended toward the bureau. "Here?"

Eyes flashing, she nodded. "There's a small case at the bottom, under my clothes."

At the case, he reached along the edges of her clothes until his fingers encountered a hard container then pulled it out. He ran his hand over the smooth surface. Curious. Red, but not red oak. Slippery, but not metal. Light in weight. "What is this strange material?"

"Garet," she expelled a deep sigh, "I'll explain about plastic later. Please bring me the little silver object."

At the urgency in her words, his gaze flicked back to the bed. The beautiful, naked woman waited.

Her lip caught between her teeth, eyes begging him to soothe her need.

As he walked, Garet pried off the lid and spied a shiny bauble connected to a small box with a stiff string. Strange.

"All you need to know is this works by energy from the little box. Move the silver bullet along the same places on my body where your tongue was."

Mouth set in a hard line, he lifted out the objects and held them in his palm. "How can this bullet do what my mouth cannot?"

"Trust me, Garet. This works. Roll the dial on the box."

When he did, the bauble buzzed as if angry bees inside had just come to life. He jumped and dropped the device on the mattress. "What in Thor's world?"

"A surprise, huh?" She giggled and shifted her hips on the mattress. "Pick it up, get used to the vibration. But hurry."

Reminded he'd left her ungratified, he scooped up the bauble and climbed onto the mattress. Between her legs, he settled into position and grabbed the jiggling object, determined to control this odd device.

In his few minutes away, the juices on her quim had dried, and he took a moment to nuzzle and lick her folds into releasing more of her sweet cream. Regret at not being able to taste her passed through his thoughts and he pushed it away. A bounty lay before him and he'd enjoy what he could.

With hesitant moves, he plied the bauble to her folds, repeating his earlier actions of running from low near her arse upward to her clitty and then back down the other side. Unable to remain inactive, he extended his tongue and flicked and circled her sweet little bud. Along his throat, he felt the device pulsing against her tender folds.

She cried out and her hips rocked, seeking the right pressure in the right spot.

The sound of her excitement ran his blood hot, and he ground his hips into the mattress, seeking friction for his hard cock. He moved his lips over her clitty and mouthed the bud, sucking hard at the same moment he inserted the pulsing bauble into her channel.

Uttering a high-pitched cry, she pushed off her heels and raised her hips.

With his free hand, he grabbed her hip and followed her movement, keeping his mouth tight on her quim until he felt her folds quiver and push back against his tongue. At the vocal proof of her satisfaction, a swelling of pride filled his chest.

Breathing hard, Truda dropped back to the mattress and clamped her thighs around his head, capturing him, holding him prisoner.

In that moment, he knew what she planned and he struggled to free his head.

But Truda was strong and her legs pressed tighter, rocking in rhythm with her release. "Ah, ahhh."

Warmth radiated from his head and neck and moved down through his body. The sensation flowed through him like heady wine, ending his resistance. On instinct, his hips flexed and thrust against the crinkly mattress, seeking release for the building tension in his groin.

With his last bit of willpower, he twisted his head until his lips pressed against her inner thigh and he bit her tender flesh.

A gasp sounded and her hold lessened.

At that moment, he stiffened his torso and straightened his arms. A sudden pain stabbed his back but he ignored it, scooting back until his feet touched the floor. His movement popped out the bauble from her channel and it landed on the mattress, its pulse tickling the side of his cock.

Dimly aware of Truda's sighs, he shifted, pressing closer to the strange device. His balls clenched in reaction and he could not resist the lure of another orgasm. Stretching to the side, he grabbed the towel from the floor, wincing at the pull in his lower back. With the towel spread over the mattress and the bauble set under his cock, he flexed his hips and thrust against the pulsing. Tightness filled his groin and he stroked his hand over his cock, increasing the tempo until he climaxed and pumped out his release. Through tight lips, he hissed out his air and then turned to her, ready to berate her for the risk she had taken. Again.

Body sagging from the restraints, her head leaned against one arm and her eyes were shut, chest rising in slow rhythm.

"Truda, are you asleep?" Already? Garet swiped the towel over his cock and let it fall to the floor. He switched off the device and dropped it on the towel. Moving to the head of the bed, he quickly untied the restraints and lowered her cold arms to her sides. Leaning a hip on the bed, he scooted her limp shoulders and then her lower body toward the middle of the mattress.

His hands lingered over her soft skin, and he wished for the chance to speak. The throb in his back had become a dull ache, but he ignored it. Warriors lived with aches and pains. He reached for the tangled bedclothes and pulled up the quilt, tucking it close around her body.

With both hands, he rubbed the skin of her chilled hands and arms. Telling himself this was to be expected for limbs suspended like they had been. As he worked, his concern grew that she did not rouse. Deep sleep did not normally come this quickly. But the light was diffuse and her features were shadowed. "Truda? Love?"

He moved to the window and raised a hand suddenly weighted and slow in movement to adjust the shutter so the moonlight shone across the bed. With weariness dragging at his limbs, he crossed the floor and slipped into bed beside her. A chill went through him and he pulled the quilt up over his chest as he studied her face. A face that had become dear in only the span of two moonrises.

Dark circles had appeared under her eyes and her skin no longer had the blush he'd seen earlier today. What she'd given him, whatever that spell or energy was, had proven too harsh on her slim body. The evidence was before him, and his chest constricted at the thought serious injury had befallen her. Tilting his head close, he listened to her breathing, assured it was steady and regular.

This time.

No guarantees existed for the next time. He needed a strategy to prevent a reoccurrence of her actions. And strategies were a warrior's forte. He vowed to figure one out. Even if he had to go back into hiding.

He reached up to caress her face and spotted the far wall through his shadowy hand. Regret weighed his movements as he drew Truda's body close and let the lassitude envelop him.

A different plan might already be set into action.

7

The trill of a songbird sounded outside the window. Truda was pulled from a wonderful dream of watching her warrior, Garet the Protector, riding toward her on a black stallion. His strong body moved as one with the powerful animal. Memories of other powerful movements flooded her thoughts and she stretched out a hand. Only cool sheets. "Garet?"

She pushed up to a sitting position and the quilt fell away, revealing her naked state. A thrill went through her at the memory of his hands on her skin. Maybe she could entice him back to the bed. Anxious to see him, she tossed aside the quilt and scooted to the side of the mattress. As she climbed down, she noticed a small bruise on her inner thigh. A smile crossed her lips. Oh yeah, Garet's love bite.

In ten minutes, she'd rushed through her morning preparations and descended the stairs wearing a flouncy skirt and camisole sweater set. "Good morning, Garet. Where are you?" In the entry hall, she spotted the pendulum clock. Eleven-fifteen? That couldn't be right. She never slept that late.

But the emptiness in her stomach told her otherwise. "Why

in the world did you let me sleep this late?" Frustrated at his absence, she went into the kitchen, grabbed a fruit smoothie and a granola bar and headed off to the office. She ripped off the wrapper and took a big bite, chewing the nuts and grains while working over the problem in her mind.

The previous night, she'd been close to figuring out what was so different about that final raid. And then she'd been wonderfully distracted. At the memory of what had happened in the stairway and then again in the bathtub, she slowed, wondering if another avenue of study was needed now.

Oh, she wished Garet would show up so she could discuss this. Her problem solving worked better with someone else to bounce around theories with. All she knew was she could somehow share her body's energy and that act made him more real. True, she felt totally drained afterward. But a good night's sleep—well, half a day's sleep—and she was back to normal.

She turned the corner into the office and immediately sensed Garet. "So, this is where you're hiding?" One thorough scan of the room told her differently but he had been here. "Okay, stay away. I've got work to do." She plopped down into the chair before the computer and twisted off the bottle top then punched the power button on the computer tower.

The screen that appeared was unfamiliar. No Wybjorn crest, no familiar operating systems icons in the lower toolbar. Probably because the system had been running when she saw the first screen. When the password prompt appeared, she typed in the symbols from the previous day. What popped up was a boldly lettered warning against unauthorized use of the system.

The password had been changed. That was obvious, but by whom? She couldn't believe a security system was in place that would change it every day. There would be no need. She tried a few rudimentary paths to go around the password prompt but her hacking skills had never been strong.

Maybe one of the files held instructions about this. She

stood and moved to the desk, her gaze scanning the files. Something was different. She'd put them into neat stacks when she'd gone through them and now they were scattered. Could the curator have returned and sabotaged her work?

Good thing she'd copied the hard drive. She walked out of the office, finishing the last of her smoothie, and climbed the stairs to retrieve her laptop and the jump drive. Backups were always useful.

Upon entering the room, she went straight to the bathroom, picked up her slacks from the floor, and dug in the pocket for the memory stick. With that in hand, she moved into the bedroom and toward the bureau where she'd laid her computer case. From the corner of her eye, she spotted a blotch on the white sheets. On the other side of the bed from where she'd awakened was a dark bloodstain.

She gasped and reached out a shaky hand. The sheet was dry. Thoughts raced through her head about the previous night. He'd become more real and had regained more of his senses. She'd been so wrapped up in the pleasure of what they'd shared that she hadn't thought about other indications of that state.

He'd also regained his old ailments, just like Truda had stated in her description to the Ingmars—"mortally injured in a raid by Swedes." The wound that put him into his weird ghostlike, suspended animation state. Of course, being the tough warrior, he wouldn't have let on to her about that circumstance. How long had he been gone from the bed? Was he lying somewhere now, alone and bleeding?

Agony clawed at her throat. "No! That can't be! Garet, I'm coming." Everything else forgotten, she dashed out the door and ran to the end of the hallway, calling his name. "Damn it, answer me. Garet!" Stopping to take a deep breath, she forced herself to think logically. *If he's hurt, he'll need medical supplies.*

Running back into the bedroom, she dumped out all the

makeup and sundry items from her cosmetic bag and tossed
back in hydrogen peroxide, Neosporin, a few Band-Aids, cotton balls, and her herbal supplements. A pitiful stash. She
slammed the case closed and grabbed the handle, then sprinted
out of the room and ran to the center of the upper hallway.
"Garet."

Opening the door to every room, she called his name, moving through the upstairs in a methodical way. At the far end of
the hallway, she heard a faint answer and her blood raced. "I
hear you. Where are you?"

"Go to the kitchen, back stairs."

In just a few minutes, she located the stairs that led out of
the back of the kitchen. Thankfully, he'd left the door open because the exterior was well disguised by a layer of stones. Every
castle she'd ever studied had similar passageways used as escape
routes in previous centuries. The hall led in both directions,
dimly lit by small round lamps high on the walls.

In her dash through the castle, she'd become confused about
where she'd heard Garet's voice. No time existed to find the
castle plans. "Which way? Up or down?"

"Climb."

She moved around a couple corners and there he was, leaning a shoulder against the stone wall. One glance told her that
he'd lost substance since the previous night. But at least, he was
still upright and on his own power. A pile of stones lay scattered at the base of the wall where he stood. "Are you okay?
What happened?"

Garet rolled to press his back against the wall and braced his
legs. His chin dipped close to his chest and he raised a hand to
the side of his head. "I thought the little troll was gone. He
must have been hiding and hit me with a rock."

Concern almost choking off her throat, she swallowed hard.
"What little troll? Where are you hit? Is this why there's blood
on the bedsheets?"

With a groan, he pulled in a deep breath and cut her a sideways look. "Truda, my head is throbbing. Go slowly with the questions."

Biting her lip to keep from blurting out any more, she stepped close and pulled on his sleeve to move his hand from his head. A bloody gash and a lump marred his forehead at the hairline. "That doesn't look too bad."

He grinned and quirked an eyebrow. "Are you a nurse, too?"

Relieved his head didn't look like it needed stitches, she set down the case and opened it. "Nope, but my mother was. Plus I have an active brother who was always getting hurt." She grabbed out what she needed and set the items on top of the case. "You'll have to sit so I can tend you." She moved toward him with an outstretched hand, intending to grab his arm.

"Do not help me." He glared and pointed directly at her. "I will lower myself—no, I can walk to the kitchen." With a hand braced on the wall, he shuffled down the hallway.

Stubborn man. She forced a calm tone into her words. "Garet, don't be silly. Rest your elbow on my shoulder."

"I said no." His words were clipped.

Her chest tightened at the cold and distant tone she'd heard only once before—when he raged the first day. "Well, all right. I'll set up at the kitchen table." Scooping the supplies back into the case, she moved ahead of him, irritation fueling her movements.

This day was not going like she'd hoped. What happened to how close and intimate they'd been last night?

She marched into the kitchen, set down the case and yanked on the hot water handle. A quick search of the cupboards produced a suitable bowl. By the time she set the bowl on the table, Garet leaned in the doorway, breathing heavily. She focused her attention on arranging the supplies to keep from rushing to his side and offering help.

The chair scraped against the tile floor and then barely creaked when he sat.

That fact scared her. He was losing substance. If she couldn't get close enough, he'd disappear. From the case, she grabbed bottles of herbal remedies and shook out several gel capsules. "Garet, you'll need to take these pills. Let me get you some water." She started toward the cupboard by the sink.

"No."

She whirled, bracing her hands on the back of a chair. "No? Why not?"

He shrugged, blue eyes half lidded and bleak. "My body doesn't work the same as yours. Not in this state, at least."

Confused, she focused on what she could do. "Okay, let me clean the wound." She dipped the edge of a kitchen towel in the hot water, but curiosity couldn't forestall the questions. "What did you mean the little troll? Who are you talking about?"

"Just clean the wound. Nothing more." He pulled back his head and narrowed his gaze on her face. "Understood?"

"Yes." She nodded, reaching the towel toward him. "Now, answers please."

"The curator Vegard. I spotted him skulking in the hall this morning."

A gasp escaped her lips. "So he was here. He changed the computer password. And maybe took some files, I'm not sure."

"Yeah, I thought he might have. But what he carried from the office was of more interest."

"This might sting, sorry." She dabbed hydrogen peroxide on his bump, then leaned close and blew on it.

"Blowing on my head is part of the treatment? Strange medicine in your time."

"An old practice I did for my brother Ander. Blowing makes me feel like I'm helping." She squeezed out some Neosporin onto a cotton ball and dabbed at the wound. "Did you say Vegard carried something from the office?"

Garet held his head still, his gaze watchful. "Have you finished your ministrations?"

That sounded like he didn't want her help. With a snap, she turned, walked to a trash can, and tossed in the cotton ball. "For now."

"Then sit." He waved a hand at the chair opposite him.

Finally, the light bulb went off over Truda's head. The man didn't know how to give the 'Don't call me, I'll call you.' speech. He'd probably intended to disappear to wherever he disappeared to and stay completely out of her way. If he hadn't been hurt, she might not have seen him again.

To keep from telling him exactly what she thought of that attitude, she pressed her lips into a tight line. The man would be receiving a short lesson on reality in the near future. With stiff moves, she yanked out the chair, dropped into it, and clasped her hands on the table. Affecting a calm expression, she returned his gaze, vowing to wait until he was finished.

"Vegard moved the brooch."

Her fingers gripped tight, she forced her lips into a smile and nodded. "Mmm?"

"I saw him carrying it out of the office, wrapping it in cloth as he walked." He leaned an elbow on the table.

She raised an encouraging eyebrow and nodded for him to continue, aware a knee bounced in agitation.

Brows drawn into a frown, his gaze searched her face. "I followed him to that hallway and watched him hide it behind a loose rock. He left, and I retrieved it. I had just reset the stone, when I heard a clunk and saw a bright light. I must have been blacked out until your voice roused me."

Ten. She'd count to ten before responding. At five, she jumped to her feet and leaned her hands on the table. "I can't believe you let me sleep through all this. Why didn't you come get me? The legacy brooch, I can't believe it. I could have been your lookout or something." She paced the length of the kitchen. "The brooch was here in the castle the whole time. You had your hands on it. Did you unwrap it?"

"No, I saved that honor for you."

She walked two more steps and turned at the end of the room. "You what? You still have it?" Her jaw dropped at the sight of him pulling a cloth bundle from the inside of his tunic.

He set it in the middle of the table and leaned forward on both forearms.

Reidun's brooch. A shiver ran over her skin but her heart pounded. She pulled the sweater tighter over her chest and wrapped arms around her stomach. Before her legs gave way, she lowered herself into the chair and just stared at the bundle. "That's it?"

"Yeah. Lucky that I pitched forward when he cold-cocked me." A grin lifted one corner of his mouth. "My weight was too heavy to allow him to take the brooch."

She slid a hand across the table then hesitated, her gaze rising to meet his. "This was yours. Maybe, you should—"

His eyes crinkled at the edges from his smile. "Truda, open it."

Shooting him a grateful smile, she pulled the bundle closer. With eager fingers, she unfolded the thick cloth and exposed the silver brooch that starred in the romantic stories of her young heart. The brooch of lost love.

The surface was rippled where hammers had shaped the heated metal, and delicate swirls surrounded a piece of polished amber. "Oh, it's so beautiful." As she ran a finger over the stone, she blinked to fight back threatening tears. "This is bigger than I imagined."

His fingers traced the edge of the stone setting. "Do you react like this over all recovered antiquities?"

Swallowing hard, she looked into his steady gaze. Was now the time to tell him of her special connection—that Reidun's brooch had an important place in her family history? "Not all, but it's happened. Being involved with the recovery of old documents or armaments or jewelry is an important part of why I became a historian."

"And the reason you came here?" His voice had an edge.

"Partly. I've been researching the legacy." She met his gaze straight on. "More because of the stories my nana told me since I was little—stories about the brooch and its legacy."

"Ha, more like a brute of a husband who scared away his young bride and then his pride made him careless." He slammed a hand on the table and struggled to push himself up. "Not much of a legacy."

How could he say that? She shook her head and leaned forward, wishing for the freedom to touch him, but knew he wouldn't allow her to. "You have no idea, but the story of Garet, Reidun, and the wedding wishes is famous." Maybe that was an overstatement.

Eyes wide, he looked as if she talked in another language. "What do the wishes spoken have to do with anything?"

"I don't think the words were wishes. I think it was a spell. Listen to the words, 'May your love prosper as far as your lands' outer reaches.'" She ran a finger over the smooth stone, the certainty growing surer in her thoughts. "On the surface, it sounds like a nice wish, but look at it from another angle. Does this have any consequence for someone who travels outside of the boundary? Does the love stop there?"

His gaze narrowed. "You mean the minute Reidun emerged from the old growth forest onto her father's lands, her love stopped."

"Or her memory of you faded. How was she transported?"

"Her father sent a messenger, but of course, I sent her accompanied by an escort."

"Do you remember who?"

"Ragnor." His eyes burned with stoked anger. "I assigned the same knight who inherited Wybjorn Castle." He slammed a fist on the table. "How could I have been so blind? He must have been in league with the troll for reasons I'll never understand."

"There's more." She fingered the edge of the metal. "I need to share something. I'm a descendant of Reidun's. That's why the brooch is so special."

"Descendant?" His eyes burned then his chin dropped and his head hung for a moment. "So, she married again."

Truda wished she could touch him. "Our family genealogy states she married Kolli the Smithy in 1630, and bore him five daughters. I'm related to Yule, the youngest."

He slumped back in the chair then immediately straightened and sucked in a breath.

"You're hurt?" The brooch forgotten, she jumped up and went around the table. "I saw the blood on the bedsheets. I know there's something wrong. Tell me."

His elbows braced on the table, he hunched his shoulders and blew out a breath. "Seems your act of sharing brings both good and bad body experiences."

"Oh, Garet." Her mind raced. His injury—the one sustained at the attack—must be evident. "Where is it?" She rested a hand on his shoulder.

His body jerked from under her hand then he sucked in a quick breath. "Lower back, left side."

She dropped to her knees and eased the fabric of his tunic up. Underneath he wore a thin linen shirt that was stained brown. At the sight of an ugly weeping scab, she gritted her teeth and told herself not to panic. This was the 21st century, and the miracle of modern medicine could cure just about everything.

Forcing her tone to remain light, she stood and swept her arm at the table. "Okay, buddy. Shirt off and lie facedown on the table. Let me look at this wound."

His movements were slow but finally he was in position.

She thrilled at seeing his strong body again. The sunlight filling the room showed off the definition of his muscles and also gave her a better look at the gash. The scab had broken open and was draining. That was good, but the fact the drainage was yellow-green was not. "I've got some stuff that will take the sting out of that wound."

"I would like that." His voice was rough, like he was drained of energy.

Quickly, she ran fresh water into the bowl and rinsed her hands. She grabbed her herbal jars and a cup from the shelf. "This will only take a couple minutes." The yellow powder from a half dozen goldenseal capsules was dumped into the cup then water mixed in to make a paste. "How are you doing?"

"Fine." His voice was no louder than a whisper.

God, he was fading. She swallowed past the lump in her throat. "Hey, Garet. Keep talking. Tell me how you knew to look for the curator."

"Up early, heard noise."

Working with quick moves, she cleaned the wound, wincing at the eruption of bubbles each time she poured on hydrogen peroxide. "Garet, this might hurt a bit but I know the paste will help. It's actually an old Native American remedy." She spread the goop over the wound, her stomach jumping every time he flinched. "I need a long bandage to wrap around your waist. There's one in my car's first aid kit."

"This is all right."

"No, I need this bandage." She bent her knees and looked him in the eye, studying for signs of fever. "I'm coming right back."

"Don't go." He tried to push himself upright but plopped back on the table.

That sight scared her, chilling her to her bones. He was weak, too weak. "Stay alert. Count my steps out to the car." Before she changed her mind, she strode to the back door and walked into the fresh air. She felt under the back fender to get the hidden key and then opened her car and grabbed the plastic case. At a jog, she returned to the kitchen and shuffled through the items to grab the boxes of bandages.

"Garet, can you sit up? I know you're tired but I can't wrap this well when you're flat."

He groaned and leaned his forehead on the table. Then he set his hands flat on the table and pushed. The faint outline of muscles in his arms and back bulged and his arms shook as he pushed himself upright.

"That's great. Here, hold this end." With quick moves, she gently set a sterile pad over the wound, then wrapped the bandage around his waist. The fact he didn't warn about keeping her distance was very telling.

Once the bandage was tied off, she backed away and studied Garet, tears stinging the back of her eyes. His head hung close to his chest and he swayed where he sat. "Can I help you climb down?"

Through hanks of hair falling over his face, he glanced at her, his eyes slitted with pain. "Don't help me. Just move that chair close." After a deep breath, he braced his hands on the edge of the table and slid onto the chair, landing with a thud. "Thor's blood, that hurts."

To keep from rushing to his side, she gathered the supplies and tucked the brooch in a skirt pocket, her throat thick with dread. Now they had only to wait for the herbs to help his wound. If only he had a reserve of them in his system. The way that she had.

"You are planning something." Leaning a forearm on the table, he lifted a shaky finger in her direction. "Promise me, no further help. If my shame is gone, nothing ties me here."

8

Fear grabbed her stomach and twisted. "No, Garet, don't talk like that." Her research couldn't have condemned him. She fisted her hands on the table and leaned toward him. "You're here and talking. I just patched up your wound. Don't even think about leaving me now."

She pounded her fists on the table, feeling hot tears on her cheeks. "I can't find the hero of my fairy tale only to have him disappear. What good is a princess without a prince?" Two strides brought her around the end of the table. "I've been half in love with you since I was six years old."

He lifted his head, his blue eyes dull and bleak. "I am . . . prepared . . . for . . . Valhalla."

"No, you're not going anywhere." Bracing herself for what she knew lay ahead, she jumped into his lap and threw her arms around his shoulders. "I love you and need you with me."

Hard wood pressed against his back and he flexed his shoulders to relieve the ache. Across his lap stretched a strange weight. What had he been doing? Blinking, he shook his head to clear his blurry vision. Sitting in the kitchen. Something about the brooch. Blackness had swirled, pulling with cloying power, and then the echo of Truda's sweet words calling him back, saying she needed him. That she loved him.

Truda!

No! He sat forward and the weight shifted. Reaching out a hand, he touched her slender back and gently shook. His chest tightened at the realization of what she'd done. Again.

"Truda?" His voice squeaked like a rusty hinge and his throat felt raw. He wrapped an arm around her middle, slid the other under her neck, and rolled her into the cradle of his lap. Her cheek landed against his chest, rapid breaths puffing against his chin. His skin heated—too fast.

One glance at her flushed cheeks and damp hair told him she'd taken on his fever. He lifted a hand to brush away the hair stuck to her cheek and stilled, his breath caught in his throat. His hand had the same substance and texture as hers.

For only a moment, he extended his arm and turned it. Skin, muscles, hair, scars. This was the arm of a human, not of an apparition.

Obviously, the woman did not listen to commands. "My turn to act as healer." He scooped her close to his chest and staggered across the floor, leaning against the doorway before tackling the stairs. "A cool bath will help." By the time he reached the bedroom, his feet dragged across the tiles but he relished the feel of tension in his muscles.

He laid her on the bed and walked to the bathroom to turn on the water. Unable to resist, he cupped his hands under the stream and splashed water on his face and chest. A laugh erupted at the sheer pleasure of feeling again. Then he sobered, grabbed a cloth from the shelf, and tossed it into the swirling water before returning to Truda.

She lay on her side, curled into a shivering ball.

His Valkyrie. She had gone to the battlefield and brought her warrior home. She was strong, she'd get through this. As quickly as he could, he stripped off her sweater and pulled the skirt off over her hips. At the sight of her tits and muff barely covered by pink underclothes, he groaned. He did not understand about these almost invisible scraps of cloth but was willing to learn.

He pulled at the ties to his breeches and stepped out of them. "Come, honnig, time to get you cool." He scooped her into his arms, the heat of her fevered skin almost branding him, and carried her to the half-full bathtub. When he sank into the water, he expected to hear a sizzle. A shove with his foot slowed the water to a trickle.

He shifted her body so the water rose to her stomach. With the dripping cloth, he bathed her face and neck, his hands awkward at this unaccustomed task.

She groaned and moved her head out of his reach. "No, too cold." Hands braced on his thighs, she tried to push herself out of the water.

Thank the gods and goddesses. She had awakened. "I must. You took on my ailment." He rested a hand on her shoulder and held her. "Be still. Let me bathe your face to break the fever."

"Oh!" she cried. Her hand scooted down his thigh and squeezed then moved higher and repeated the action. She rubbed her shoulders against his chest. "I can really feel you." Twisting in his arms, she looked up, her gaze searching his face, water droplets in her lashes. "Are you human again?" A hand rose toward his face then hesitated.

He cupped his hand around hers and brought it to his jaw. "At least for now." The softness of her touch against his skin felt wonderful. One glance at her hopeful smile and the shiny look in her green eyes made his mouth go dry.

Her body rubbing against his brought on other reactions and he shifted his hips away. "Sit forward so I can splash your back." He gently grasped her shoulders and turned her, testing that her skin did feel cooler. With cupped hands, he scooped water onto her back, watching it run in twin rivulets on the sides of her backbone.

"Ah, that feels good." She grabbed the edge of the tub and moved toward the opposite end. Suddenly, her head disappeared under the water.

"What? Truda?" He lunged forward and grabbed at her body, one hand landing on an arm, the other grabbing a handful of soft tit. He hauled her out of the water and against his chest. "Are you all right?"

She settled against his chest and laughed. "I was just getting my head wet. That's the secret to breaking a fever." With a wiggle, she pressed herself against his hand. "But you may have something else in mind."

The pleasure she offered was tempting. Too tempting. He moved his hand to her stomach and splayed his fingers, holding her tight against his body. The pressure of her ass against his cock made him wince but he gritted his teeth and warned her. "Do not scare me again."

"I'm sorry. I didn't mean to." She twisted her head and looked up through her eyelashes. A sigh escaped. "I can't believe how handsome you are in real life." She stretched upward and brushed his cheek with an open-mouthed kiss, swirling her tongue between her lips.

His brain said no, but his body had been denied for too long. He reached up and cupped a breast, flicking a thumb over her nipple. "Truda, you should rest."

"I will, right after we have sex." She turned, sagged against his chest and twined her arms around his neck. "Come nap with me."

He shook his head, warring with his true wishes. "You are weak."

"I've waited long enough. I'm strong enough to get myself dry and to the bed. I'll show you." She pushed away and climbed out of the tub, swaying only a bit.

He pretended not to notice. Instead, he took his time in watching her towel off her delectable body. Even in the cold water, his cock was rock hard and he fought to keep his hips still. Without letting on, he watched her carefully for any signs of shakiness then climbed out and took the towel when she was finished.

The sight that waited for him was a shock, although he didn't know why. This woman was like none other he had met. She faced the bathing chamber, chin on hands and elbows propped on the mattress, her upper body lying on the mattress. "I'm a bit more tired than I thought. But in this position, I have lots of support."

"All the more reason to get into the bed and sleep." He walked toward her, intent on scooping her onto the mattress. When he spotted her pale ass cheeks with legs spread, he couldn't resist caressing the rounded flesh. One caress led to another.

"Mmm, that's nice." Her hips swayed. "But I want hard and fast."

Had he heard her right? He cupped her ass then slid his fingers along the crease at the top of her leg down to her inner thigh. Two fingers stroked her pussy lips and came away slick with her juices. His willpower gave way. Into her channel, he plunged his middle finger and, with the other, tickled her clitty.

"Oh, yes." Her hands plopped to the mattress and grabbed handfuls of the quilt.

The sweet sound of her urgency pressed him forward. He rocked his hips but his cock scooted in the crevice between her cheeks. A nice sensation but not what he had in mind either.

"You are too low." He leaned down and pulled out the trundle bed a few inches. "Stand on this."

With a smile tossed over her shoulder, she stepped up and again offered her backside to his touch.

The blood pumped through him, hot and primal, and he cautioned himself against moving too fast. No repeated mistakes from the past. With one hand on her hip, he stepped close and nudged the head of his cock along her slippery folds. He pressed, easing his thickness into her warm channel and waited for her to adjust to his girth.

Truda circled her hips and pressed back, accepting more of his length. "Garet, this is not my first time. You won't hurt me."

Instinct took over and he thrust deep, his other hand going around her side and palming a breast. He pulled back and plunged again, wanting to give her as much pleasure as she provided him. The tension in his balls built higher with each thrust.

"That's what I wanted, my warrior." She arched her back, rising off the mattress on straightened arms.

He pumped until he saw her body stiffen and heard her cry. Then he plunged in one last time and shot his seed deep into her body, his breath rasping from his throat. When he could breathe again, he leaned over and kissed her shoulder. "Ready for your nap now?" Not that he relished being separated from her luscious curves, but every line of her limp body screamed exhaustion.

With a groan, she turned her head on the mattress and glanced from the side of her eye. "Do I have to move?"

He chuckled, skimmed a hand around her waist and lifted her to the mattress. "Slide under the covers."

As slow as a turtle, she dragged herself to the head of the bed and pulled the quilt over her. "You, too."

At her insistence, he climbed in and held her close until she finally slept.

But he was too restless to remain. With careful moves, he slipped from under the quilt and moved to retrieve his breeches. The sight of the garment he had worn for too long made him shudder. He turned to the carved wooden armoire and opened the double doors. One of these costumes had to come close to fitting him. After finding a new set of breeches and a loose shirt, he rummaged around the bottom for shoes.

Once the idea of walking Wybjorn's grounds crossed his mind, he knew he couldn't settle down for the night until he'd breathed the air outside the castle walls. With each step down the hallway, his excitement grew as did the strange hollowness in the pit of his stomach.

Hunger. He'd deal with that next.

At the castle entry, he rested a flat hand against the door and took a deep breath. Centuries had passed since he'd felt pasture grass under his feet or smelled the dust of a rocky trail. Finally, he could walk from his prison. He threw the bolt to the side and yanked open the wooden door. A breeze blew into the opening, enveloping his body in clean fresh air.

In the east, the sky was darkening to a rich purple-blue, and stars twinkled above the canopy of trees. He stepped forward and was pushed back, windmilling his arms to keep upright.

Had he stepped on a stone that upset his balance?

The threshold looked level. He tried again but got the same result. Frustration building inside, he slammed the door and started across the entry, his long strides eating up the distance to the kitchen. At the back door, he experienced the same invisible barrier.

Twenty minutes later, he stripped off his clothes and climbed into bed, fitting his body along Truda's back. He rested the back of his fingers against her neck and her forehead, grateful the fever seemed to have broken. With an arm around her middle, he drew her close, wanting to enjoy her for as long as she'd stay. His limitations should not become hers.

Tomorrow's conversation about this new obstacle would not be pleasant.

Truda came awake slowly, aware of two things—her bladder was overfull and the previous day's fever was now centered in her back.

A low snore sounded.

Ah, not an illness fever. Garet—a different kind of fever.

She slipped out of bed to use the bathroom, surprised that she wore a nightgown. When had that happened? One look in a mirror had her diving for her hairbrush. But no amount of brushing could fix her wavy hair after it dried naturally.

"I like it curly."

She jumped and turned. "No fair. You can still move as quiet as a ghost."

"Your turn is over." He jerked a thumb over his shoulder. "Depart."

A smile spread her lips. Seeing, really seeing, his face made her so happy. "No sharing the space?"

"Nope." He crossed his arms and stared.

Just one look, she told herself. But she couldn't stop the long slow perusal of his naked body.

He raised an eyebrow, his mouth drawn into a tight line.

She ambled past and squealed when he swatted her ass.

"Minx." Then the door closed with a thud.

With a running leap, she landed on the bed and wiggled her arms and legs in silent celebration. Garet the Protector, a man of legends, was human and in her bedroom.

She raised her head and glanced around. Actually, she was in his.

The doorknob rattled. She scurried to the head of the bed and reclined against the pillows.

Then the door opened and he stood framed in the doorway. The magnificent specimen of a warrior. Hair tousled and brushing his shoulders, muscles bunching and flexing as he walked, a thick, but flaccid, cock that bumped along the top of his thigh. He stopped at the side of the bed. "We need to talk."

"Come closer." Affecting a frown, she cupped a hand around her ear. "I'm having trouble hearing you. Maybe from the fever."

At her last word, he crawled across the mattress and brushed a hand against her skin, brows drawn into a frown. "You don't feel hot."

With a twist, she captured his hand and pulled it toward her crotch. "Test me here."

"Truda—"

"No talking." Using her grip as leverage, she covered his mouth and shook her head. "Not a single word, unless you're telling me what position to be in. I want you, Garet, all of you." With her hands cradling her jaw, she drew his head close and planted kisses over his chin, lips and nose. The fact she felt resistance against her lips thrilled her all the more.

He groaned and flopped onto the bed, pulling her on top of his body, a hand trailing over her lip. "How can I resist?"

"Don't try." She extended her tongue to lap at the nub of his male nipple, then closed her mouth over it and sucked.

A low, deep groan rasped from Garet's throat. "I must feel your skin." His hands yanked at the hem of her nightgown and pulled it up and off her body. On the downward stroke, he ran his hands along her raised arms, circling his thumbs along the outside of her breasts.

She twisted until she brushed a tight nipple against his moving thumb. At the contact, a moan of satisfaction hissed from her lips. "This time, I want to see your face. I hope you're okay with me on top."

"You are giving me a choice?" He chuckled.

An experimental wiggle of her hips and she pressed against his lengthening cock. Good, he was halfway ready. Being able to touch his strength was intoxicating. This man had worn a suit of armor and ridden into battle, the accounts of which she'd studied. She gave a fleeting thought to his wound but assumed since she'd recovered, he must have too.

Later.

Now was for sensual pleasure. To complete the lovemaking they'd started the previous day. She leaned low enough to brush the tips of her already tight nipples across his chest, circling them to tease his male breasts. The friction sent tingles straight to her pussy and her dewy juices seeped.

Under her fingers, steely muscles shifted as his arms came around her sides and his big hands caressed her back.

"Your skin is as soft as doeskin." He turned his head and kissed a trail along the inside of her arm.

"Hmm, we'll work on those analogies." Her thighs rode on his tight waist and she scooted down until her crotch bumped his cock. His impressive, rigid cock.

Need spiraled low in her womb. Damn, she'd wanted to linger this morning but her body wanted satisfaction. Trailing her hands from his shoulders, she clamped them around his ribs and eased her knees beside his hips. Keeping her gaze locked with his, she pulled her wet pussy along the length of his cock. With a slow slide, she circled her hips. "Are you ready?"

"For you, always."

By flexing her thighs, she rose a bit and centered her throbbing pussy over his cock then eased down enough to capture him. "Come get me."

His embrace tightened and his hips flexed, engorged cock plunging inside with one long stroke.

At the sensation of being filled completely, she hissed in a breath, excitement spiraling in her womb.

With a thrust, Garet sat up, his arms tight around her back. "Wrap your legs around me."

When she did as he asked, their connection was lost. A whimper escaped, and she steadied herself on his shoulders.

Strong hands clamped on her hips, lifted her then slowly lowered her onto his cock, his blue gaze staring into hers.

Warmth spread through her chest and she bit her lower lip. This was really happening. Her warrior was right here with her and was here to stay. To counter his thrusts, she moved her hips and felt his cock rub against her G-spot. Ripples of tension built and she threw back her head, letting Garet guide the tempo. When she felt his lips close around a nipple and suckle, she cried out, her completion throbbing around his cock, pulling him deeper, wanting to hold him tighter.

With frenzied pulls, he moved her in opposition to his strokes. His mouth dropped kisses across her breast and, with one last thrust, he let out a groan as deep and harsh as a battle cry.

She wrapped her arms around his neck and rested her temple against his, their puffing breaths tickling each other's shoulders. The fact she felt him a testament to his reality. "Ja, that's a good way to wake up."

With a slow twist, he fell back to the mattress, cradling her head. When their breathing returned to normal, he ran a finger along her hairline and down the side of her face.

"Another fever check?"

"Just enjoying my newfound sense of touch."

"Oh, yes." A glint in her eyes, she wiggled against his body. "I'm enjoying it, too."

He touched her forehead with his. "We need to talk."

"Uh-oh, that sounds serious."

"First—haven't you ever heard of meat? I plundered the kitchen last night and what you bought didn't amount to much."

"Didn't?" She shifted in his arms. "As in it's gone."

"What I found fit to eat. That sack with grains and nuts looked like chicken food."

"No problem. We'll go to that little café for breakfast." She leaned forward and ran her tongue along his collarbone. "Or maybe for brunch." When he didn't respond, she looked up and saw bleakness in his expression. Her stomach clenched. "What's wrong?"

"I am still bound to the castle." He ran a finger along her cheek.

"What?" She sat upright. "How can that be?"

"I tried walking through every doorway but was stopped."

"Stopped?" The change from the afterglow of lovemaking languor to solving a puzzle caught her off guard. "By bars? The whole castle is locked?"

"No, I can see nothing of the barrier."

"I don't understand." She jumped out of bed and dashed to her suitcase, rummaging through her clothes until she found yoga pants and a T-shirt. "Show me. Did you have the brooch?"

"No, why?" He jammed a pillow behind his head and leaned against it. "How will that make a difference?"

"Don't ask, just get dressed. We have to try." She yanked the shirt over her head, pulling her hair free. "Where's my skirt from yesterday? I stuck the brooch in the pocket."

"On the floor by the foot post." He moved off the bed and grabbed the breeches and shirt from a nearby bench.

Ten minutes later, they stood in front of the entry door. Truda couldn't keep herself from stepping out into the sun, just to make sure she wasn't trapped. She turned and shaded her eyes with a hand to see into the dim interior. "Okay, now you try."

In one hand, he held the brooch and walked toward the opening. Suddenly, he stumbled back.

She gasped at the sudden movement, searching for physical signs of what held him back. "Are you hurt?"

A hand rubbed the middle of his chest. "Just feel stupid."

Her thoughts raced. "What if you have to say something? Try repeating the legacy."

"Tell it to me."

She squinted an eye at him. How could words that had become so important to her be forgotten by the person who'd been so affected? "May your love prosper as far as your lands' outer reaches."

He tried again with the same result. This time he banged a knee. "Are you sure those are the right words? I thought there were more."

"Oh, we have to figure this out." She paced and waved her hands in the air. "There is a connection, I know there is. Everything connected to a troll is not as it seems."

"That day, I had my suspicions, but let my happiness overshadow my caution." His eyes burned at her determination, but he forced a smile. "Maybe the Trust will give me a job as a tour guide."

"Don't joke." She squared off opposite him and jammed her hands on her hips. "We didn't go through all this for you to be stuck here."

"What if this is where I belong?" His arm swept the interior of the room.

"Don't say that! You belong with me." Eyes blinking rapidly, she stepped close and threw her arms around his waist, wishing her confidence could transfer through her embrace. "I have our life all planned. We'll move to the family farm I inherited last year. You have experience with crop management. Maybe we'll grow herbal plants like echinacea and goldenseal."

She tilted her head so she could gaze upon his handsome face. "I'll rewrite your story to correct the obvious inaccuracies. But maybe I'll turn it into fiction so I can exaggerate the juicy parts." With a devilish smile, she lifted on tiptoes and stretched to press a hard kiss on his lips.

* * *

Throat tight with emotion, he brushed his knuckles across her cheek. "My little Valkyrie, you can't control everything."

"Don't use that tone of voice." She rubbed against his hand. "I'm not giving up. Let's go read the inscription on the wedding tapestry. I know this is the key to unlocking this puzzle."

Wanting to believe she was right, he grabbed her hand and strode to the Great Hall with Truda at his side. This felt right—them side by side, working on a problem together. "Okay, the inscription reads, 'In your true love's hand, may your love prosper as far as your lands' outer reaches.' I knew there were more words."

"What?" She gasped and grabbed his forearm, her fingers holding tight. "Ah, I never heard that first phrase. All I ever knew was the other part. Maybe you need to be in the same place where you first touched the brooch."

For a moment, he relished the sensation made by her tight grip. If this was all he was granted, he believed it was enough. This strong woman believed in him, believed in their bond. "That would be here in this room." He squinted as he looked around the area and then moved a few feet to one side. After repeating the inscription, he walked across the room and tried to nudge a knee through the closest exit door. He was stopped short—again. Disappointment weighed his steps back to where Truda was.

"This has to be tied to Reidun." She paced, running a hand through her hair. "So, maybe you need to be where you saw her last. Where were you when she left that day?"

Standing opposite the tapestry, he studied the inscription. "One word is hard to read, the stitching is not clear. If I remember correctly, I heard the troll say, beloved, but this reads, genuine or true."

"Not much of a difference." She shrugged. "I don't understand. I think we need to change locations."

The words tumbled through his mind. Beloved or true. Past

or present. Realization hit hard, and his chest tightened. Truda was right—the location was the key element. "Come, I know exactly where I need to be." With growing confidence, he grabbed her hand and headed back toward the entry hall.

She had to run to keep up with his long strides. "What did you discover?"

Up the stairs, he dashed, pulling her behind him then he approached the short wall overlooking the castle's entry door. "This is what is important. The brooch is here from the past, you believe in the words, and I believe in you."

Bracing a shoulder against the wall, he half turned and extended his hand. "Hold this with me, Truda Borg." His hands surrounded hers with the brooch clasped inside. "I need to stand here in the spot where I first saw you. 'In my beloved's hand, may my love prosper as far as my lands' outer reaches'. You are the one I've been waiting for." He paused, thinking a special feeling would wash over him.

Tears filled her eyes and her lips trembled. "Oh, Garet."

At the love shining in her eyes, he felt his throat tighten. Thor, he hoped this worked because he would not want to live if he had to watch this woman walk away. He clasped her to his chest, lowered his mouth for a sweet kiss and then strode down the stairs and yanked open the door. At the last moment, indecision overtook him and he hesitated.

"This is it, I feel it," Truda's voice was confident. "Walk outside, Garet."

After a final look at her smiling face, he closed his eyes. Holding the wish for a future with Truda close in his heart, he stepped over the threshold. A crunch sounded as his boot ground on loose dirt on the concrete step. He took another step, setting his other foot down on gravel, then opened his eyes and looked around.

The castle's wooden door was four feet behind him. Drawing deep breaths of fresh air into his lungs, he spread out his arms and spun in a circle. "I am free."

Truda ran and jumped into his arms, wrapping her legs around his waist. "No, you're mine."

Sweet kisses rained on his face. Lightness filled his heart, and he grabbed her in a tight embrace, spinning them both until they grew dizzy. "I can live with that."

Keket's Curse

Shayla Kersten

Prologue

Temple of Hathor, Dendara, Egypt, 1123 B.C.

The night air teased Jamila's skin through the fine linen robe. Just thinking about the warrior Bomani sent damp fire through her core. Her body ached for him with an insatiable lust. No other man attracted her this way. His hard body and thick sword would soon claim her once again.

Given to the temple at the age of five, Jamila grew up surrounded by luxury and debauchery in equal measures. The goddess Hathor granted her temple maidens freedom to love where they wanted. Introduced to the art of pleasure at eighteen, Jamila learned her lessons well. Now twenty-three and one of Hathor's handmaidens, she could have her choice of lovers. And she chose Bomani.

Jamila leaned around the column where she hid, seeking sight of her lover. The clear night sky cast the light of a thousand stars over the courtyard. Anticipation whetted her desire. Secrecy only heightened the erotic nature of their meetings. Three weeks had passed since her last tryst with the tall, muscled warrior. Three weeks too long.

A shadow moved toward her. The soft swish of linen accompanied silent footsteps.

Intense pleasure shivered through her body leaving her panting. Bomani must have seen her. His stride quickened.

"Bomani!" The soft gasp was muffled by his lips on hers.

Hard muscles pressed her against the temple column. Already erect, his cock pushed into the soft flesh of her stomach.

"I want you now." Bomani's hoarse groan fanned the fire in her pussy.

"Yes . . ." Jamila tugged the edge of his linen tunic up until her hands found the thick, swollen shaft. Grasping his cock in one hand, her fingers not quite closing around the girth, she stroked him. "I need to feel you in me. Now."

More than any other man, Bomani stirred her desire. She dreamed of his thick veined flesh plunging deep in her aching pussy. Thoughts of his arrival had held her on the edge of orgasm for days. Now, with satisfaction imminent, she almost came just from touching him.

Rough calloused hands grabbed her ass and squeezed. Frantic fingers rolled up the sheer material until her gown bunched around her waist. Pushing her against the limestone column, Bomani grabbed her thighs and pulled her up.

Jamila released his weeping cock and flung her arms around him. Her legs circled his waist. The blunt head of hot flesh nudged her wet, aching hole. His thick shaft slid deep in one hard stroke. She bit the tight muscle of his shoulder to keep from screaming her pleasure.

The cool evening air contrasted with the heat of his cock. His soft linen tunic caressed her breasts through her near-transparent robe. Her nipples tightened to hard points. She rubbed the sensitive nubs against his heavily muscled chest.

Intense pleasure rolled through her body as his long, hard

cock withdrew before plunging again. The hard column bracing her against her lover grated against her back.

His musky scent blended with the heady aroma of her own juices. He once again impaled her with his thick sword. Her body shuddered with pleasure at the invasion.

Muffled groans combined with the wet slap of flesh. The dank smell of the Nile delta mingled with the pungent scent of arousal. Pleasure burned through Jamila as her body raced toward ecstasy. A few more strokes would be all she needed to quench the fire in her body.

"Bomani!"

The icy voice of the priestess Keket washed over Jamila like a sudden cold shower. Even her obvious fury didn't cool the fire in Jamila's loins.

Jamila's legs tightened on Bomani's waist to keep her lover from pulling away. "No," she moaned. Her determination was no match for his strength. The hot flesh she'd desired for weeks slipped free of her aching cunt. She tottered off balance when her legs dropped and her feet hit the ground. "No!"

Caught having sex with Keket's lover, Jamila should have been afraid. Her lust-driven mind wouldn't recognize the seriousness of her situation. Jamila could be banished from the temple.

Little did she know the power the high priestess Keket wielded.

1

New York City, Present Day

Fire burned in Jamila's body. Flames danced over her skin, flickering into the pit of her stomach. Burning, acidlike clarity pulsed through her cunt. Insatiable desire drove her, had driven her, for the last 3000 years. For the millionth time, her mind damned Keket's Curse as her body careened out of control with need.

Aaron Freiberg was the perfect solution to her immediate problem. A fit, hard body and an even harder dick pressed against her as they rode the elevator to his apartment. A cocky young man, he didn't question her request for no-strings-attached sex. He accepted her offer as if it were his due. He didn't even waver when she insisted on no kissing, at least on the lips.

His hungry mouth bathed her neck with warm strokes of his tongue. The chill air cooled the wet streaks making her overheated body shiver.

Jamila's impatient libido screamed for satisfaction. Her skirt hiked up, she wrapped one leg around his hip. Grinding her pussy against the hard flesh straining against his fly, she growled at the sweet friction. If the doors didn't open soon, she would demand he fuck her here and now.

A slight lift and drop signaled the elevator had reached the floor. The doors swooshed open to reveal a lavishly decorated hall. Jamila pushed her amorous lover toward the open doors. She needed him and she needed him now.

They stumbled from the elevator.

"Which way?" she demanded

Aaron grabbed her arm and tugged.

He didn't have to encourage her. She followed, pushing him to hurry his steps. Her whole body ached with an unquenchable fire. His cock deep inside her would only slightly cool the burn.

Nothing could put out the eternal flame of her desire.

The jangle of keys matched the ringing in her ears. She'd waited too long. She'd pushed herself to the limit of her endurance. She needed sex now.

The broad shoulders blurred as lust consumed her. Darkness teased the edge of her vision when the door finally swung open. Only the man in front of her mattered. And really only one part of him.

Aaron slammed the door behind her. Darkness engulfed her, then movement registered right before light stabbed her eyes.

"Now . . ." Her voice growled like an animal. A cat in heat.

Aaron's dark eyes flashed from lust to fear and back to lust.

Then Jamila lunged for him. Her hands tore at his shirt. Need made her fingers clumsy as she ripped at his belt.

"Now!" Her tone rose from a growl to a howl.

"All right, lady." Aaron's hands joined hers and the buckle released. "Shit, what did you do? OD on Ecstasy?"

"Shut up. I'm here to fuck." A rough shove at his hard chest sent him reeling back.

The coffee table skittered to the side and glass crashed. Aaron fell to the floor hard. Flat on his back, he gasped to regain his breath.

Jamila didn't wait.

His cock bulged against his briefs through his open pants.

Jamila yanked her dress up and tore her panties off. Straddling Aaron's thighs, she pulled his briefs below his balls. Just enough to free his cock.

In spite of having the breath knocked out of him, his erection stood proud. Hard and already leaking, thick and circumcised, the tip swollen and red.

Barely aware of his moan, Jamila scrambled to position her pussy above him. Her breath caught when the blunt tip slid against her clit.

"Yes," she whispered, sliding down. The hard flesh pierced her cunt. Flashes of light blinded her. The sound of cars from the street, of doors slamming in the hallway, everything except the wet slide of his flesh into her, faded into the distance.

His skin felt cold and clammy against her overheated sex. The burning in her groin eased slightly. But it was not enough. It never was.

Her muscles clenched around his cock. She rose up letting the thick cock slide almost free before she slammed back down. The long dick filled her, touching her womb deep inside. She ground her swollen clit against his coarse pubic hair.

As the explosive tension subsided, relief washed over her like a cooling breeze.

"Yes," she moaned. Feeling returned in other parts of her body. Strain quivered through her thigh muscles. Aaron's moans joined hers, reminding her of his presence. Her muscles found relief when he bent his knees and his thighs supported her back.

His hips arched to meet her downward thrust. His feet planted on the polished wooden floor provided leverage for powerful strokes.

"Yes, more, harder . . ."

"You like it rough, huh?" Aaron's voice echoed as if far away.

Calloused hands rubbed her thighs, cool against her feverish skin. Rough fingers teased her clit. Pleasure shot through her.

One hand moved to an aching breast. Her nipples strained against the material of her dress. A twisting pinch sent an electrical shock straight to her cunt.

"You want it hard and rough, bitch?"

Her reply came out a moan. Words wouldn't form. The heat blistering her body drained toward her pussy, focusing in anticipation of relief at last.

"So close . . ." The whisper slipped from her lips. Eyes closed, she concentrated on the rising wave of ecstasy. A little more, a little harder . . .

The exquisite ride to pleasure ended when Aaron's hands grabbed her waist. With a painful twist, Jamila found herself on her back, the hard wooden floor cold beneath her.

"You want to play rough, I can play," Aaron's body moved over her.

Her hips arched trying to regain contact. Heat flashed through her body again, worse for the sudden interruption.

Aaron's hands pinned her wrists. His cock slid across her clit but he avoided her frantic attempt to capture him.

"Not yet," he growled. "I want to play this game too."

His heavy body pressed her down, hands immobilized. His lips brushed hers.

"No!" She struggled harder. "Stop. You don't know what—" She turned her head to the side. "Please don't! You can't do this—"

One strong hand released her wrist and grabbed her hair. Jamila fought to keep her head turned in spite of the sharp pain but his strength overpowered her.

"Please . . . No—" Hard lips muffled her cry. Bruising force knocked her teeth against her lips and the copper taste of blood filled her mouth. Her free hand clawed at his face.

"Bitch!" His hand untangled from her hair and grabbed her jaw.

Forcing her mouth open, Aaron took her mouth, his tongue thrusting between her lips.

"No . . ." Jamila's moan turned into a whimper.

The hard body stilled, the inquisitive tongue ceased its probing and the light of anger and lust faded from Aaron's eyes.

David Craise just wanted a quiet evening, a cold beer and, for once, a good night's sleep. At least he was getting the cold beer.

Seated on a stool at the end of the dark wooden bar, David ran a finger up and down his glass. The trails of condensation fascinated his tired mind. Fortunately, the pub wasn't busy. Only a few customers gathered at the other end of the bar. David couldn't deal with a crowd right now.

For three nights in a row, calls from the station interrupted his sleep. Why couldn't people kill each other at a decent hour?

David bowed his head, regretting the thoughts. He was just tired. He rubbed his eyes hard, sparks of lights flying around the inside of his eyelids. The vision of the dead woman last night would haunt him for a long time. From what David put together, the husband had been pissed his dinner wasn't ready, so he killed his wife and cut her up with a butcher knife.

The case wrapped up fast since police found the husband sitting in his wife's blood mumbling about missing dinner.

A shudder ran through David. Maybe he needed a break from homicide. A man could only handle so much death before he broke. But then his sense of justice and responsibility kicked in. He couldn't walk away. He just needed some sleep. And maybe a life outside of work.

Since his fiancée had called it quits two years ago, David

couldn't seem to find the time or energy to think about dating. Getting laid would be nice though. He spent too many nights with only his right hand for company.

"Long face, tall beer and you, my friend, look like you could use someone to talk to."

David looked up at the sound of Joshua's voice. "Hard day."

Joshua Preston tossed his coat on a stool and eased onto one around the corner of the bar from David. "Bud on tap," he said to Tina, the blond bartender.

"Coming up," she said with her perpetual smile.

David watched her walk away from them. "I need her job," he mumbled.

"What? The life of a big city detective getting boring?" Joshua's finger hooked the edge of the bowl of peanuts in front of David and pulled it toward him.

David snorted a not-so-amused laugh. "I want boring."

"You'd call it quits in a week." Joshua scooped some of the nuts from the bowl and tossed them in his mouth. "Maybe you just need a vacation."

David smiled at his portly friend. As medical examiner for nearly thirty years, Joshua had seen more death than David ever would, but he still kept a jolly Santa attitude. He laughed at the image of his gray-haired mentor with a long beard and a red suit. "Maybe a vacation would be a good idea." David snagged the peanuts back.

"Find some place warm and sunny with bikini-clad women. You should get laid."

David choked on his peanuts. Grabbing the beer, he took a long drink to clear his throat. Joshua always seemed to know what David was thinking. "Thanks for the advice. I think."

Tina slid a beer in front of Joshua but she directed her smile at David. She sauntered back down the bar to another customer.

Joshua's voice dropped to a whisper. "She'd jump your bones."

David let his gaze rest on Tina's retreating figure. Long blond hair pulled into a high ponytail swayed back and forth. Her nice ass, tightly packaged in faded jeans, kept time with her hair. Not a bad idea . . .

"No, bad idea. I don't want to deal with another relationship."

"Who said anything about a relationship? You don't have to date someone to sleep with her." Joshua grabbed the bowl of peanuts again. "You need to do something to relax before you explode."

David shook his head and closed his eyes. As good as the idea of a willing female body against him sounded, his ex had left him too burned. Even after two years, he wasn't ready.

Joshua took a long drink of his beer. The glass returned to the counter half empty. "Gotta go. Elizabeth will be wondering where I am."

"Tell her I said 'hi'."

"Always do. See you tomorrow. Try to get some sleep." Joshua grabbed his coat and put it on as he headed toward the door.

David watched him until the door shut behind him. He was still staring at the door when the woman walked in. Exotic almond-shaped eyes and coal-black hair. She glanced around the room with a frantic wild-eyed look.

David couldn't help staring. When her gaze met his, he tried to look away but he couldn't. Dark eyes glittered like onyx with a hungry, predatory look. She moved with the grace of a cat on the hunt and he was her prey. A shiver raced through his body, and blood rushed to fill his cock.

Her long black coat flapped open with each step, revealing a short, emerald-green dress. Although her eyes captured his gaze, the slim body still registered in his mind. Full breasts pushed against the tight green material and legs, long legs made to wrap around a man's body.

When she'd moved within a few feet of him, her delicate nostrils flared. A flash of tongue wet her lips and her black eyes narrowed.

David now knew what an animal felt like trapped in a car's headlights. His mind yelled at him to do something, but his body wouldn't cooperate.

She circled him. His head turned to follow her movement. Hot breath caressed his ear.

"I want *you*. Now."

A shudder swept through David's body and took up residence in his groin. His cock strained against his pants and his balls tightened. If she touched him, he might come where he sat. He breathed deep, hoping to calm his racing heart. Her scent filled his senses. *Exotic spices and dry heat.* He shook his head to clear the strange thought, and his mind.

As if she knew the effect she had on him, she trailed one sharp nail down his spine.

"I . . . We . . ." His mouth worked now but his brain couldn't supply a coherent sentence. His suspicious nature swept some of the fog from his brain.

"Look, lady. I'm a cop. You're skirting with solicitation here."

"Don't want money. I just want you to fuck me. Now. Here." A raspy purr whispered in his ear.

David drew a ragged breath. His mind screamed but he said, "Here?" His voice cracked and his cock jumped.

This had to be a setup. Would Joshua do something like this? David couldn't believe it. Besides, when Joshua passed the woman on the way out of the bar, there had been no indication of recognition.

"Now you're talking about indecent exposure." His voice might be objecting but his dick had a mind of its own. His aching cock strained against his slacks.

"Follow me," she growled.

The woman tugged at his sleeve and the stasis holding David

released. Sliding off the barstool, he stumbled after her. He couldn't believe he was doing this but he followed her anyway. His only focus was on the dark figure in front of him. For all he cared, they were the only two people in the bar.

A door opened, light blinded him for a second after being in the dimly lit bar.

The bathroom. The door clicked behind him and the lock snapped into place.

"Now!"

Her black coat slid to the floor. She fumbled with his belt. Warm hands tugged his shirt free before fingers released the button and zipper on his pants. Cool air caressed his aching cock when she yanked his briefs down.

"Look . . ." He needed to stop this. Fucking a strange woman in a public bathroom? He'd lost his mind.

"Shut up and fuck me."

Once again, the forceful growl made his mind cloud with lust. He reached for her but she eluded his grasp.

With her back to him, she raised the hem of her dress until it bunched around her waist. Black lace, boy-cut panties slid to her ankles. One delicate foot kicked free of the sexy material. With her hands against the wall, she stood spread-eagled.

"Now."

His mind left the building and his cock took over at the controls.

Presented with a sweet tight ass and unblemished skin the color of café au lait, David couldn't stop himself from obeying her command.

He tugged her hips to adjust her position, his mind barely registering the silken smoothness of her skin. His balls ached with need. The tip of his cock met satin wetness.

"Now!" Her anguished cry accompanied a backward push.

His hard flesh sank into her tight depth. Heat overwhelmed his cock. With each stroke, she pushed back to meet him. Wrapping his arms around her waist, he nuzzled the fragrant skin of her neck.

His body was on sensory overload. She smelled of spices and sex. The soft skin of her stomach, the intense heat of her cunt sent his mind reeling. His skin crawled with static as if he'd plugged into an electrical current when he connected with her body. And he couldn't get enough of her.

"Oh, yes." The muffled words sounded loud but he didn't have the breath to do more than moan.

This, whatever this was, wouldn't last long. Tension built with each plunge into the wet heat.

"Harder." She growled the word over and over.

He was hers to command. Straightening, he grabbed her hips. Long, hard strokes slammed her toward the wall but she begged for more.

"Oh, yes!" His cock erupted, releasing the tension in the pit of his stomach. A hard shudder racked his body as he ground his groin against her.

She pushed against him with equal force. Her cries of ecstasy letting him know he hadn't left her behind.

More than just passion racked her body. Gut wrenching sobs shook through her.

"Are you okay?" He shook his head to dislodge the lust-induced cobwebs in his brain.

She pulled away.

His cock slipped free sooner than he wanted.

"Fine," she mumbled. Without turning to face him, she leaned over, threaded the lacey material over her freed foot, and yanked her underwear up. Bending over again, she snagged her coat from the floor.

Before David could get his cock tucked away and his pants zipped, she'd unlocked the door and fled.

"Wait!" As he was still fumbling with his pants, his cell phone rang.

In his dazed state, it took a minute to realize what the noise was. The caller ID revealed the precinct number.

"Damn," he mumbled. He flipped opened the phone. "What?"

With the phone precariously perched on his shoulder, he finished dressing.

The captain's voice spoke on the other end of the line. "There's been a murder."

David stifled a groan. "I've been up since two this morning. Can't you call someone else?"

"Not for this case. It's Councilman Freiberg's son, Aaron. I need you on this one."

By the time David got the bathroom door open, no sign of his mystery woman remained. And he had no time to search.

2

Jamila leaned against the ladies' room door. Her heart raced with fear and the relief her orgasm had given her. The blond Adonis satisfied her in a way she hadn't known in over a thousand years. But the stupidity of taking a man in a public place! And a cop!

She'd been too far gone to stop when he revealed that little tidbit of information. In less than an hour, she'd killed a man and fucked a cop.

She rapped the back of her head against the door. If she'd been caught or if something had gone wrong . . . Tears filled her eyes as she shook her head.

Something had gone wrong. Aaron was dead. She should never have waited so long to find a man. Keket's Curse always won in the end. She knew better than to delay the inevitable.

The slam of the men's room door made her jump. Her fingers double-checked the lock. Hopefully, he would think she'd left the bar. His muffled voice penetrated the door. She'd heard the cell phone ring. Maybe whoever was on the other end would draw him away. Her gaze roamed over the tiny bathroom. She couldn't hide in here forever.

Warm seed mixed with her own juices, soaking her panties. She pushed away from the door and moved to the toilet. With toilet paper and a wet paper towel, she cleaned up as much as she could in a public bathroom.

Staring into the mirror, she examined her face. Not for the first time, she wondered why her features didn't reveal her evil nature. The killer in her should mar something, should create an imperfection or flaw. If the eyes were truly the window to the soul, shouldn't hers reveal the depths of her depravity?

A knock at the door startled her out of her self-pity. She'd brought this on herself. She'd betrayed Keket by sleeping with the priestess' lover, Bomani. Punishment she deserved—but forever was overkill.

"Hey, are you ever coming out of there?" The woman's voice was loud and slurred.

"Almost done," she called out. Jamila didn't need to draw more attention to herself. She tossed the soiled paper into the toilet and flushed.

With a deep breath, she opened the door.

The woman barged past her and into the tiny room.

As Jamila hurried through the bar, her gaze lighted on the spot where she'd found her lover du jour. Several bills sat next to the half-empty glass of beer.

David left his car at the bar. The murder scene was only two blocks south. The cold night air helped clear the last of the fog from his brain.

He'd just had sex in a public bathroom.

"Shit."

But the woman . . . She'd woven some kind of spell over him. Even now the spicy scent of her perfume lingered on his clothes.

Flashing blue and red lights brought him out of his thoughts. Two police cruisers and an ambulance were already on the scene.

David pushed aside the memory of his sexy mystery woman. Work beckoned.

He flashed his badge at the uniformed officer in the foyer, slipping the lanyard over his head so his shield rested on his chest. "Which apartment?"

The young man scrutinized the badge before jerking his head toward the elevator. "Six-b."

"Has the medical examiner been called?"

"Yes, sir. ETA fifteen minutes."

"Thanks." The security door was propped open. David stepped through and headed for the elevators. The doorman stood behind a desk talking to another uniformed cop. David's trained gaze checked out the lobby. No security cameras that he could see. For now, he'd let the uniform handle the doorman.

The tight confines of the building's single elevator enhanced the lingering fragrant scent of the strange woman's perfume. Her memory flashed through his mind making his cock twitch. Fortunately, the ride didn't take long. The doors slid open, and he once again suppressed thoughts of his erotic adventure.

Another uniform stood guard in front of an open apartment door. David nodded to him. The man moved aside allowing David to enter.

A sturdily built blonde knelt next to the body of a well-dressed man.

As David drew closer, he noted the parts of the man left undressed. The victim's pants were pulled down his hips with his half-erect penis exposed.

David frowned. "Hey, Susan. They called you out too, huh?"

His partner stood and nodded. "Looks like a rape gone sour for the perp."

"From the evidence," David cleared his throat, "I'd say he didn't get to finish what he started."

"Good for his victim." Susan's words carried a touch of satisfaction.

David frowned. "Hey, ease off, Susan. We don't know for sure if that's how it went down." His partner's personal experience with sexual assault slanted her views. "Any evidence of robbery?"

"Other than signs of a scuffle here, the rest of the room looks untouched. I'm waiting on the medical examiner before I turn him over to check for his wallet." She flipped through a couple of pages on her small notepad. "The next door neighbor called it in. Said he heard a woman screaming and then silence. He saw a woman in a dark coat with a scarf over her head in the hall a couple minutes later."

"Didn't see her face?"

"No, he was watching through the peephole. Didn't see hair color, race, nothing. Said she was about five-seven and slender but that's it. The doorman didn't see her face either."

"Any idea about cause of death?" David knelt next to the body. Looking for bruising or other signs of trauma, he was careful not to touch the body.

Susan sighed. "Not a thing. No blood, no sign of ligatures on the neck, no bruising. Only the scratches on the face."

David looked around the room, searching for clues. The coffee table was cockeyed from the couch. A broken glass vase on the polished wooden floor, with water and flowers scattered.

"But signs of a struggle." David stood and turned slowly around the room. Neat, expensively furnished. What he'd expect from the son of a wealthy city councilman.

Squeaking gurney wheels from the hall caught his attention.

"David, I thought you were going to get some rest," Joshua said as he entered the room.

Paul, the ME's assistant, followed, pushing a gurney topped with an equipment case.

"Yeah, so did I, Josh." The other part of their earlier conversation sent a slight flush burning across his face. He stepped away from the body so Joshua could do his thing.

"Looks like our friend here went out with a bang." Joshua's gloved hands turned the victim's head from side to side, examining his neck. He closed his eyes and his nose wrinkled as he drew a deep breath. "Smells like sandalwood. Unusual cologne for a man. Maybe a woman's perfume."

David hadn't smelled anything, but he couldn't get the unusual fragrance of his earlier encounter out of his head.

"Make a note." Joshua nodded at his assistant.

Paul had already started writing.

Joshua reached over and picked up the dead man's hand. "Lividity hasn't started, neither has rigor." Sure hands inserted a temperature gauge into the dead man's lower stomach. Nodding, he looked up at David and Susan. "With the liver temperature, I'd say our victim's been dead less than two hours." With practiced hands, he checked the body where it lay. "Did you get all the pictures?"

Susan nodded. "You can move him."

Paul set aside his clipboard and helped Joshua roll the dead man over.

Susan stepped forward. "Is his wallet there?"

"Yes." Joshua pulled an expensive-looking leather wallet from the man's back pocket. He flipped it open and examined the driver's license. "Aaron Freiberg." He handed it to Susan.

She rifled through some cash. "Lots of money. Robbery wasn't the motive." Susan handed the wallet to David.

"Next of kin, Eliot Freiberg." David shook his head at what lay ahead. Councilman Freiberg was one of the NYPD's harshest critics. This wouldn't be an easy case even though it appeared a cut-and-dried case of self-defense. "Let's talk to the doorman. See if we can get anything more out of him."

The doorman wasn't happy, his face alternating between pale and flushed. His forehead beaded with sweat. Having someone murdered in his building evidently didn't help his résumé.

"The woman kept her face down, both coming and going."

"Was it unusual for Mr. Freiberg to bring women home?"

The man frowned and shifted his weight back and forth.

David took that to mean no, but wanted him to say the words. "Mr. Schiller, please answer the question."

"No." Schiller shook his head and released a huge sigh. "Mr. Freiberg considered himself a bit of a player. A lot of women came through here. I don't remember too many repeat customers."

Susan moved closer to Schiller before David could ask another question. "Did he ever seem violent with any of the women, any gossip from his neighbors?"

Schiller's eyes narrowed. "I don't know what you're talking about."

"Come on, the doorman in any building knows more about the residents than anyone," Susan insisted. "Do you know of any complaints?"

"Are you saying it was self-defense?" The man fiddled with a button on his jacket. His gaze refused to meet either of theirs.

David interrupted before Susan could say anything else. "No, we're just gathering background information." He shot Susan a glare to make her back off.

The man pulled his hat off then ran his fingers through his hair. "There was one woman. A couple of months ago. She wasn't real happy when she left and her blouse was ripped."

David didn't miss the gleam in Susan's eyes. She obviously had her mind made up.

"Thank you, Mr. Schiller. If you think of anything else, please call me." David handed the doorman his card then herded Susan toward the exit.

Jamila let the hot water run over her long after she'd scrubbed her body clean. Tears mingled with the shower water. She hadn't wanted Aaron dead.

Hands spread against the cool tiles, her position brought back the memory of her encounter in the bar bathroom. The blond man's face replaced Aaron's dark dead eyes. Both faded into a collage of all the men. So many men . . .

"Damn you, Keket. Enough is enough."

Sobs racked her body. Her legs trembled as she slid to her knees.

Three thousand years of punishment with no end in sight. The cool desert night flashed through her memory and Keket's angry, dark eyes as she pronounced judgment over Jamila.

Endless lust, unending life, until Jamila knew pain equal to Keket's. Only true love betrayed could free her. And until then, Jamila's kiss was deadly.

So many men had died in the beginning, until Jamila understood the true nature of her curse. Each man had been someone she'd cared for, if not loved. But when the lust engulfed her, she had no choice but to seek out a lover.

After several years, she recognized a pattern to the episodes. The longer she waited between men, the worse the desire. This time, six days had passed without sex. Too long, and she'd lost control.

Another man was dead.

She also knew the longer she could wait, the greater the satisfaction. The man in the bar sent her further into ecstasy than any other in a thousand years. He guaranteed at least a few days' respite from her hunger.

The water began to cool. Jamila reached for the faucet and

shut it off before she stood. After wrapping one towel around her body then another around her hair, she stepped from the bathtub. She dried off quickly, grateful the steam-filled room hid her reflection in the mirror.

After tugging an oversized T-shirt over the towel on her head, she let the one around her body drop to the floor next to the clothes she'd stripped off earlier.

Exhaustion ached through every muscle. She closed the bathroom door behind her, leaving the mess for tomorrow. With her wet hair still wrapped in soft terry cloth, she climbed under the thick blankets of her bed. The cool sheets sent shivers through her water-warmed skin.

With her body curled in a tight ball, her last thought before sleep settled her was hope for a dreamless night.

"I understand. I'll talk to you in the morning." David snapped his cell phone shut. Staring out the window of his apartment, he shook his head. This case was definitely going to be a bitch.

Anthony Jenkins, David's precinct captain, wasn't a happy camper. He'd volunteered to make the notification to Councilman Freiberg, and to say it hadn't gone well was an understatement.

Freiberg's accusations against the police force started almost as soon as the words had left the captain's mouth.

The evidence at the scene hadn't really pointed to murder, and now with the victim's father a vocal public figure. . . .

David could only hope Joshua found something solid to go on. Cause of death wasn't obvious. Even if the autopsy did reveal something, from what they knew so far, the younger Freiberg got what was coming to him. If the son tried to rape a woman and she defended herself, the councilman wouldn't be happy with the outcome.

No woman should be treated like that.

The dark-haired woman in the bar insinuated herself into

his thoughts. He shook his head at the memory of her, spread-eagled and demanding. So subservient and yet so dominant.

His balls tightened and his cock perked up. "Down, boy." He needed sleep, not another session with his right hand. Besides, he wasn't sure he wanted to cloud the memory of tonight with a quick jerk off.

Granted, ages had passed since he'd had sex, but the woman tonight was just . . . Wow. He'd had his share of women but no one had ever turned him on quite like her.

He shook himself away from his thoughts. "I need a shower. A cold shower." After closing the blinds, he headed for the bathroom. "After that . . . sleep."

So much for sleep. The next morning, David walked into the medical examiner's lab a little after seven. Wild dreams of his mystery woman had made for a restless night.

Joshua straightened from his position over a microscope. "You're early."

"Yeah, I could say the same for you."

"The chief of police made a personal request." Joshua rubbed his forehead. "Sounded more like an order."

"Couldn't you get someone else to do the autopsy?" David worried about his friend. At almost sixty, Joshua didn't need the long sleepless nights.

"Not according to the chief."

"So did you find anything?"

"Not much. Still waiting for toxicology. But I already know the cause of death."

"Which was?"

"Heart attack."

"What? He was twenty-eight." David couldn't believe the cause was that simple.

"A ninety percent blockage on the aortic artery. Unusual in

a man so young but possible. The stress of fighting his victim could have brought on the attack."

"So you think it was an attempted rape?" David didn't think this would make the case any easier. Convincing the councilman of his son's culpability would be difficult.

"Could be. He hadn't ejaculated. The scratches on his face are indicative of defensive wounds. There's some bruising around his hips and thighs where she could have kneed him." Joshua ran his hand through his hair. "All in all, it could have been rape. I sent the fluids for DNA analysis, not that the results will help without a suspect."

"Morning." Susan entered the room with a tray holding three cups of Starbucks coffee. "I decided we needed the good stuff this morning."

David grinned at his partner. He took the offered cup. "Thanks." Susan had a serious Starbucks addiction and used any excuse to splurge.

"So, anything interesting?" She nodded at the body on the table.

"No, just more mysteries." David quickly ran through the facts as Joshua had presented them.

"Where do we start?" she asked.

David sighed. "Pull his credit card information and see if we can figure out where he was last night."

As a temporary curator, Jamila entered the museum through the staff entrance. Her expertise with ancient Egyptian artifacts made her a decent living. Not that she needed it. She'd accumulated considerable wealth over the last three thousand years. However, she needed something to fill the empty days and a way to blend into society.

The usual guard on duty was nowhere to be seen. Even though it was early on a Saturday, someone should have been there.

Frowning, she made sure the door locked behind her, then headed toward the elevators. The quick trip to her subbasement office didn't reveal anyone else. Eerie silence didn't ease her jittery nerves.

Visions of Aaron's dead eyes and her blond Adonis' blue ones had punctuated her restless sleep. When the cop's face appeared as dead as Aaron's, she gave up on sleep and decided work would help to clear her mind.

Ancient Egyptian artifacts cluttered her office. Being surrounded by the trappings of her youth usually made her feel young again. This morning, the gold and jeweled items just reinforced her despair.

Picking up a Canopic jar found at a burial site near her original home in Dendara, she settled in to translate the writing. Not a hard process since she knew exactly what it said. Her mind had time to wander.

Something about the cop tugged at more than just her desire. He was different from the men she usually picked up. Someone she could feel something for besides lust. Avoiding entanglements was the only way she survived her curse. Any long-term relationship would only end with a dead lover. She normally chose men who wouldn't think twice about sex with a stranger and even less about her leaving without a word.

Shaking herself like a wet cat, she forced her thoughts aside. Remembering an e-mail from yesterday about a new artifact, she headed to the vault to check it out. Maybe something different could occupy her mind in a more productive fashion.

Ancient memories whispered to Jamila while she wandered through the maze of archives. Three thousand years wrought so many changes, but her youth was fresh in her mind. She could *still* smell the hot desert air and feel the breath of cooling evening breezes.

Sometimes, the past was clearer than the present. But the here-and-now was all that mattered.

Lost in her rambling thoughts, Jamila didn't hear the guard until she walked around a corner. The man who should be standing at the staff entrance was inside the vault rifling through precious antiquities as if they were children's toys.

Without thinking, Jamila marched into the vault. "What are doing?"

The guard jumped and turned to face her. His eyes narrowed from wide-eyed surprise to suspicion. "Nothing. Why are you here today?" He shuffled toward her, his face impassive.

"You know you're not supposed to be in here." Jamila's indignation over the mishandled artifacts faded into unease. No one would hear her cry for help. Dying wasn't a fear, but she could and would feel pain if he attacked her. "You should leave now." Her voice wasn't as strong as she wanted it to be. "Get back to your duties."

"I'm afraid I can't do that." He continued his slow stalk toward her.

Fear teased the hair on the back of her neck. "Stay away from me." Jamila backed out of the door. She knew the archives well. A maze of shelving and larger pieces, she could probably lose him, if she could get a head start. Or at least find something to use as a weapon.

Her heart beat in her throat. She just needed to get past the shelves on either side of the vault door before she could run. Not taking her eyes off the man, she picked up her backward pace.

"Oh, no, you don't."

He lunged, almost tackling her just as she turned to flee. His fist grabbed the hem of her skirt. A hard yank sent her sprawling facedown. Her shoulder slammed into a shelf before she fell to the floor.

A heavy body trapped her legs but she tried to kick anyway, hoping to hit a soft target. One hand flailed on the bottom shelf seeking a weapon of any kind.

When the guard rose up and began to crawl up her body. She struck hard, her foot kicking backward. The harsh grunt let her know she hurt something. Not enough.

Fingers curled in her hair and jerked. Pain shot through her head and neck. In spite of the dizziness, she wasn't going down without a fight. A sharp swing of her arm and her elbow made contact with soft flesh. Another grunt and a sharp exhale of air gave her painful satisfaction.

"Bitch," the man mumbled. He managed to straddle her waist in spite of her resistance. "You're gonna have to learn some manners."

Jamila's neck popped when her head was yanked back again. She didn't have time to respond before her forehead hit the concrete and the world went dark.

3

Throbbing pain in her head dulled Jamila's awareness. Her body ached all over. Tightness in her chest constricted her breathing. Painful memory returned but she was on her back, not facedown. Realization snapped her eyes open.

The body of the guard was responsible for her breathing trouble. Motionless and glassy-eyed, his dead weight covered her.

With a frantic shove, she rolled the man's body over, so that it rested against one of the shelves lining the wall.

Jamila breathed a sigh of relief when she saw his pants were still buttoned and zipped. Her skirt was bunched around her waist and her underwear was shredded but he hadn't had time to rape her. Her thighs ached from her earlier resistance.

Sitting up renewed her dizziness. Grabbing the post of a shelf, she hauled herself up off the floor. She had to get back to her office. She couldn't be anywhere near the body when someone discovered it.

Her mind raced as she stumbled toward the exit and the elevators. She stopped short of pushing the call button. Raising the hem of her skirt, she punched the button with a cloth-covered finger. Her fingerprints would be all over the archive, but her access wouldn't be questioned. However, her print as the last one on the elevator could be.

A sigh of relief forced the air from her lungs as the doors opened. The car was empty. She moved inside, thankful for the absence of security cameras in the elevators.

Her mind focused solely on getting to her office. Once there, she would be able to think clearly, figure out what to do next.

David held the door of the upscale eatery until Susan passed through. "Definitely looks pricy."

"It should with three hundred dollars charged on his card." Susan stopped in front of the reservation desk.

A snooty looking man in a tuxedo looked up from his book. "Reservations for?"

"For this." Susan smirked, flashing her badge. "We have some questions."

"Yes, Officer?" The man looked down his nose as if he smelled something bad.

"That's *Detective* Brennen. And your name is?"

"Maurice DuVall."

"Were you working last night?"

David stood back observing the man while Susan questioned him.

"Yes." The man's disdain rolled through the word.

"Did you see this man here?" Susan held up a photo of Aaron Freiberg.

DuVall squinted at the picture. "Yes. That's Mr. Freiberg. He's a regular."

"Was he with anyone?" Susan tucked the photo in her jacket pocket.

"Several of his gentlemen friends."

"No woman?" David jumped in. "Dark coat and scarf?"

The man looked at David, his eyebrows arched. "No, she met him outside."

"Did you get a look at her face?" David moved closer to the man.

"No. As I said, she met him outside. Her head wasn't covered though. Her hair was dark, almost black, shoulder length and very straight. Why all the questions?"

"Mr. Freiberg died last night. We're trying to trace his steps." David pulled a notepad from his pocket. "Do you know the names of the men he was with?"

"Murdered? By that woman?" The shock on DuVall's face overcame the haughty attitude.

"We're not ruling out murder but right now we just want to find out his movements last night." David looked up from his pad. "The names?"

Jamila sat at her desk staring at the Canopic jar. Her mind had shut down, almost as numb as her body. For 3000 years, she'd craved sex, slept with countless men, but never had a man forced her. If anything, she'd been the one forcing her lovers.

A glance at the clock showed almost two hours since she'd returned to her office. No outcry, no uproar. How long would it take for someone to find the body? Even on the weekend, someone should notice the guard missing at the staff entrance.

She glanced at her reflection in the computer screen. The bruise on her forehead had already begun to fade. Serious injury was possible but she healed very quickly. Fortunately, the only damage from this encounter was bruises.

Her underwear had been unsalvageable. They were tucked in a zippered compartment in her purse. A casual observer wouldn't notice a small tear in the seam of her skirt near the hem. She'd managed to straighten out her rumpled appearance.

Should she leave? Go home?

The security cameras in the main part of the museum would show the police she'd been here. Also, she'd signed in at the desk. But since the archives didn't have cameras, no one would know she'd done anything except work in her office.

Taking a deep breath, Jamila shut off her computer then headed out of the museum. She'd been here over two hours. When asked, she would claim she never left her office. No one could prove otherwise.

David tossed down his notepad and looked across at the desk facing his. Tugging at his already loosened tie, he growled his disgust. "That was the last one. All of Freiberg's friends said the same thing. He was evasive about his after-dinner plans. A couple of them thought he was bluffing about a hot date, and that he was going straight home. No one saw the woman."

Susan looked over the papers she had been reading. "So now what?"

The phone rang before David could answer.

Susan grabbed the receiver. "Brennen." She nodded as she listened to the person on the line. "Yes, sir. We're on our way."

"A break?" David stood, grabbing his jacket.

"Another body. Museum guard at the Metropolitan."

David slung on his jacket. "Maybe this one will have a few clues."

Susan leaned over David's shoulder while he examined the body. "More clues, huh? Can I say 'famous last words'?"

"No, you can't." As much as he cared about his partner, sometimes Susan's sense of humor got on his nerves. David couldn't find any apparent cause of death. Nothing. Just like Freiberg. "But the museum has security cameras. Maybe the video will reveal something."

Susan straightened and looked around the cluttered room. "Doesn't look like any cameras here."

"No, but maybe we'll see who came down here besides the guard."

Joshua's voice halted their conversation. "David? Where are you?"

"Over here."

Joshua mumbled about mazes while making his way to the crime scene. "What have we got?" he asked once he rounded the last corner of shelving. With the snap of rubber gloves, he knelt by the body before David answered.

"Mark Simmons, museum guard. Came on duty at six this morning. Looks a lot like Freiberg. No marks, no obvious cause of death, but it doesn't really look like any sign of struggle."

Joshua grimaced. "In other words, you've got nothing."

"Pretty much," Susan said.

"We're going upstairs to the security office to check out the surveillance tapes. Let us know if you find anything." David glanced around the area one more time as if a clue would magically appear.

"Will do."

David motioned for the guard who found the body to lead the way. The man was standing as far from Simmons as he could and still be in sight. He was visibly pale. David doubted the man had ever seen a dead body up close and personal. Or maybe the deceased was a friend.

After winding their way through the archives and into the elevator, David asked, "Did you know Mr. Simmons?"

Susan followed them in and punched the button for the ground floor.

The guard leaned against the far wall of the small space. "Not well. He was kind of new and usually worked the night shift. He only moved to day shift a few weeks ago."

"Was checking the subbasement part of his regular duties?" David asked.

"No. I don't understand why he was down there. He was on duty at the staff entrance. It's not supposed to be left unmanned even on weekends." The elevator bumped to a halt on the main floor. The tension in the guard's neck and shoulders visibly relaxed when the doors swished open. Before they completely parted, he rushed out.

"You don't like the archives?" Susan asked.

"No." He took a deep breath and released it slowly.

Susan's eyes narrowed. "Any problems down there before today?"

"No. No." Shaking his head, the guard frowned. "I just don't like being down there with dead things."

"You mean Mr. Simmons?" The ill-lit area didn't make David nervous but he could understand the guard wouldn't like being around a body.

"No, well, yes. That too. But," the man's voice dropped to a whisper, "there are rumors some of that stuff is cursed."

David held up a hand behind his back to silence the snort of disbelief from Susan. "Cursed?"

"Yeah. People have died from just touching it."

"Okay." They came to a stop in front of the security office door. David handed the man his card. "We'll want to talk to you some more later. Don't leave the museum until then."

The man nodded and fled.

"Cursed?" Susan asked when the guard was out of hearing.

"Hey, haven't you ever heard about the Curse of King Tut? Supposedly everyone who entered the tomb died young and under strange circumstances." David shrugged. "It seems like he's a true believer."

Susan shook her head and made a very unladylike noise. "Bull."

Laughing, David opened the door to the office.

"Come in, detectives." A tall heavyset man walked toward them.

David shook the outstretched hand. "Are you Sergio Calabria?"

"Yes, head of museum security. I have the tapes set up and I've already reviewed them. Not much help but you're welcome to look at them."

"What did you find?" David sat in the chair Calabria indicated.

Susan took the other.

"Only one person entered the staff entrance this morning. Jamila Aten is a visiting curator from the Egyptian Museum in Cairo. She came in a few minutes after seven and left at 9:30. Simmons was missing from his station when she arrived." Calabria started the tape rolling. "She looked around, probably for the guard then signed the book and headed to the elevator. Her office is on sublevel two."

David managed to keep the shock punching through his veins from showing on his face. His mind had a million thoughts but his mouth couldn't force them out.

On the monitor, a woman in a red coat walked across the screen.

Different coat but the same woman. His mystery woman.

"Jamila Aten," he mumbled.

"Why do you want to do this alone?"

David wanted to scream. Susan wouldn't drop it. He couldn't explain why he didn't want her around when he met with Jamila Aten. Just seeing her on the video monitor made his cock sit up and take notice. A reaction like that in front of his partner wasn't a good idea and David wasn't sure he could control himself.

Then again, if Susan wasn't there . . .

David threw his hands in the air. "Okay, fine. I just thought it would be more efficient to split up. You check out the rest of the staff while I talk to this woman."

Susan followed him out of the museum. "I think it would be better to stick together."

The look Susan nailed him with made him realize she was on to him. He must have given something away in spite of his best efforts.

"Whatever." Nonchalance now probably wouldn't work, but her piercing glare eased off.

Jamila stared out her apartment window. Her hair was still damp from a long shower, and her bathrobe was loosely tied around her naked body. Maybe she should plan to leave the country. Her current passport listed her as an Egyptian citizen. The job at the museum was only visiting curator. It wouldn't be hard to leave. Any harder than leaving a thousand other places.

Despair tightened her throat. She wasn't ready to leave New York. Only here for less than a year, she had been happy. Or at least as happy as she could be under the circumstances. The museum afforded her the luxury of working among familiar things from her past, and the city was ripe with horny men willing to fuck without questions or strings . . . or kissing.

The blue-eyed cop swam through her memory, his face haunting her. The ache in her pussy had nothing to do with the curse. Cream pooled between her thighs and her nipples tightened. She ran her fingernails across her breasts, the sharp edges catching the tight nubs.

Only a few times in thousands of years had a man made her feel this way. Sex wasn't for pleasure. It was a necessity of her endless life. Long ago, Jamila had given up on anything resembling love. But once in a long while, the rare man came along who made her wonder what life could have been.

The idea of a kiss, a deep, tongue-tangling, soul-searching kiss, made tears well. The lush full lips of her blond lover from last night pressed against hers, his rough mouth taking hers, the scratch of his beard against her skin . . .

A knock on the door startled her. No one came to her apartment. She held herself aloof from everyone. Letting anyone get close was dangerous. It had to be the police.

Jamila checked her reflection in the window. She smoothed her robe before she walked to the door. Peering through the peephole, she saw a blond woman and . . .

"Oh, shit."

"Police, ma'am. We need to speak with you about the museum," David answered in response to the woman's voice behind the door, his shield held up to the peephole.

He hoped his voice didn't sound strange to Susan. His throat tightened with anticipation and all the blood in his body made a run south. He didn't dare look at Susan to see her reaction.

The door opened slowly. The dark eyes looked curious but David couldn't see any sign of recognition.

"How may I help you?" Her soft words were so different from last night's hoarse demands.

"I'm Detective David Craise. This is my partner, Detective Brennen. May we come in?" David knew this was the same woman, but she seemed so docile and meek compared to their first encounter.

"Of course." She opened the door wide and stood to the side.

A dark red silk bathrobe hugged her body, revealing the luscious curves he remembered from last night. The pungent scent of her spicy perfume flooded his senses. His cock ached within the tight confines of his slacks. He pushed aside the thought of grabbing her for a repeat performance. He was grateful when Susan spoke.

"There was a death at the museum. You were seen on the security video. We just need to ask a few questions."

"A death?" Jamila's eyes widened with surprise. "Who? How?"

David found his voice. "The security guard on duty at the staff entrance, Mark Simmons. Did you see him this morning?"

"No, when I came in, no one was at the door." Jamila motioned for them to sit on the couch.

"You never saw him?" Susan's voice seemed a little rough.

"No, I worked for a little while on a translation of a Canopic jar and then I went home."

David nodded while making notes on his pad. "What's a Canopic jar?" Her soft, musical laugh made him look up.

"It's a funerary jar used to hold the internal organs of the deceased in ancient Egypt. That's my specialty, ancient Egyptian artifacts."

"And you never left your office?" Susan's tight voice made David glance her direction.

Jamila shook her head. "No, not until I left the museum. The guard still wasn't there."

David shifted in his seat, tugging at his jacket for strategic cover. His hard-on was getting worse just from being near her. The scent of her perfume overwhelmed him. If Susan hadn't been there, he didn't think he'd be able to control himself. Visions of Jamila spread-eagled against the wall kept thrusting into his mind.

"Okay, Ms. Aten. If we have any more questions, we'll be in contact with you. And if you think of anything, please call." David handed her his card.

Her fingers caressed his before she plucked the card from his grasp. Heat flushed through David's body.

"Thank you." He needed to get out of there fast. Much longer in the woman's presence, and he'd end up doing something about the ache in his groin. He wouldn't care if his partner watched.

Susan followed without saying a word.

With the door safely closed behind them, David breathed a sigh of relief. When Susan did the same, he turned to glare at her.

"She got to you, too?" The words slipped from David's lips without thought.

"Shit, yes!"

The fact that Susan was a lesbian never bothered David before, but right now a jolt of jealousy rampaged through his body. The idea of Susan touching his woman . . .

Whoa. He cut the thought short with a shiver. Where had that sudden rage come from? His cock was so hard David was surprised it hadn't torn a hole in his slacks.

At first, David was grateful the elevator doors closed them away from Jamila's floor. Then the scent of female arousal wafted over him. His initial irritation returned.

"She's a suspect," he growled.

"She is?" Susan glared at him. Her shoulders rolled back in defiance. "Why? Because she was there? Or because you want her off limits to me."

David clenched his fists. "She's off limits to you anyway."

Susan's stare hardened. "Why? Because you want her?"

"No!" he growled. Irrational rage swept through him like a wildfire out of control. His partner's glare reflected a flicker of fear as his fists clenched at his side. Reason flooded back into his mind. "Oh, Susan, I'm sorry. I wouldn't . . ."

Susan's shoulders slumped and she leaned against the back

of the elevator. Her eyes were wide with shock, her face pale. "I know. I don't know what's wrong with me."

He had been ready to fight his partner over a strange woman. A woman who was, for all he knew, a suspect in a possible homicide.

The elevator doors slid open and they bumped shoulders in a rush for the street. The doorman opened the door before they reached it. Cold air washed over David, relieving little of the heat consuming his body.

Once outside, Susan stopped and turned. "David, I'm sorry." She still looked wild-eyed. "I don't know . . ."

"I know. Me too. Let's just forget it." David pulled the keys to the car out of his pocket.

"I need some time. I'll catch up to you at the station." Susan didn't wait for David to reply.

"Susan?"

"Just go," she called out, her hand waving him away.

With the door still open, the key in the ignition beeped. He watched Susan retreat down the block but he couldn't bring himself to start the engine.

With her forehead pressed against the door, Jamila listened to the sound of her heart race. How bad could her luck get? The cop she fucked was now investigating the death of the museum guard. She shook her head in disbelief. Her whole body hummed with arousal from his mere presence.

And it wasn't the burning frenzy of the curse at work. This was something different, something approaching normal attraction, something she hadn't felt in three thousand years. Not since her ill-fated affair with Bomani.

Slowly banging her head against the door, she tried to get her breathing under control. A clear head was required. Being forced into the detective's presence could complicate her situation. Even his female partner seemed shaken.

"Great. Another one."

It wouldn't be the first time her sexual pheromones attracted a woman. A few times Jamila had used a woman for sex, but it never gave her what the curse demanded. She still needed a man to quench those fires.

She was still leaning against the door when a knock vibrated through her body. She glanced through the peephole and gritted her teeth.

She should have known.

Opening the door wide, Jamila asked, "Did you forget something, Detective?"

4

Intense blue eyes stared at Jamila. A frown marred a pale forehead.

"Did you need something else, Detective?" she repeated. He stumbled toward her as she retreated into the apartment.

"You—" was the strangled reply.

"Then maybe you should close the door." Jamila wished her voice sounded calmer. Although it was too soon for the curse to return, Jamila wouldn't have known it from the flames engulfing her.

David slammed the door and he rushed forward.

Walking backward, she barely kept ahead of his frantic pace. "No kissing. I don't kiss. Understand?" The thought of those deep blue eyes faded and glassy in death almost made her ask him to leave. "Say you understand!"

David nodded and kept moving toward her.

The coffee table smacked the back of her knee, sending her off balance. She sat down hard on the sturdy oak furniture and didn't bother to get up. Her seat offered the perfect vantage point to watch his long fingers undo his belt.

The button and zipper were next. The soft white cotton briefs bulged, revealing damp evidence of his arousal.

The sight sent shivers through her. Moisture pooled in her core. Her hands reached across the short distance separating them. Fingers curled into the elastic. She pulled him forward at the same time she pushed the thin cotton down.

Their previous encounter hadn't lasted more than a few minutes. She probably wouldn't get another chance and Jamila intended to make the most of today.

His thick leaking cock jutted out through the opening of his shirt. A glance up revealed blue eyes glazed with passion.

Jamila pushed both his slacks and briefs down to his knees. Her nails combed through the hair on his legs as she trailed her fingers back up to his ass. Moving around to his shirt, she made quick work of the buttons and pulled the material out of her way.

The collar pulled free of his already loosened tie. He yanked the still-buttoned cuffs over his hands. The soft sound of tearing material indicated one cuff hadn't survived his haste. His hands moved to rest on her shoulders.

Licking her lips, she leaned forward. Her hands once again found his tight ass. Her mouth encircled the tip of his cock. His pungent salty flavor exploded on her tongue.

His fingers dug into her flesh as he gasped for air. His hips pumped forward a fraction of an inch.

She could feel his ass tighten in an attempt to control his thrust. Her fingers stroked the lines of his muscles. Digging her fingers into the hard flesh, she pulled him forward. His cock pushed deep into her mouth. The girth strained her jaw but she still urged him closer.

Her lips tickled with her own moan. She leaned back a little, easing the fullness in her mouth, then pushed forward.

His body caught the hint and he began rocking back and forth slowly.

As he fucked her mouth, she explored his hard body. One hand slid up his back, tracing the tight tendons, weaving patterns with her nails. The other kneaded a tight cheek until her fingers couldn't resist exploring the crevice of his ass.

His thrusts moved faster with the prodding. The thick flesh swelled against her lips. More saltiness spurted across her tongue.

For so long, sex had been a necessity. But with the curse so recently sated, Jamila wanted this to be about pleasure, his as well as hers.

She slid her hand down his back, around his hips and between his legs. The warm sac tightened further at her touch. Capturing the soft flesh in the palm of her hand, she massaged with slow strokes. The fingers of her other hand parted his ass cheeks and teased his puckered hole.

Frantic thrusts nearly gagged her. When her fingertip pushed past the tight anal muscle, his balls tightened and a loud moan warned her. Warm thick fluid pulsed across her tongue. Another sharp thrust and more hot liquid hit the back of her throat.

His fingers gripped her shoulders hard as the last of his seed spurted into her mouth. His body shook through the aftermath.

Easing her head back, she released his cock with a slight pop. Her almost numb lips didn't keep her from smiling at his expression.

Eyes closed, mouth open, breath panting and his skin flushed . . .

Jamila's heart ached at the sheer beauty of his expression. A rush of excitement flushed through her body and straight to her pussy.

As if in slow motion, his knees bent, and he sank to the floor between her parted legs. His hands, still on her shoulders, moved to cup the back of her neck. His face pressed forward.

Quickly, she covered his mouth with one hand. The other

hand, fingers spread, pressed against his chest. "No kissing," she whispered. She wondered if her regret sounded as clear to him as it did to her.

One hand slid from her neck and down her robe to her breast. His calloused fingers teased her curves through the sheer silk robe before settling on her nipple. A sharp tweak pulled air from her lungs. She hadn't realized she had been holding her breath.

"No kissing?" he mumbled into her hand. His lips nibbled her palm. "Just on the lips?" His tongue teased her skin.

Unable to find the breath to speak, Jamila nodded.

His tongue poked between her fingers and curled around her middle finger. The wet warmth matched the gush of juice between her legs.

His fingers trailed from her neck to her forearm. Pulling her hand from his mouth, he smiled. "So I can do this . . ." his voice trailed off as he kissed her wrist.

Her "yes" came out a whimper.

The tip of his tongue traced her wrist. His other hand stayed busy tormenting her nipple with gentle tugs.

She moaned when his hand moved away.

His knuckles teased the other breast.

Her eyes rolled and her eyelids drooped. She forced them open. She couldn't chance taking her eyes off him. If she let her guard down, more than she already had, he could have his mouth on hers before she could stop him.

"Is this okay?" His whisper ended with moist heat engulfing her middle finger. A hot tongue tangled around her knuckle.

What she would give for that mouth on hers. . . . But she wouldn't give his life. She shook the fantasy from her mind.

Her finger slid from his mouth. His hands moved to the tie of her robe. Freeing the thin piece of cloth, he pushed her robe off her shoulders. Leaning forward, he captured a hard nipple between his teeth.

Her back arched, pushing her breast into the heat of his lips.

Gentle sucking replaced his teeth. His hand circled around her waist, calluses scraping her skin and sending shivers through her. His other hand dipped to her mons. A finger gathered the dripping moisture before circling her clit.

Jamila spread her legs wide. Her hips arched, seeking more than the teasing pressure. "Please . . ."

He released her nipple. A breath blew on the wet flesh. "What do you want?" His teasing finger left her clit. Rubbing her juices on her lips first, he sucked his finger into his mouth.

"I need . . ." How could she tell him she needed to be mortal? To have sex without fear of death?

He pulled his finger from his mouth then ran it around her lips. "Let me taste these." He didn't move closer but the plea filled his eyes.

"No . . ." She shook her head. Tears welled in her eyes. "No."

"Then I'll have to settle for these lips." A rough shove sent her sprawling down the length of the coffee table. His hands yanked her thighs up. Burying his face in her cunt, his tongue laved her clit.

"God, yes," she moaned. Her nails raked a trail across his scalp then her hand clutched his blond hair.

Fingers parted her clit, giving him full access to her swollen sex. A thick thumb pushed into her hole. Her cunt clenched and heat pooled deep in the pit of her stomach. "More," she whispered.

The thumb left her, replaced by two fingers. Short strokes and enthusiastic tonguing left her breathless and so close to the edge. Her hips arched in time to his strokes.

"So close." But not enough. She needed more.

His mouth clamped on her clit and sucked hard. With two fingers in her cunt, a third nudged her ass.

"Yes . . ."

The third finger, slick with her cream, pushed past the tight anal muscle. Finally . . . She rode the crest of orgasm. Her hands clutched the sides of the coffee table. The rough scrape of his beard against her thighs only added to the fury ravaging her body.

Hard hands forced her legs open. Cool air rushed against her overheated sex. The chill didn't last long. Hot blunt flesh pushed against her hole. The thick cock pushed into her in one hard stroke. Searing heat filled her.

Still quaking from her first orgasm, his abrupt entry sent her over the edge again. She clutched the table for balance then raised her legs up and wrapped them around his waist.

His fingers dug into her hips. Hard long strokes pounded her flesh. Each time their bodies met, his pelvis ground against her over-sensitive clit. Waves of pleasure kept coming until she thought she would drown in exquisite sensation.

Flexing her legs, she struggled to match his pace. Her thighs quivered from lust and stress.

His chest shone with a glaze of sweat. The muscles in his neck strained. His tie flopped against his skin with each frantic move.

The slap of skin on skin mingled with moans and grunts. The smell of sex permeated the room. A rising tide of ecstasy flooded her body. And then she was there again, muscles clenching in ecstasy. Lightheaded weakness flooded her body.

David's body jerked, his seed exploding within her, pouring more heat into an already raging fire.

"Oh, yes," she gasped.

His body leaned forward, covering hers. Lips nuzzled her neck while his sweat-slicked chest rubbed against her breast.

One arm wrapped around him. Her free hand automatically covered her mouth. Sorrow welled up in her throat. She wanted his lips on hers. She wanted the intimacy of a long lazy kiss, of tongues tangling, of tasted breath. And more than anything, she wanted a relationship that lasted longer than a quick fuck.

"Please leave," she mumbled. "Go." She needed him gone. She needed to grieve for what could never happen.

David dunked his head under the faucet. The cold water made him gasp. The funk clouding his mind eased a little. The whole incident seemed a dream or a drug-induced hallucination.

Her throwing him out was the last thing he expected from her after fantastic sex. And he swore there were tears in her eyes.

The door to the men's room swung open. David blinked water from his eyes and looked at the new arrival.

"Hard day?" Joshua asked as he walked toward the urinals.

"Yeah, kind of." David reached for the paper towels. "Any information on our security guard?"

"Nope. Another heart attack. Strange coincidence."

The urinal flushed while David towel-dried his hair. By the time he finished, Joshua stood in front of a sink washing his hands.

David shook his head. "Heart attack. Again." Disbelief warred with irritation. A simple murder would be nice. A long hot shower wouldn't hurt his mood.

The sound of the towel dispenser brought his wandering mind back.

"Well," Joshua said before he tossed the paper towel, "I'm looking into possible foreign substances which might cause heart attacks. So far toxicology hasn't found any of the usual suspects."

"Thanks. Let me know if it does."

* * *

Wrapped in a towel, Jamila sat on the couch staring at her red silk robe still draped on the coffee table.

The curse didn't explain her actions today. With a normal cycle of at least five days, she hadn't needed a fix. Something about David's presence . . . No, the memory of last night combined with seeing him again explained part of it. But why this man? And why did he have to be a cop?

Definitely time to move on. Two dead bodies and fucking the cop investigating one of them . . .

She looked around the large, well-lit room. This apartment had been a dream find. The same with her job at the museum. The idea of leaving after less than a year hurt. She hadn't been this comfortable with her life in a long time.

And David.

She rolled over and curled up into a tight ball. She refused to let her mind wander down that trail. A normal relationship wasn't possible.

Loneliness gnawed at the pit of her stomach. So alone, so long. The only cure for the curse required risking a man's life. Something she wouldn't, couldn't do. Not intentionally.

A vision of David's eyes, cold and lifeless, staring, accusing, flashed in her mind.

Time to leave.

Jamila sat at her desk, staring at the computer screen. The e-mail from the Egyptian Museum contained an enthusiastic response to her inquiry. A new find in the area of Jamila's expertise made the head curator more than happy she'd consider coming back.

The big problem now was getting out of New York without looking like she was fleeing. A knock at the door made her close the e-mail.

"Come in."

The last person she expected to walk through her door was David.

"Hi." He ran his fingers through his hair.

Her stomach did flip-flops at the memory of his skin against hers, his hold on her, fucking her. The turmoil settled in her groin, reigniting the fire from yesterday. "Hello. How can I help you?"

"I needed to follow up on our case." David threaded an ink pen through his fingers, back and forth.

She kept her smile to herself. His jitters eased her discomfort. "I told you everything I knew."

He leaned over her desk and peered at the artifact on her desk. "The Canopic jar?"

Jamila nodded. "The head is a representation of the god of embalming, Anubis." She used a pen to point to a drawing of a baboon. "This represents Hapi, one of the four sons of Horus. He was guardian of the lungs."

"There're lungs in there?" David straightened up.

"Used to be. The seal was broken long ago. Probably by grave robbers. The contents have long since gone to dust." The idea saddened her. She shook her head. "But you didn't come here to talk about Canopic jars."

"No, I didn't." He paced the small space in front of her desk. Coming to a stop in front of her, his stare pierced her heart and sent tremors through her cunt. "To tell you the truth, I don't know why I'm here."

"Look, yesterday and the night before were mistakes. It can't happen again, *won't* happen again."

David's eyes softened. "Why the other night, in the bar?"

"I . . ." What could she say? She'd killed the man who was supposed to service her before she got what she needed? Oh, yeah, that would go over well. "I'd had a fight with a man I was dating. Caught him with someone else. I needed payback. You were—you were just there." The lie stuck in her throat. She shouldn't have said that much.

"And yesterday?"

"I don't know." Her voice caught. "Please leave. This has nothing to do with your case. Just go."

She sighed with relief when he turned for the door, but it was short-lived.

He whirled around, his eyes wild. "I want to see you again."

"Not possible. I told you, it was a mistake." Her pussy pulsed at the lust plainly written across his face. But a hint of something else in the deep blue eyes sent her heart racing. The possibility of more than sex. "Leave . . ." She meant to sound forceful but the word came out as a plea.

At first he hesitated, his mouth opened to say something. Then he nodded and stalked out of her office, slamming the door.

Jamila turned to her computer and opened the e-mail from Cairo, typed a quick reply, and hit SEND.

5

"Detectives Craise, Brennen, my office!"

David winced at the irritation in Captain Jenkins's voice. He glanced at Susan for a hint of what was up. She just shook her head.

Popping his head around the door to the captain's office, he asked, "What's up?"

Jenkins motioned for him to come in.

When David moved around the doorway, he spied a tall, thin, older man—Councilman Freiberg.

"Detectives Craise and Brennen, this is Aaron Freiberg's father. He would like an update on the case."

David took a deep breath before he spoke. "Sir, I'm very sorry about your loss. But there's not much to tell yet."

"Why not?" Freiberg didn't bother to hide his disapproval. His frown narrowed his close-set eyes. "I was told by the mayor that my son's murder would be this department's highest priority."

"I'm sorry, Councilman, but we haven't been able to rule it a homicide yet." David wasn't sure how much to tell the man, and the captain's passive face wasn't giving him any clues. "The autopsy report showed the cause—"

"Yes, yes, I've already heard the bull about a heart attack." Freiberg's voice remained impassionate, as if he were discussing the weather. "My son was young and healthy. There is no history of heart problems. He had to have been poisoned or something. His was not a natural death."

"So far, toxicology hasn't revealed anything." David kept his voice neutral. "Dr. Preston requested some additional analysis but we haven't received the report yet."

"Why not?"

David glanced at Susan but she just shook her head slightly. "I'll call Dr. Preston and see if he's heard anything since this morning."

"Phone calls? Reports? This is all you can offer? I know there was evidence of a struggle. Have you found the other person?"

David's gaze darted toward the captain.

"No, Detective, your captain didn't tell me. The *chief of police* was kind enough to show me the files." Freiberg's voice finally showed some emotion and it wasn't grief. Glowering, he moved toward David. "Find the person who did this or I'll have your badge." He turned to the captain. "And yours as well."

Freiberg brushed past Susan and stomped out of the office.

Drawing a deep breath, David shook his head.

"I don't know about you two, but I happen to like wearing a badge." Jenkins flopped down in his chair.

David clenched his fists. "Captain, the evidence doesn't point to murder. What are we supposed to do? Make some up?"

Susan moved closer, her hand touched his arm. "Maybe the additional tests came back with something. We need to talk to Joshua."

Jenkins ran a hand over his nearly bald head. "What about the museum guard? Having another young man die the same way doesn't peak your interest in the slightest?"

"Of course it does, but we're at the same dead end. Nothing leads to the conclusion of foul play, except possibly on the part of the guard." David sat down in a chair with a sigh. "Simmons shouldn't have been in the archives. The museum is doing an inventory to see if anything is missing. They said it could take a few days to account for everything."

"With two similar deaths, have you checked to see if there's a connection?" The captain's penetrating stare must have read David's expression. The frown showed his disappointment.

"No, I haven't," David admitted. Jamila had him wound so tight, he'd screwed up. He should have thought of a possible connection. "We'll get on it. Right now."

"You do that." Jenkins' tone left no doubt about his displeasure.

David stood, then hurried from the office. With the door safely closed behind him, he let out an exasperated sigh.

His mind needed to be on his job, not some sexy piece of ass. Jamila meant nothing to him. Two hot encounters and his brains had drained out through his dick.

"You okay?" Susan's voice interrupted his pity party.

He couldn't stop the growl in his voice. "Fine. We've got work to do."

"Well, don't bite my head off," she snapped. "I've been here trying to make some sense of Joshua's reports. I can only imagine where you've been."

David stalked across the short distance to his desk. "What's that supposed to mean?" He yanked off his jacket and tossed it on the back of his chair.

"You disappeared. What am I supposed to think?" Susan glared across their joined desks. Her voice lowered to almost a whisper. "You went back there, didn't you?"

David couldn't lie to her, so he ignored her question. Right now, he needed to clear Jamila from his thoughts. "Have you found anything?"

Susan opened her mouth then shut it. Two files slid across the seam separating their desks. "Nothing," she mumbled. "See for yourself."

David picked up the file. "Do we know of any connection between the two men?"

"Not much. Different social circles, educations, careers. The only connection I saw was the museum. Freiberg's father is a heavy donor. Junior gave as well but not on the same scale." Susan shrugged. "Like I said, not much."

The museum where Jamila works. David shook his head against the sudden thought.

Not possible.

"Did we get a composite sketch from Freiberg's neighbor and the doorman?"

"Ah, yeah," Susan mumbled as she rifled through a file. Yanking a piece of paper out of the manila folder, she held it up. "Just the clothes. No identifying features." She leaned across her desk to hand the sketch to him.

Blood rushed from his head. His hand shook. The coat and figure matched Jamila's from their encounter at the bar.

"What have you got?" Susan stood up, then walked around to stand next to him.

"Nothing." He couldn't tell her about his bar bathroom scene. "We need to check into the museum connection."

Shoving open the precinct door, David let the cold air wash over him. A deep breath eased some of the tightness in his chest. He trotted down the stairs toward the sidewalk.

Susan was more than happy at his offer to go for coffee, and David would willingly pay for her exorbitant Starbucks fix to get out of there.

Somehow, Jamila was in the middle of both deaths. She had to be. Freiberg's apartment was two blocks from the bar. The sketch was a perfect match.

He didn't believe in coincidence. Turmoil roiled through his stomach. The idea of her involvement had him on edge, and he wasn't sure why. She didn't mean anything to him. Sure, their encounters had been unbelievable, something straight out of *Penthouse*. The fact he had sex with her could complicate the investigation. But it had just been sex. Hadn't it?

And what about the murders? She seemed involved, even if only by association. His career stood on a precipice and he tottered on the edge. Still he couldn't get the smell of her perfume and the heat of her body out of his mind.

Jamila expected the museum director's knock, but when it came, she still jumped. The head curator in Cairo hadn't wasted time in requesting Jamila's return.

"Dr. Bosta, please come in." Jamila waved the older woman toward the only guest chair in her office. "How can I help you?"

"I've heard from the Egyptian Museum. Why do you want to leave?" With her brow furrowed, she seemed genuinely upset as she sank into the chair.

"They need me on a new find. I didn't request to leave." The lie flowed off Jamila's tongue easily. With three thousand years of experience, lying wasn't difficult. However, she was fond of Dr. Bosta and regret was harder to play down.

"Does it have anything to do with Mr. Simmon's death?"

Jamila shook her head. "No, ma'am. Although it's tragic, it doesn't have anything to do with my decision. The new find at Dendara is too tempting. You know my fondness for artifacts from that area, especially since they believe the tomb is Twenti-eth Dynasty."

"Yes, I understand." Dr. Bosta smiled. "It just seemed so

sudden. I wanted to make sure of your reasons. We'll miss you."

Jamila's eyes clouded with tears. Leaving usually wasn't this difficult but she'd be leaving behind more than just friends this time. "And I you. But maybe I can come back in a few years."

The older woman smiled as she stood. "I hope so. You're expected back in Egypt next week. How will you have time to settle your affairs here before you leave?"

"I'll hire someone to pack up the apartment. I won't need much if I'm on a dig anyway." Jamila stood, then walked around her desk, her hand extended. "I want to thank you for everything."

"We'll see each other before you leave." The woman enclosed Jamila's hand in both of hers. "I'll have to come up with something suitable for a going-away party."

"You don't need to do anything. Please don't make a fuss." Jamila meant what she said. She hoped to disappear without too many questions.

"Nonsense. I promise to keep it small."

Jamila watched the door close behind the woman before she sat again. One task down, a million to go and a week to do them in.

Pulling a phone book off her credenza, she turned to the section for moving companies.

Three days and no further along in the investigation than the day the two men died. David threw Freiberg's financial records on his desk. "This is ridiculous." His growl was more to himself, but it caught Susan's attention.

She flicked her gaze toward him from the paper she was reading. "Too bad. We don't have a choice."

David took a deep breath. They didn't. After the captain got through chewing their collective asses again this morning,

David was sure his pants fit looser. "What the hell does he expect us to find? These two men didn't know each other. So far, it doesn't look like they even had any acquaintances in common."

Susan snorted her amusement. "But we keep looking."

Grabbing the scattered papers, David held them in front of his face. He pretended to read them as he blocked Susan's smirk.

She didn't seem to care that they were stuck with a never-ending case.

And David couldn't get Jamila out of his mind as long as these two files took up permanent residence on his desk. Her delicate features haunted his dreams. The almond-shaped eyes, her dark full lips. And her body.

He bit the inside of his cheek, hoping a little pain would ward off the threatened arousal. A constant state of horniness didn't help his concentration. In spite of nightly jerk off sessions, his cock never seemed to deflate past half-mast. The mere thought of Jamila resulted in a raging hard-on.

The precinct bathroom really wasn't a great place to masturbate. However, he'd done it yesterday out of desperation.

This time, when his teeth caught the side of his mouth, he tasted copper. He welcomed the slight distraction the pain afforded.

Susan's voice cut into his thoughts. "Hey, here's something."

He pulled the papers down enough to peer over the top. "What?"

"This phone number. I recognize it." Susan stood and moved around her desk. "Here. I've seen it on Simmons' usage detail. A lot. That's why it was familiar."

David shifted a pile of paper off the top of another file and rummaged around for a few seconds. Pulling a sheet of paper out, he compared the two lists.

Susan was right. The phone number showed up as an incoming call on Freiberg's records twice—two days before his death. But the same number was on Simmons' list several dozen times.

"I wonder who it belongs to?" David mumbled. His fingers already hovered over his keyboard. Quickly pulling up a menu, he typed the number. "The museum."

"Another dead end? They both have ties, although Freiberg's are minimal."

"I don't know. It's not the main number. We need to see which office the line belongs to." David stood with a mixture of dread and elation running through him. A reason to go to the museum or an excuse to see Jamila. He pushed the second idea to the back of his mind. "Let's take a ride."

Jamila put on her best smile and nodded to each person entering the room. Dr. Bosta had gone all-out for the party and invited every employee in the museum. So much for a small, quiet affair.

Murmured regrets about her departure registered in her mind, but she was too numb to say more than simple pleasantries. The press of bodies in the warm room created a myriad of scents, some pleasant, some not—some almost erotic. Several of the men appeared aroused by her close proximity.

The curse would rear its ugly head shortly. Her pheromones were getting close to peak. She should have objected more to the party or found a willing man last night.

The idea of anonymous sex so soon after David made her shudder.

"Are you chilled?" Dr. Bahir Abu Kadir whispered near her ear. "I have a cure for that, you know." His fingers trailed down her spine.

Jamila jumped away. She hadn't realized he was so close. Normally, she avoided Kadir. Something about the man's nearness set her teeth on edge. Not that he was unattractive. Quite the opposite—a classic tall, dark, and handsome—but he knew it and felt no woman would turn him down. He pestered her endlessly to go out with him, and each time she refused. Even if she hadn't found Kadir repugnant, sex with someone she knew was out of the question.

"I'm fine. Thank you." She moved toward the food. Circling the table looking at the selection, she stayed out of reach of Kadir's roaming hands and lecherous gaze.

She wondered how soon she could escape without people talking. She really needed some fresh air. The mingling odors of food and people were getting to her.

Pausing for brief chitchat here and there, she finally arrived at the open door. She didn't see the man on the other side until too late.

Bumping against his hard body sent a rush of adrenaline and arousal through her. She recognized his scent before she looked up to see David's amused blue eyes staring down at her.

Lust filled his gaze. Searing heat jolted through her body straight to her cunt.

"Leaving the party so soon? Looks like it just got started." David's smile seemed forced.

"I just need some air." She backed away from the heat of his body. "It's a little stuffy in there."

David's right eyebrow quirked up. He glanced over the top of her head into the room. "Looks like more than one kind of stuffy, too."

Jamila couldn't help but laugh. "Yes, that too."

"I'll walk with you."

Bad idea, but she didn't resist when his hand grasped her elbow and tugged. His partner glared at him as they walked past her.

"Susan, you go ahead. I'll be back in a few minutes."

His partner narrowed her eyes at Jamila but didn't say anything. Moving through the doorway, Susan disappeared into the crowd.

"Where's she going?" Jamila craned her neck to look over her shoulder.

"Talk to a couple of people. Nothing to worry about." His scent left no doubt of his arousal.

The curse went from a slow simmer to full boil. As if he could sense her hunger, his fingers tightened on her arm. "Where?"

"What?"

"Where can we go? Some place private?"

His low growl sent a fresh surge of moisture to the apex of her thighs.

Her mind raced. Her office would be too dangerous. If anyone noticed her missing, that's the first place they would look for her. The staff elevator caught her eye.

"Here." She pulled away long enough to punch the call button.

His body stopped so close to her, she could feel heat radiating off him.

Fortunately, the elevator doors opened immediately. Rough hands pushed her forward, but she needed no urging. The curse controlled her actions now. If they didn't find somewhere private soon, she'd fuck him in the middle of the museum, on display for all the patrons.

His body pressed against her back as soon as the doors started to close. The heat of his cock branded her ass through their clothing.

Her finger hovered over the controls. The EMERGENCY STOP button tempted her, but she pressed the sublevel for the archives instead. With all the archivists occupied at the party, the place should be empty.

A hand roamed up her stomach while David arched against her back. Her nipples, already tight and pointing with desire, ached when his fingers reached her breasts. His other hand slid south, covering her mons through her dress.

"Touch me," she whispered. Torn between pressing backward against his cock or forward into his hands, she settled on swaying back and forth.

His thumb and forefinger tweaked a hard nub of flesh. His other hand pressed tight against her groin.

Her clit, swollen with anticipation, throbbed in time with her racing heart. The swoosh of the opening doors caught her by surprise. Pulling away from David, Jamila grabbed his hand and led him into the poorly lit area.

A storage room a few feet from the elevator would work. She fumbled with the doorknob while David played with her breasts. The creak of the door startled her but she didn't hesitate to pull him into the darkness with her. Her hand felt for the wall and found the light switch. Fluorescent lighting blinked, then steadied.

Still behind her, David pushed her against the cold wall. Fingers pushed her collar down and a hot mouth suckled the tender skin of her neck.

"I want to kiss you," he murmured, his voice hoarse with need.

"No!" Softer, she whispered, "No, you can't. Please don't ask again."

His lips nibbled along the line of her neck until he reached her collarbone. Warm moist flesh traced the hollow dip then moved to her throat. The rough scrape of stubble sent shivers through her body.

"Cold?" he murmured. Soft amusement caressed the word.

"Not exactly," she teased. As she pushed back into him, the feel of his hard flesh generated enough heat to warm a small city. "But I am a little impatient."

"Hmm . . . Well, you know patience is a virtue." His mouth sucked her ear lobe.

"Who said I was virtuous?" Her forehead pressed against the cool wall.

His laugh sent warm air against her skin.

"Can we move this along? I'll be missed soon." She really

didn't care about the crowd upstairs. Her body ached to be filled.

The jangle of his belt buckle then the ripping sound of his zipper made her gasp. She reached for the hem of her dress. Hiking the tight material up high, she tugged at her panties.

Rough fingers helped pull the silky material down her thighs. Callused hands grabbed her hips, yanking her back. His fingers brushed through her parted cheeks. With her legs restrained by her panties, the blunt tip of his cock pushed between her thighs and nudged her wet cunt.

"Hurry." Her hands pushed against the wall.

A soft chuckle was his reply. But he pushed deeper, his hot shaft penetrating her moist core at a maddeningly slow pace.

Relief flowed out on her exhaled breath when he finally filled her. But his torture wasn't finished. Rocking slowly back, he withdrew. Just as slowly, he reentered her depths.

Her body shuddered with each anticipated move. Her teeth caught her lips to keep from screaming. Pain didn't diminish the intense pleasure shooting through her cunt. Her juices lubricated the juncture of her thighs, aiding the slow sliding cock with each stroke. Her fingernails tore at the rough wall.

The unusual build-up of pleasure left her panting. So different from her usual encounters. And so good. "So good . . ." she moaned.

He leaned forward, his breath teasing her ear as he spoke, "One of these days, I want you in bed. Laid out against the covers, completely naked."

"Oh, yes . . ." She knew it couldn't happen but the idea of cool soft sheets and hot rough sex . . . "Yes."

"My bare skin against yours." His whisper was so low, she had to strain to hear him. Throughout his soft words, his body never broke the steady exasperating rhythm.

Biting her lips, she groaned. She wanted everything he said, more than he would ever be able to understand.

"Somewhere I could kiss every square inch of your flesh. Taste your sweet cream." His sensuous words teased her as much as his hard body.

Kisses fluttered across her shoulder. One hand slipped from her hip. Fingers brushed her swollen clit. And the long even strokes never stopped. The pressure against her mons increased. Soon his fingers matched the movement of his hips.

Exquisite release caught her by surprise, dragging all the breath from her lungs. Her body tightened around his cock.

His pace increased, slamming into her once, twice, then he joined her in breathless moans. He leaned against her back, his arm wrapped tight around her waist. Frantic kisses covered the side of her neck.

"Jamila . . ." he whispered.

Before he could finish his words, the muffled sound of voices penetrated the door.

6

David froze for a second then pulled away from the comforting heat of Jamila's body. He stifled a groan when his cock slid from her dripping cunt.

Shit, what was this woman's allure? Once again, he'd just fucked her in a public place. He had to get this obsession under control.

Jamila scrambled for her underwear, yanking them up before tugging her dress back in place.

"Do you recognize the voices?" David whispered. Leaning his ear against the door, he strained to hear coherent words. Two masculine voices murmured but he couldn't make out what they were saying.

She mimicked his stance. With her body close to his, the scent of her exotic perfume mixed with the smell of sex.

The enticing aromas distracted him.

"No." She barely breathed the word.

The sounds receded farther into the archives. His rapid heartbeat drummed in his ears. He took a deep breath and shoved his dick in his pants. Tucking in his shirt, he zipped and buttoned up. He needed to get out of here and clear his head.

Jamila turned to face him. "We need to go."

The storage room where they hid was close to the elevator, but if the car had already left this floor ... "Where're the stairs?" They could get to the next level then take the elevator.

"Around the corner from the elevators, to the right," she whispered. Her breath was still rapid, either from passion or fear. Or both.

"You ready?"

She looked up at him and nodded. Her eyes looked glassy and distant.

"Let's go." He pulled the door open enough to peer out. No signs, no sounds. Grabbing Jamila's hand, he eased the door open then tugged her out behind him. He had to catch her when she stumbled. "Are you okay?"

She regained her balance then pointed in the direction of the stairs. "That way."

Moving faster, they rounded the corner. David pushed the bar carefully to avoid noise. Rushing Jamila through the opening, he slid in behind her and closed the door softly.

Jamila still looked dazed, but she started up the stairs at a rapid pace.

David trailed along behind her. With immediate danger of discovery past, his mind wandered back to his obsession with this strange woman. Nothing had ever been more important than his job. He knew what he was risking, but whenever she was near, his mind stopped working and his dick took over.

And how the hell was he supposed to question her after fucking her?

They paused on the landing of the next floor. Jamila's eyes glowed with an indescribable aura. Her skin still flushed with rosy heat. She pulled her hand out of his.

He hadn't realized he was still holding on. The warmth of her touch immediately dissipated. He missed it.

"We have to talk. About the case." He clarified quickly. "Where can we go?"

A frown creased her soft look of satisfaction. "My office. It's on this level."

He matched her pace but stayed a couple of steps behind her. His mind raced with the conflict of having to interrogate a woman he . . . He what? A sick feeling settled hard in the pit of his stomach. How could he love someone he'd only known for a few days? And the only way he'd *known* her was in the biblical sense.

He nearly plowed into Jamila when she stopped suddenly in front of the door to her office.

"So is this about the guard?" she asked as he closed the door.

"It's not about the guard."

Her frown deepened. "Then what about the case?" She dropped into her chair and glared at him across the desk.

"Do you know this man?" He placed a picture of Aaron Freiberg in front of her. His gaze never left her face.

She picked up the photo by one edge and stared at the image. After a brief pause, she replied, "He looks familiar. Maybe?" She shrugged. "I see a lot of people through the museum. Who is he?" Her eyes lifted to meet his.

"He's another dead man."

She didn't flinch or look away from his gaze. No indication of lying. Or was she just really good at it?

David took the photo from her. "And he was seen with a woman matching your description the night of his death."

"Murdered?" Jamila kept her voice impassive in spite of the turmoil in her stomach. If he connected her to Aaron, then suspicion for the guard's death could rest on her as well. Her flight left in two days. Under scrutiny in two deaths, she'd never get out of the country.

"So far, it looks like natural causes but there are some suspicious circumstances surrounding both deaths." David eased into the guest chair. "And you appear to be connected to both men."

"I don't know him. And I didn't know the guard except in passing. So how am I connected?"

He held up the picture. "This man's apartment was two blocks from the bar. He died the night you . . . The night you and I . . ."

"Fucked in the bathroom." Her words came out much harsher than she intended.

He simply nodded. "You were close to the scene and more than one witness described you."

Jamila knew she'd kept her face covered when she met Aaron and when she left the apartment. How could anyone have her description, other than her clothing? Or is that what he was basing his accusations on?

"You said you had just left a boyfriend, caught him with someone else. What's his name?" Intense blue eyes almost begged for her answer.

"I don't want him involved." Jamila turned her chair so she wouldn't have to face him. She sighed and shook her head. "I don't know the dead man. Can't you trust me on this?"

David moved around the desk and grabbed the arms of her chair. The wheels squeaked as he pulled her closer. "Trust you? Based on what? Our longtime friendship? Our three quick fucks?" His eyes narrowed. "I'm risking more than you can understand here and I'm just supposed to trust you?"

Jamila shrank against the back of the chair. "I can't help you. I didn't murder anyone. Please leave."

His mouth opened but whatever he started to say, he must

have changed his mind. He pushed the chair, sending it rolling back against her credenza then stormed around her desk to the door.

He paused at the door, his hand hovering over the door-knob. "If you're involved, I'll find out. It would be better if you cooperated."

"There's nothing to tell. I'm sorry." And she meant it. She was sorry for everything but regret couldn't help her. She waited for the clichéd 'don't leave town' but it never came.

The muscles in his back relaxed with a sigh. "I'm sorry too." He pulled the door open slightly then shut it. "I thought there was something . . ." He shook his head. Then, yanking the door open, he left.

Jamila jumped as the door slammed shut. She wanted to run after him pleading to know what the something was but she stayed glued to her chair. Even if he had feelings for her, her past held her future hostage.

She had killed two men, and the man who stole her heart was a cop. "Thanks again, Keket."

David looked around the sea of people mingling with drinks and food. Susan's bright hair should be easy enough to spot but his mind really wasn't on finding his partner. He'd stopped in the men's room to wash up and collect his thoughts. The cleaning up worked. His thoughts were another story.

Jamila was a drug, and he was addicted. In spite of the risk to his job, he'd almost told her he had feelings for her. His involvement with her already strained his relationship with his partner.

Susan had kept him at arm's length since the interview at Jamila's apartment. She guessed he'd gone back and must have known what happened when he had.

His life was diving into the toilet in the short span of a few days and he didn't know how to stop it.

"Looking for me?" Susan's voice hovered behind him.

"Yeah." He turned around to see her with an older Middle Eastern man.

"This is Dr. Bahir Abu Kadir. He's the curator of the permanent Egyptian exhibit. I've been talking to him about the phone calls to him from our victims." Susan turned to the man. "This is my partner, Detective Craise."

Something about the man made David's skin crawl but he took the offered hand. Maybe it was the fake smile plastered across his face.

"Did you know both men?"

"As I was telling your lovely partner, yes, I did." His smile broadened as he glanced at Susan.

Mentally, David chuckled. *Barking up the wrong tree.* "What was your relationship with them?"

"Mr. Freiberg I knew only casually. Mark, however, I had struck up a friendship with. I was stunned by his death. We all were. But I was under the impression it was natural causes and not murder."

"We are simply exploring the possibilities." David noticed the curious stares of some of the other guests. "Why don't we take this conversation somewhere less populated?"

Kadir nodded. "This way."

David and Susan followed him through the crowd to a different door than they had entered. The noise of the crowd dimmed to a murmur as the door closed.

Kadir led them into a gallery filled with displays of Egyptian artifacts. David almost smiled at the series of Canopic jars in a large glass case.

Controlling his expression, he turned back to Kadir. "So

why did Freiberg call you? Was he interested in Egyptian artifacts?"

The man laughed softly. "Not exactly. More like he was interested in a certain Egyptian woman."

"Who?" David steeled himself for the answer even though he knew already.

"Jamila Aten."

A sharp pain stabbed at David's gut.

"And was she interested in him?" Susan asked.

David was grateful for her intervention. He wasn't sure he could keep his disappointment out of his voice.

"I don't know." Kadir shrugged. "He had met her at a museum function a few days before his death. He wanted to know more about her."

Susan's expression mirrored David's confusion. "If you only knew him casually, why would he call you?"

"I don't really know. Aaron and I had met at a dinner several months ago at his father's house. And at the museum the night he met Ms. Aten." Loathing dripped from Kadir's lips when he said Jamila's name. "He'd seen me talking to her, so maybe he felt he could impose on our tenuous acquaintance."

David's dislike for the man grew with each word he spoke. An overall air of arrogance combined with his obvious animosity toward Jamila.

David cut Susan off before she could respond. "You don't like Ms. Aten?"

"She claims to be an expert on ancient Egypt but I hadn't heard of her until the museum hired her. And she's very young to be in her position. I doubt her credentials. I don't know her personally well enough to like or dislike her." Kadir narrowed his eyes at David. "But you appear to be smitten with her. I saw you leaving the party together."

"I was questioning her. She claims she didn't know Mr.

Freiberg." David's imagination conjured the smell of sex and Jamila's perfume. At least, he hoped it was all in his head.

"Well, I know she's met him. How far Aaron got in his pursuit of something more, I wouldn't know. But he seemed determined, and if he was anything like his father, he wouldn't let it go until he had what he wanted."

David hesitated and he was grateful when Susan jumped in with a question.

"So you know the councilman well?"

"Not well. I've been trying to convince him the city needs to fund a new exhibit of Twentieth Dynasty Egypt. He's not easy to convince." Kadir made a show of looking at his watch. "I have to return to the party. So if you have no further questions . . ."

"What's the party for?" Susan asked.

From the way she looked past Kadir at him, David knew she already had the answer.

"Jamila Aten's going-away party. She's returning to Egypt in a few days." Kadir nodded at David then Susan.

The words hit David in the pit of his stomach. She was fleeing his jurisdiction. And his life.

Jamila sent an apologetic e-mail to Dr. Bosta explaining she had to leave the wonderful party to attend to moving issues. Grabbing her purse and coat, she left the museum through the staff entrance.

David was bound to find out she was leaving. The party was a dead giveaway. With him already suspicious, he'd be back and she needed to make sure she wasn't here for him to find.

Cold wind buffeted her as she hurried down the street. She decided against trying to hail a cab and headed to the subway station. She disliked the subway but she didn't want to risk David and his partner catching her as she waited for a taxi.

A rush of air blew up the stairs of the station accompanied by the screeching of brakes as a train entered the station. She wouldn't have time to get a token and make the train. This time of day, the next one would be several minutes away.

Her heart raced as she pushed her money through the small opening in the token booth. She kept her head down, avoiding eye contact with the clerk. He flicked a token and her change back through without saying anything.

The warning ding of closing doors greeted her as she pushed through the turnstile.

"Hold the door!" She ran toward the train but no one paid any attention to her cry. Within a few steps of the train, the doors closed.

The train pulled away slowly, almost mocking her. Jamila swallowed the rising lump in her throat. Her life had turned upside down in just a few days. The cold deserted subway station emphasized the emptiness of her life.

Three thousand years of meaningless sex all because she couldn't keep her hands off one man. Bomani hadn't been worth this.

And now there was David. The first man in so long to spark more than just lust. He could be her downfall. Or she could be his.

She stared at the subway tracks. Over the centuries, she'd been injured, seriously at times, but she healed with phenomenal speed. She'd wondered what would happen if she lost a limb or if she suffered decapitation. Would she miraculously regain the necessary parts?

Despair had never moved her enough to test her theories. The rumble of the next train echoed down the dark tunnel. Jamila moved closer to the edge of the platform. A single step and she'd drop the short distance to the tracks. If she timed it right, the train's engineer wouldn't have time to stop. Maybe it would all be over. Her meaningless life finally over.

Standing on the top of the stairs in front of the museum, David welcomed the cold wind. He'd been fooled, led around by his dick. Jamila knew both of the dead men and she'd lied. Why lie if she had nothing to hide? And why would she leave the museum in the middle of her own party?

"David, what's wrong?" Susan's hand warmed a small spot on his shoulder.

"She's involved. I'd hoped it wasn't true." He winced as the last few words slipped out. He didn't want to reveal that much of his turmoil.

"I'm sorry, but you don't know if she had anything to do with the deaths. We still don't have any evidence of foul play. Just a circumstantial connection between the victims. No more or less than Dr. Kadir. He knew both men as well."

David turned to face his partner. "True." He shook his head. "But why would she lie if it was an innocent coincidence?"

"I don't know. We need to keep looking and we need the test results from Joshua."

"Yeah." He nodded. The sympathy in her eyes actually cheered him.

Their relationship meant a lot to him. Partners for five years, he considered her his best friend. For them to be on the outs with each other, especially over a woman, wasn't right.

"We should find her though. She has more questions to answer."

Susan squeezed his arm. "Agreed. She had to go home. If she's really involved and planning to flee, she'd need at least a few things from her apartment. We can call Joshua on the way."

They moved down the stairs and toward the car. They'd parked in the no parking zone near the subway entrance.

A scream and the screeching brakes of the train echoed out of the station.

David and Susan glanced at each other and then ran toward the subway. David took two or three steps with each stride, leaving Susan behind.

He flashed his badge at the token booth and they buzzed him through the gate.

Several people stood around jabbering at the conductor.

Holding his badge up, he waded into the middle. "What happened?"

One man, pale and shaking, shook his head. "She almost jumped. If I hadn't grabbed her coat . . ."

"Who?"

The man just kept shaking his head, his eyes wild.

David turned to the conductor. "Did you see anything?"

"A woman, dark haired, slender, in a long red coat, was standing too close to the edge of the platform when we entered the station." He pointed to the still shaking man. "He grabbed the back of her coat and pulled her away. She got away from him and ran out the south entrance."

Jamila. The description could have been anyone but his heart insisted it was Jamila.

Susan arrived in time to hear the conductor's words. Her gaze met his. One graceful eyebrow arched.

Two uniformed transit police hurried onto the platform. "What's happening?" one of them asked.

David walked toward the south entrance as Susan explained all they knew. This was the transit's territory. They could handle the crowd.

What would cause Jamila to try to kill herself? Guilt. His heart sought another answer. Was the woman addictive? He'd only known her a handful of days and he didn't want to face the truth. She had to be connected to the deaths.

He jogged up the stairs into the cold. The intersection was crowded with the normal rush of pedestrians and vehicles. Turning in a slow circle, his gaze sought the red coat the conductor described, the same one that had been hanging on a coat rack in Jamila's office. A few caught his eye but the wearer wasn't her.

Footsteps echoed up the stairs behind him. "Why would she try suicide if she wasn't guilty of something?"

"I don't know." David wondered if she'd try again. He had to find her and make sure there wasn't a next time.

7

David tossed his jacket on the chair near his front door. He needed sleep but he didn't think it would come easy even if it was almost ten. He'd been up since six and a good night's sleep was rare lately.

He found no sign of Jamila, and the captain was on his case for losing a probable suspect in a high profile case. Fortunately, Jenkins agreed to keep this latest development out of the report for the time being. The captain resented the chief passing on information to Councilman Freiberg so he wasn't hard to convince. Not to mention, the old man might leak the information to the public. If Jamila hadn't fled already, news stories about her would definitely send her running.

If she hadn't succeeded in killing herself. David shook the thought out of his mind.

He grabbed his phone and dialed her number. Again. He had it memorized already.

The answering machine picked up on the second ring.

"Ms. Aten, this is Detective Craise again. Please contact me as soon as possible." The same message he'd left several times before. Impersonal, so if it ended up in evidence he could claim it was strictly business. His finger hesitated over the END button. Against his better judgment, he put the phone back to his mouth. "Jamila, please call me."

In her dark apartment, Jamila was curled up in an over-stuffed chair in her bedroom. She listened to David's cold message. Afraid the police would be watching her building, she'd snuck in through the delivery entrance. With the lights out, no one would know she was there. But it was a temporary solution.

A small overnight bag sat open on her bed with a few clothes hanging out. She had her escape route planned, a short walk to the subway then Amtrak out of Penn Station to Washington, D.C. She could get a flight out of D.C. to Europe then on to Egypt. She didn't think she'd made America's most wanted yet. Their evidence was circumstantial at best. She shouldn't have any problem catching an international flight.

She just had to finish packing a few belongings but she couldn't force herself to move.

If that stranger hadn't stopped her, she wouldn't be worrying about what would happen. She didn't know whether to be grateful or angry at his interference.

After a brief pause, she'd heard David's voice soften. "Jamila, please call me."

As bad an idea as it was, she wanted to see him one more time before she disappeared for good. She stood, stretching the kinks out of her back and legs. She'd been sitting there for hours without moving. His business card was next to her cell phone on the dresser. All she had to do was get his number and dial it.

The phone rang just as David set it on the table. He snatched it up and answered, barely managing to keep from saying Jamila's name. His heart raced as he spoke. "Hello."

"David, it's Susan. Joshua got the toxicology reports back."

"And?"

"Are you at home? I want to bring them over. I've also got some interesting information you need to know about."

David sighed. "Yes, I'm home. Come on over." His disappointment over not finding Jamila on the other end of the line dampened his curiosity. He didn't wait for Susan's response before he flipped the phone shut. Whatever she'd found, her information probably damned Jamila and he didn't want to think about it just yet.

The phone rang again and he almost didn't answer it. Susan probably forgot something. He looked at the unfamiliar number on the caller ID. "Hello?"

"David?"

"Yes." He forced his breathing to remain normal. "Jamila? Are you okay?" Relief washed over him.

"I want to meet you. I need to explain."

"Of course, why don't you meet me at the precinct?" The cop in him tried to assert itself.

"No! Just you and me. If you bring anyone else, I won't be there."

"Okay, fine. I won't bring anyone else. Where? When?"

"Wollman Rink in Central Park. In one hour. And please come alone." Her voice cracked as she stressed the last word.

The silence on the other end of the line confirmed she'd hung up but David checked the display anyway. One hour, and Susan should be at his apartment any minute. The precinct wasn't far. He'd have time to look at the reports and whatever else it was she had and still meet Jamila. It'd be close. The trip to Central Park would take a few minutes, but this late, traffic would be minimal.

Nervous energy forced him to pace the floor. If Susan didn't get there soon, he'd appear suspicious asking her to leave before she could tell him what she found.

And what could she have found? Did the tox reports show poison? Had she found more information on Jamila?

When the knock on the door came, he leaped for the door.

Susan looked surprised when he yanked it open. "In a hurry?"

"Just tired. I need to get some sleep." He motioned for her to come in. "What have you got?"

She sat down on the couch and spread some papers out on the coffee table. "The tox report revealed a substance called *letum viscus*. It's very rare and usually associated with Egyptian tombs." She picked up one of the papers and held it out.

David's impatience for her to leave lessened. He grabbed the paper and sat next to her on the couch. "Causes sudden death by acute myocardial infarction . . ." He looked up at Susan.

She nodded. "Heart attack."

"Deliberate?"

"Joshua doesn't think so. There's very little information on the substance or its effects on the human body. However, Crime Scene found the same substance in the archives of the museum and in Freiberg's apartment."

"But he doesn't think someone used this substance to murder the two men?"

"Well, combined with some information I dredged up, no." Susan rummaged through the paperwork. "I really didn't like Kadir. And he seemed to be putting a seriously bad spin on Jamila's connection to Freiberg. So I checked him out." Susan glanced at the page in her hand. "After we left the museum, he made a series of phone calls." She pointed to a highlighted phone number. "This number is a known fence of antiquities. The Major Case squad has never been able to pin anything on him that would stick. If Kadir is calling him in a panic . . ."

David shook his head. His mind was on the ticking clock and couldn't focus on how this related to the two murders.

"That may be great news to Major Case but how does it help us?"

"Well, if some of the artifacts were contaminated with *letum viscus* and they passed through certain hands . . ."

"The guard. He wasn't supposed to be in the archives. That would explain his death but what about Freiberg?" David needed Susan to have a rational explanation.

"If there was any residue on Jamila's clothing and she met him . . ."

David stood then paced the floor. "Then why didn't it kill her? Or me?"

"You?"

David rubbed his eyes with the heel of his hands. "Me." With a sigh, he turned to face his partner. "That night, the night Freiberg died, I met her. I stopped at Murphy's for a drink. She showed up there." He turned away and walked toward the window. His image reflected in the frosty glass. "I . . . ah . . . She kind of seduced me."

"Damn it, David! You should have said something before now." Disappointment colored the anger in her voice. "You could have compromised the whole case."

"I know."

"Oh, shit. You did go back to her apartment that day, didn't you?"

He just nodded. There really wasn't much he could say. His behavior was inexcusable. He wanted to tell her he was meeting Jamila tonight but he hesitated. The memory of Jamila's pleading words kept him silent. "I think I'm in over my head."

"Are you in love with her?"

With his back still to Susan, David shook his head. "No. How can I be? I only met her a week ago." He knew the words were a lie as soon as they slid off his tongue. Why else would he risk his career, maybe even his freedom? He took a deep breath and turned to face his partner. "So why wouldn't it have killed me?"

"Maybe only certain people are susceptible to it?"

"Do you think this evidence will exonerate her?"

Susan shrugged. "I don't know, David. She's acting suspicious enough to make me wonder if she's part of it somehow. Maybe collaborating with Kadir? If she hadn't planned to leave the country on such short notice . . ."

"The museum director said she was asked to come back by the Egyptian Museum."

"I know but it seems too convenient."

"The evidence at Freiberg's apartment still supports the theory that he tried to rape someone. If he died in the middle of the attack, Jamila could have been traumatized." A spark of hope ignited with the thought. "She could be running from the incident, not because she had killed him."

"Too many 'ifs', David." Susan gathered her paperwork then stood up. "Major Case is picking up Kadir for questioning. Any time a museum curator contacts a suspected fence, they get interested."

"Susan, are you going to say anything about my relationship with Jamila?" David knew he'd have to come clean with the captain but he wanted to have the chance to do it himself.

"Are you?"

David nodded. "I will. Tomorrow."

"Good. I'll let you know if Major Case calls back."

"Thanks." David stared out the window as she left. He knew he should have told Susan he was meeting Jamila tonight but he wanted a chance to talk to her alone. Then he'd bring her in for questioning.

Cold wind buffeted Jamila as she looked out over Wollman Rink. Leaves swirled around her ankles teasing her skin. Drafts of frigid air ignored her long coat and puffed up her skirt.

A few straggling skaters braved the cold and the late hour. She watched one doing intricate spins and twirls in the middle of the ice. Jamila's world mimicked the skater's movement. Torn in so many directions, her life spun faster and faster out of control.

She was a few minutes early. Too early. It gave her time to reconsider. David was a cop and she was a murder suspect. Why would he agree to meet her alone? Her trust in him had no foundation. Her gut said he wouldn't betray her but her mind called her a fool.

A dark figure moved up the sidewalk, tall with broad shoulders and a determined pace.

In spite of the chill, heat pooled between Jamila's thighs. Passion, true passion and not remnants of the curse, swept through her body. Her heart ached for David, for the good-bye she had to say without speaking. He must know she planned to leave New York. The museum director wouldn't have seen a need to hide that information. Still, she couldn't say good-bye.

"Jamila?"

She stepped out of the sheltering shadow of the trees. "I'm here."

Warm arms enveloped her. Automatically, she lowered her head to avoid his lips but she gave herself completely to his tight embrace.

"You're safe." His tight voice conveyed more feeling than she wanted to hear. "After the subway . . ."

Her heart skipped a beat. "How could you know?"

"I just do. Why?"

His arms squeezed her so tight she had trouble breathing. "I don't know." How could she explain the millennium of despair that possessed her in that moment? "It seemed like the right thing to do at the time."

"And now?" His lips caressed the side of her neck.

"Maybe it wasn't such a great idea."

"Jamila, I want to help you." His hold on her loosened. One hand moved to the side of her face. In spite of his cold fingers, his touch warmed her cheek. "But you have to be honest with me."

"I want to be. I want to tell you everything, but I can't."

The dim light from the skating rink highlighted the disappointment in his eyes. "Did you kill Aaron Freiberg?"

Jamila opened her mouth to answer but her words were cut short.

"David!" Susan's voice shot through the darkness. "Step away from her."

Instead of obeying his partner, David shoved Jamila behind him. "Susan, not yet . . ." His words sparked like electricity in the air.

He had betrayed her. She should have trusted her reason and not her heart. Pain racked her chest, turmoil roiled through her stomach. Tears welled up and spilled over, leaving trails down her face. Then she ran.

"What the fuck are you doing?" David yelled at Susan.

"Trying to save your ass. I came back to tell you Major Case caught a break and I saw you leaving." Susan started past him to follow Jamila.

David grabbed her arm. "Leave her to me."

"No." Susan yanked her arm free.

This time David grabbed both arms. Susan was a strong woman but his anger fueled him. "You followed me. Why?"

"You can't see past a pretty piece of ass, so I have to handle it for you. Even now, you're letting her get away."

Shock flowed through David. Jamila had at least a block head start because of him. "Damn it, Susan. She was about to tell me what the hell is going on." David released his partner and ran down the path after Jamila. When he came to a fork in the path, he stopped.

Susan almost ran into him. "Which way?" she panted.

"They both lead to the East Drive."

"According to motor vehicles, we know she doesn't have a car. She'll have to find a cab." Susan looked at her watch. "This late, she won't have much luck in the park. I'll go this way." She pointed at the path on the left.

"Okay." David started toward the other.

"David, you have to bring her in."

"I know." He turned to stare at Susan under the streetlight. "I would have. You just couldn't wait."

"I'm sorry but we're wasting time."

David didn't waste anymore saying good-bye. His heart beat in time to his footsteps as he raced down the path. He almost didn't hear the rustling leaves of someone sheltered in the woods off the path. He stopped and listened for the sound again.

Soft sobs and gulping breaths whispered to him. He retraced his steps listening until the rustle of leaves revealed her position.

"Jamila . . ." With slow steps, as if approaching a wild creature he didn't want to frighten, David walked toward her. Leaves and twigs crunched under his feet.

"You said you'd come alone." The ragged accusation pinpointed her exact location. She was moving again.

"Jamila, you have to come with me. We need answers."

"Stay away from me. I didn't kill anyone but I won't go with you. I have to leave."

Anger burned out his patience. "If you're innocent of a crime, then why won't you just tell me what happened?"

"You wouldn't believe me. No one would. And I can't be locked up. I'd rather die."

"So that's why you tried to jump in front of a train?" He kept moving toward the sound of rustling leaves.

"Yes. And I'll do it right next time. I can't go to jail."

David lunged for where he thought she was. Exultation rushed through him as his hands closed on her coat. Yanking her toward him, her back thudded against his chest. "I won't let you kill yourself." He wrapped his arms around her.

Her fingernails dug into his hands. Flailing kicks landed sharp blows to his shins.

"Stop it! I'm not letting you go." Her struggle threw him off balance. Stumbling backward, David slammed into something solid. "Damn it, Jamila." He swung her around and pinned her to a tree. "We'll figure this out. If it was an accident, I can help you."

Her resistance fled and she slumped against the tree. "You don't understand. I'm a lost cause. I have been for so long."

David's anger melted at the resignation in her tone. "You're not lost anymore. I found you."

"All you've found is the shell of someone who existed long ago. I should have had the courage to end it years ago." The clouds cleared and light from the full moon spackled her face with dots of pale light. Her black eyes glittered in the darkness. "At least you've given me that."

"I won't let you hurt yourself. Haven't you figured it out? I've risked everything trying to believe in you." His head dipped toward hers. "Do you know why?"

"Don't kiss me!" Her struggles turned frantic.

His emotional roller coaster swung around another bend and his anger flared again. He pushed her hard against the tree. Her no kissing game was getting old. Three times she'd let him fuck her but she denied him a simple kiss?

His body kept her pinned to the tree while one hand grabbed at her hair. With a tight grip, he angled her head up.

"No! Please, no!"

Her lips kept pleading as he covered her mouth with his. His tongue tasted the cold lips but he wanted more. With a yank of her hair, her lips opened. The sweet delicious heat of her mouth beckoned. He ignored her struggles and took what she denied him.

8

"No . . ." His mouth swallowed her howl of fear and frustration. A warm tongue swept deep in her mouth. She gave up her struggle and waited for him to die. Her path to her own death was clear. She couldn't live knowing she'd killed him.

His curious tongue teased her pallet then down to touch hers. He was still alive. She tried to push him away but she stayed wedged between his hard body and the rough bark of the tree.

She chanced a small moan as pleasure replaced the fear and joy chased away her despair. He was alive and kissing her. Heat spread through her body. She wrapped her arms around him and she fell into his kiss.

Warm lips and a hot mouth with a living body, kissed her. Burning heat pooled between her legs. She raised one leg and hooked it around his thigh, pressing her aching cunt against his rising erection. She kissed him hard. Her tongue wanted to taste every part of his mouth.

"Oh, God, so long . . ." she moaned. "Need you . . ."

"Yes," he mumbled against her lips.

Without moving her mouth away from the heat of his, she slid her hands between them and fumbled with his belt and button.

His hands tugged at her skirt, bunching the material as it slid up her legs. Cold air teased but didn't cool the heat burning through her pussy.

Sliding his zipper down, Jamila pushed her hands into his briefs. A sharp grunt was David's only reaction when her cold fingers wrapped around his hard cock. One hand yanked his pants down enough to free his hot flesh.

His hands grabbed her waist. He pulled her off her feet. Steadying her against the tree, he rubbed his cock against her wet slit.

She pulled the crotch of her panties aside to allow him access to her aching core. "Yes, I need you. Now." She moaned around his tongue. "Fuck me."

His hard flesh filled her in one fast stroke. Her head rolled back in ecstasy and she almost lost contact with his mouth. Her arms wrapped around his neck and she renewed her fervent kiss.

Their awkward position kept his strokes slow and short but she didn't care. Keket's Curse couldn't compare to the burning need firing her now. Joined mouths and his cock inside her was all she desired. The rolling thrusts were all she needed.

The curse was over. His betrayal, bringing his partner when he promised to come alone, had ended her torment. What happened after tonight didn't matter.

"Don't let me go," she moaned between biting kisses.

His arms tightened on her, his cock slid deeper. "Never. I love you."

"Oh, God, yes . . ." She took his mouth hard. Three thousand years of limited passion, three thousand years without feeling the warm mouth of a man against hers. She flexed her legs around his waist, meeting each of his thrusts with her own. The pungent scent of her cream filled her nostrils. The juicy slap of skin on skin serenaded her. "Love . . . you," she mumbled.

The cold world around her retreated and she was young again. She could almost smell the desert air and the exotic fragrances of the temple incense. The dark curse lifted and her spirit renewed. The man holding her, making love to her in dark frigid woods, was all she needed now.

David's mouth left hers and trailed down her neck. She shivered as the cold breeze touched her damp flesh.

"Need you." He grunted. His body moved faster. The short stokes lengthened. "Need. You."

"Yes, harder . . ." The ache in her stomach melted into her cunt. Heat radiated through her groin. So close.

His hands slipped under her thighs. Holding her against the tree, he thrust hard. Pounding flesh warmed her very soul. A wave of pleasure spread from her core and washed over her. "Kiss me! Please kiss me!"

His mouth covered hers in a long hard kiss, full of passion and promise. The warmth radiating through her cunt spread to meet the heat filling her from his kiss.

With a jerk of his hips and a groan, his seed filled her. The deep kiss grew shallow. Small kisses, biting of lips, teasing tongues.

So lost in him, Jamila almost didn't hear Susan's shout.

"David!"

Jamila moaned as his heat slid free of her. She'd already gotten more than she ever expected but it wasn't enough. He planted a quick kiss on her lips as he lowered her feet to the ground.

"Don't worry. We'll figure it out," he whispered. "Come on."

Jamila straightened her underwear. His seed and her cream mixed together dampened the silk material as soon as it covered her pussy.

David quickly tucked away his softening cock and fastened his pants. "Ready?" He held out his hand.

She let his hand close over hers. "For anything."

* * *

David led Jamila out of the darkness of the shadows and into the light of a street lamp. Her change in attitude seemed miraculous but he was too grateful to question it. Now to clear her of the possible murder charges.

"Over here, Susan."

His partner, flanked by two uniformed cops, headed toward him. "Why weren't you answering your phone?"

David slapped the pocket where he usually kept his cell phone. Empty. "I must have dropped it somewhere." His hand tightened on Jamila's as he glanced at the two uniforms. "You didn't need to call backup. I have things under control."

"I didn't. They were patrolling near the park. When I couldn't find you and you wouldn't answer your phone, I flagged them down to help search for you." She turned to the two officers. "You guys can go. Thanks for your help." Susan nodded at Jamila. "Ms. Aten."

Jamila acknowledged her with a similar nod. "Detective Brennen."

Susan waited for the other two men to leave before she turned back to David. "Kadir has confessed to a smuggling operation. Joshua seems to think the *letum viscus* was transferred from man to man through the smuggling ring."

"Freiberg was part of it?"

"Smuggling?" Jamila looked from Susan to David.

Susan nodded. "Egyptian antiquities."

"Kadir? That son of a . . . He's no better than a grave robber!"

David couldn't help but smile at Jamila's anger. She was beautiful when she was mad. Hell, she was beautiful when she wasn't. "Calm down. He's in custody."

"Yes, Freiberg, the guard, and Kadir were all part of the plot and with this development, I'm sure Freiberg's father will be more than happy for the case to close." Susan chuckled. "I'm sure he doesn't want the scandal to touch him in next year's elections."

"I'll bet not." David pulled Jamila into the circle of his arm. "But I have to know, Jamila. What was your connection to all of this?"

Her shoulders tensed under his arm and then relaxed as she let out a long sigh. "I went out with Aaron. We ended up at his apartment. Things got a little out of control. I fought him but he was too strong." With her body pressed close to him, David felt her shudder. "Then suddenly, he was dead. I didn't know what to do. I just left."

"And the guard?" Susan asked.

Jamila nodded. "I found his body. I was afraid to say anything. It was the day after Aaron . . . I was scared."

Susan reached out and squeezed Jamila's shoulder. "It's okay. The evidence points to accidental poisoning while in the commission of a felony. It's over."

"It's over." Jamila's voice cracked.

When David looked down, her face glistened with tears. "Come on. We can go down to the precinct tomorrow to get your formal statement. Let's go home."

Epilogue

David smiled at his choice of programming. A year ago, a documentary on an Egyptian temple wouldn't have made his list of must-see-TV.

The announcer's clipped British accent droned on about the new finds at the Temple of Hathor in Dendara. "The ancient writings tell of a woman cursed by the high priestess Keket for stealing her lover. Until she felt betrayal equal to that of Keket, the woman was destined to suffer eternity with unending lust. However, like the medieval legends of the succubae, her kiss was deadly. This painting of the victim of Keket's Curse was uncovered last year at Hathor's temple. An exquisite find in almost perfect condition of the woman known only as Jamila."

David stared at the painting of the woman on the screen.

The resemblance was uncanny. And the no kissing thing . . . Jamila had never really explained her objections. At the time, David hadn't cared. But now . . .

The living breathing counterpart of the image walked over and turned off the TV.

"You watch too much TV." Jamila sauntered across the room and climbed on his lap. "Kiss me."

Her lips didn't wait for him to shake off his shock.

Turn the page,
and Tawny Taylor
will introduce you
to a WICKED BEAST!

Coming soon from Aphrodisia!

Lander Cornelius smiled to himself as he walked, despite the abuse he was taking from the woman draped over his shoulder—or perhaps in a small way because of it. He put up a silent thank you to the witch who'd sent him into his captive's strange world as he carried his prize back to his lair.

When the witch had first appeared to him, he hadn't known how powerful his quarry's magic would be, how wonderful. How could he? Who missed what they'd never known?

Thanks to Cailey, he could now smell. Taste. Feel. The world was no longer cloaked in shades of gray. Empty and odorless. Two-dimensional. Oh, the joy.

Yet the witch had given him an even greater gift. Once the woman on his shoulder had fully submitted to him, he could possess the power to change the past, the present, and the future. He could alter the events that had occurred years ago and those yet to come.

He thought of the possibilities, the disasters he could prevent. Tragedies. Deaths. Yes, this was the ultimate gift to a king.

Cailey. She was the key to this power, for she possessed a

magic greater than even the witch. He could control it, once he had her complete submission. At least that was what the witch had told him.

Oddly, he sensed a strange connection with his prey, an invisible tether ferrying thoughts and emotions back and forth. He only had to open his mind to hear her gentle voice in his head. To share sensations, emotions, and the occasional thought.

It was distracting, disturbing.

He shifted her weight back a bit, allowing her to breathe easier. "Not much further."

"Fuck you."

He swallowed a growl.

Cailey was nothing like the lionesses he admired most. Sure, she was intelligent. And, of course, there was no denying she was beautiful. Stunning golden waves cascaded down her back and over her shoulders. Expressive eyes lent what some men might consider an ordinary face unrivaled radiance. Her body was soft in the right places, but also strong and well-proportioned. He couldn't wait to see her completely undressed. That would be soon, but definitely not soon enough.

But she was also outspoken, independent, headstrong.

His gaze momentarily dropped to the erection tenting the front of his black pants. Because of his nature, he was never too keen on wearing clothing, although not particularly negative. He'd never had a choice in the matter. But at the moment, the garments were bunching in the wrong places. He needed to make an adjustment. Quickly. Or to get rid of them entirely.

As he stepped up his pace, Cailey continued to beat his back with her fists, kick, and squirm. The pain didn't bother him. In fact, he was grateful to feel her blows. But he feared her wild thrashing might cause an injury. To her. His treasure.

He didn't want to think about the consequences.

Thankfully, his home was not far from the portal between their worlds. By the time he had her safely inside, she was breathless from her exertion and, gauging from the slowing pace of her punches, just about worn out.

Good. Her exhaustion would work to his advantage.

He took her straight to his bedroom and set her down on her feet. As expected, she immediately broke into a run, heading straight for the door.

It didn't take her long to figure out it was locked.

When she turned around, she drilled him with a furious glare. "How dare you! Let me out. Now!"

Clearly, she had no idea how to address a king. He realized, painfully, how difficult it would be to train this goddess to submit. No gift came without its price.

Control. She must always realize who is in control.

He leaned to the left, resting a shoulder against one of the eight-foot pillars at the corners of his bed. "But don't you want to know why I brought you here?"

"No."

She was lying. He sensed it in her voice.

"Or who I am?" he prodded, intensifying his gaze. "Aren't you the least bit curious to know who I am?"

"No! I don't give a damn who you are."

Another lie.

It was hard, but he forced himself to maintain an emotionless mien, even though the vixen had fought him since he'd snatched her from her home. His every nerve was stretched thin.

Adding to the tension was Cailey herself. Her beauty. The scent of her skin filling his nostrils. The sound of her voice humming through his body.

There was a lot to do. Sobering business. If he was going to train Cailey to use her magic for his purpose, she needed to learn to speak the truth. She needed to learn to respect him. And she needed to learn to admire both him as an individual and the strength and majesty of his kind.

He was king of the Werekin—shapeshifters of all species. He merely had to guide her to these truths—with an adequately firm hand.

She stood mute, her back to the door, her arms crossed over her chest. Her anger hadn't eased yet. He could smell it. Spicy and sweet. Delightful. Nearly as intoxicating as the sight of her lush lips and the ivory swell of her breasts, rising and falling with each breath.

Did she know how much he wanted her? How quickly his desire was building? Could she sense it the same way he could feel the longing and fear warring within her? He hoped not. If she did, she might use his desire against him.

He had to maintain control. Always.

He took a single step forward, but she tried to fend him off by lifting her hands and glaring.

"Don't come any closer or I'll scream," she warned.

He had no doubt she would shriek. She'd tested the limits of her vocal chords once or twice—or ten times—already. His eardrums had worn thin, thanks to the high-pitched screeching.

But there was no one to hear her now. At least no one who would do anything about it.

He studied the tension in her body, the stiffness in her limbs as he took a second step toward her. The tang of terror filled his nostrils. The aroma stirred his instincts to chase. Capture. Take. "You don't know our kind," he said.

"What 'kind'? What are you talking about?" She flattened herself against the door.

He stopped directly in front of her, using his size to his advantage. "I'm Lander Cornelius, King of the Werekin."

Recognition slowly touched her features, one by one. Her eyes widened. Her lips parted. The lower one trembled. "Oh. My. God," she muttered in a breathy voice.

"You will learn to respect me." He lifted a hand to her face but before his fingers made contact with her skin, she jerked her head to the side.

"Don't."

"Yes, I will touch you," he said, "whenever and however I wish. You are mine. My possession."

"No, no, no!" She shook her head. "It's impossible. I just started that story. It isn't published. I haven't posted it on the internet . . . how? Did you hack into my computer and steal it?"

Her question confused him. What was a computer? And then he realized she was suggesting he had stolen something from her. He took several slow, deep breaths and cleared the rage from his face and voice. "I don't have to steal anything. Computer? Internet? Story? I don't know what you're talking about."

Her confusion and fear hummed along that invisible line between them and vibrated through his body. The sensation intensified the need swirling within him. Regardless of the anger, frustration, and rage, he ached to touch her, to get closer. Why did he react to this . . . infuriating . . . woman this way? He reached again, this time for her arm.

To his surprise, she didn't jerk away. Her gaze was down, fixed to the floor. She drew her eyebrows together and pulled the corners of her mouth into a frown. But she didn't run. Didn't flinch. Didn't move.

When his fingertips finally made contact with her warm skin, a blade of wanting ripped through his body.

Her gaze shot to his face.

Did she sense something? The bond between them? The hunger charging through his system? The desperate need she stirred in him? Her lips parted again. Her tongue darted out, tracing a slick path along her lower lip before slipping back into the sweet depth of her mouth. Damn, he wanted to taste her.

She would let him.

He tipped his head and met her gaze. "I do not have to steal anything. As king, it's my right to take what I want." The little gasp of surprise he heard roused the predator within him.

Seize. Dominate.

"You're not really a king. You're some kind of obsessive fan ..."

"Fan of whom?" He lowered his head, until little puffs of warm, sweet breath cyclically caressed his lips. Soft like the stroke of a feather.

"... who stole my story and wants to act it out ... or something like that," she muttered, her voice shaky, her words disjointed.

"Act out a story? Why would I do that?"

"I ... I don't know." She sighed.

A sign of submission. Progress.

It wouldn't be much longer. He would have complete submission. She would give it to him freely. And then he would possess the ultimate power and free his people of all tragedy.